THE
GARDEN
OF
BLUE
ROSES

MICHAEL
BARSA

Underland Press

This is U032, and it has an ISBN of 978-1-63023-061-6.

Library of Congress Control Number: 2018931839

This book was printed in the United States of America, and it is published by Underland Press, an imprint of Resurrection House (Sumner, WA).

All that we see or seem
Is but a dream within a dream.

Edited by Melanie Hart
Book Design by Mark Teppo

First Underland Press edition: April 2018.

Underland Press
www.underlandpress.com

THE
GARDEN
OF
BLUE
ROSES

For Kim, Sacha, and Katja

Resistance to something was the law of New England nature; the boy looked out on the world with the instinct of resistance; for numberless generations his predecessors had viewed the world chiefly as a thing to be reformed, filled with evil forces to be abolished, and they saw no reason to suppose that they had wholly succeeded in the abolition; the duty was unchanged. That duty implied not only resistance to evil, but hatred of it. Boys naturally look on all force as an enemy, and generally find it so, but the New Englander, whether boy or man, in his long struggle with a stingy or hostile universe, had learned also to love the pleasure of hating; his joys were few.

—*The Education of Henry Adams*

Roses red and roses white
Plucked I for my love's delight.
She would none of all my posies—
Bade me gather her blue roses.

— Rudyard Kipling, *Blue Roses*

I WAS A GREEK THAT NIGHT. NOT SLICK-TONGUED SINON BUT A SOLDIER on the inside, in the belly of the Horse. One of the murderous 40—Calchas or Teucer or Neoptolemos, killer of Priam. Girded with a short sword, a leather breastplate, a helmet formed of boar's tusks, I was excited and terrified to be shut inside, in the humid blackness, and wheeled to the gates of Troy. Would it work? I peered at myself through a magnifying glass. My wooden face was blank. I closed my eyes and imagined it, the face of someone who wasn't sure if he was a hero or a fool. Then I selected my thinnest brush—a Windsor Newton of Kolinsky sable, the finest miniature brush in the world—and bent low over my modeling desk with its scalpels and paint pots and crane-arm lamp. I blended flesh—cinnabar red, yellow, white, olive green— and dipped the brush's tip. Now the final touch. To breathe life into my lips. But no. I paused. Snow blew against the study's window, forming a constellation of cold white dots. They had a pattern—I sensed it even then—and like the ancient Greeks I began furiously connecting them. A horse. A soldier. A car hurtling wildly out of control.

The telephone was ringing.

I pictured the device in the kitchen, a clanging monster as old as the house itself, and wondered: were people *more* deaf before rock concerts and bulky pounding headphones? Suddenly it stopped. Relief. Silence, but not quite—the wind howled, floorboards creaked. I heard my sister: "W-what? That's impossible. How . . . ?"

The Greek slipped through my fingers. He lay there, vulnerable and faceless as a larva, while Klara cried out, then slammed the phone. Rapid footsteps. The door swung open. Her hair was a black frazzled mess, her woolen pants streaked with dust. It must have been from the attic, the only place our housekeeper Marta didn't clean.

"Has something happened?" I managed.

She nodded as if the words were stuck in her throat and she was trying to shake them loose. She leaned against a hook. This was where Father had once dangled a human head. It was shrunken to the size of a grapefruit, with mottled purple skin and a puckered mouth—a curio from a long-ago trip to a writer's conference in Peru. "There's been an accident."

An icy ravine. Police cars. A spotlight on Mother's Volvo, crumpled into a wall of snow. Klara collapsed in sobs, while I glanced about, unsure if this strobe-lit scene was real or one of Father's novels come to life. Father was John Crane. *That* John Crane. *"The most unusual and acclaimed horror writer of our time."* This was a lie. His books were trash. Full of gimmicks. They littered checkout lanes in supermarkets and were taught in lesser community colleges, where his trademark style—*"the Master of the Slasher who writes in rhyming couplets"*—might seem profound. Still I couldn't purge them from my mind. I peered into every corner of that ravine, searching for ominous shadows or a glinting devilish eye, and into the car itself for the slightest otherworldly stir:

> He sensed it in the wintry night,
> A whiff of fresh undead, a rotting putrid blight
> That told him what had happened here
> Upon this smoking, charred, and empty bier.

Did the officers sense anything amiss, anything strange about the scene? No, they were dull and provincial—they just wanted to get things over with. One of them silently drove Klara and me to the station. A young policewoman greeted us there with cups of coffee and a clipboard thick with forms. Klara filled out the forms in a distracted hurry, while I gazed at a wall full of admonitions: NO SMOKING, NO EATING, NO RADIO PLAYING.

When no one was looking I tucked my cup beneath a plastic chair. I cannot tolerate caffeine.

The bodies were in the basement, on slabs of steel—Mother with shards of her sunglasses still nestled in her platinum bob and Father in his tweedy, seedy best. "I think I see Father breathing," I whispered to Klara. She gave me a stern look and told me to hush. I would not. Instead I began poking him in the face to wake him up. Even when his head flopped to one side and his jaw hung open crookedly, I laughed and said: "What an actor!"

I didn't trust his death. Father was an author. He was words. You can't kill words—can't lock them up and drive them off a cliff. That night I peered into their room—at the roll-top desk and fireplace and four-poster bed, at Mother's brush clotted with glittering loops of hair and the ladder to the attic where Father wrote. While working he was like an apparition, only descending in the dead of night for his special visitations, as he called them. In my secret diary I called them something else; I called them *moods*, as in: *Father came to me in one of his moods tonight.* Afterwards I'd stumble to my window and see him wandering the grounds—a thin hunched figure flitting between the trees. I pictured all the evils of his books—buried bodies and Satanic rites, communes with witches and animal sacrifices and the weird obstetrical needs of half-human births—as I wondered: *What did he do out there?*

"Milo?"

I whirled around. Klara lurked in the vast stone hallway, arms folded over her nightgown, her face waxy with grief. She had Father's nose—a hawkish protuberance—and she was breathing heavily through it.

"I think he's still up there," I gestured. "In the attic."

She glanced past me. Even as a young girl she'd sneak up to see him, claiming to be his *amanuensis*, proud of herself for knowing what that meant.

"Close the door," she said.

I couldn't. She had to do it herself. A bare pale arm grazed my chin. I remembered her dusty pants.

"What was he was working on, Klara?"

"It doesn't matter now."

I knew she was lying. As a boy I'd once burst into her room with a kitchen knife, reciting a passage from his fourth novel, that infamous psychological horror that catapulted him to world-wide fame:

> *Keith's virgin killing was sublime,*
> *A young man's thrill, a murder just in time*
> *For art school graduation. What were classmates for*
> *Except to help achieve our dreams? His name was Franklin, poor*
> *Kentuckian, a lover of Picasso (self-promoting, compromised)*
> *And all clichés in art, which Keith despised.*
> *So there he was, tied to a chair,*
> *The ultimate artistic feeling: being scared,*
> *While Keith made of his throat a blood soufflé*
> *That puffed and oozed and rasped away,*
> *And Keith, his fingers black, said "look" and licked the gore*
> *And thought of many, many more*
> *Artistic turns he'd make, like Cubism for real!*
> *Or landscapes full of bodies! Battlefields*
> *Had always turned him on, so make it new!*
> *Oh yes, he would, he saw them now,*
> *Those necks and arms and bellies and pricks*
> *And eyes devoured by candle sticks.*
> *He dropped the knife and left his friend, so keen to make*
> *The kind of art that would forever slake*
> *His need for full divine transcendence—*
> *Supreme and shining incandescence.*

She was furious. Not about the knife but about the book itself. *A Portrait of The Artist As A Young Psychopath.* It wasn't yet in print. So how had I known it? Had Father bestowed his precious verse on me first? I refused to answer her questions, even as she boxed my ears and knocked me to the ground, and I sensed the same jealous impulse now—the same desire to keep his memory for herself—as she turned and walked away. I didn't protest. I let her have it—let her have all the frail dead parts of him locked away up there. I knew it would never be enough for her. Father had always been her idol, her colossus. Now she had nothing— just a few relics and the myth.

It snowed on the day of the funeral. The cemetery was hushed and still, almost beautiful under its fresh white blanket. Icicles hung from mausoleums and the trees were like crystal shrouds. It was one of the oldest cemeteries in southern Vermont, on a small knoll near Bennington College where students communed with the dead and spooked their girlfriends into skulking, wide-eyed sex acts. Now they were all crowded behind a distant barricade, these students, waving and gawking at the suddenly boxed-up famous writer and his cold, grieving children. ("*There they are! The kids! Not really kids anymore, eh?*") I tried to ignore them. It was impossible. They were everywhere. At one point, just as the coffins were lowered into the ground, a band of black-clad teens snuck into the cemetery with copies of Father's sixth novel, *We Are the Dead*, which they ignited using cigarette lighters. They chanted lines about how "the dead never die" (it was a vampire novel) before tossing the flaming volumes into nearby shrubbery. Klara was just then reading an obscure passage of Milton. She had to stop until the groundskeepers extinguished the conflagration and chased away those zit-covered pyromaniacs.

Afterwards the haze and smoke lingered, as did the crowds. Everyone had come for a carnival: they sang and raised their own lighters and wrapped pine branches around their necks as in *Killer Trees*. Everyone except one, that is. I noticed him near the ceremony's end: a still point amid the topsy-turvy tableau, a figure in a dark overcoat leaning against a fence. And the strangest part was that I recognized him, he was *familiar*, though with all the hubbub I couldn't remember how, couldn't reconstruct a past.

Then he was gone. Or perhaps I lost sight of him. My sister hastily finished reading and hurried toward me. She looked exhausted, like a painting by Gustav Klimt, Adele something-or-other, her eyes drooping and her hair in a rounded heap. "Come," she said. We drove home in silence. As we climbed out of the car she leaned

5

against me, hunching so she wouldn't tower over me. I allowed my hand to slip around her waist. I didn't think she'd mind. I was trying to be *supportive*, as people say. Still I looked at her, just to be sure. Her lips were pressed together as if she'd just stubbed her toe, and she was gazing at the spindly woods behind the house, whose grey stones and peaked rooftops glowed in the dying light. "You know that Mother always dreamed of doing something with this property," she whispered.

"Such as?"

"Hiring a gardener. Making it beautiful."

It seemed like an offhanded comment, a way to dull the pain, and at first I let it go, puff, into the bone-chilled air, too preoccupied with holding her up to imagine any connection between these words and that mysterious figure (whom I'd already decided had been a *mirage*). I was conscious of being the sort of brother I'd never been: caring, attentive, *present* to her needs. Amazing what tragedy can do.

"Well it's certainly not the season now," I said as I guided her across the icy driveway.

"I suppose you're right."

The next day I forgot about him entirely. We were visiting the lawyer. Father had been rich enough to hire the best law firm in New England, but he stuck with an old shyster who worked out of a ramshackle cottage on the outskirts of Manchester. We sat around a kitchen table he'd made himself and ate hot scones and cheese. He talked almost exclusively to Klara. He only ever addressed me to shout: "Look at you! All grown up!" But I didn't care. I noticed how distracted Klara was. She was nibbling a scone. Then she paused and wiped away the crumbs. Suddenly she was concentrating intensely on something the lawyer was saying. "Would you mind repeating that?"

He did. That's when I understood, after several blinking moments, what had just occurred. Legal title to our property, over a hundred acres, had passed to her alone, to manage as she saw fit, while I merely received the right to live there "for the duration of my natural life." I was stunned. What about the other assets? The money? These were held for Klara in a complicated trust, while I received a stipend like a college student, along with the right to object if she "wasted" assets in a way that was "detrimental to the estate."

"That's it?" I said.

The lawyer put down the will and scrutinized me over his gold-rimmed reading glasses. "You're lucky to have such a responsible sister," he said. "I wouldn't worry about a thing."

So *she* would take care of *me*, I supposed he was saying, and it might have worked out that way—might have been lovely, in a way. But Klara then leaned forward with a troubled frown. You'd think she was the one left with nothing but a right to protest. "What about the insurance?" she asked in a low voice.

"That's paid to both you and Milo outside the will. Assuming it was an accident."

Assuming? I felt like the Trojan Horse, my belly a sudden hollow full of murderous enemies. "What do you mean?" I asked.

"The police report hasn't been finalized. We should know more in the morning."

I couldn't wait. As soon as we got home Klara lunged up to her room. She looked more devastated than ever. I said I wanted a glass of water and closed the kitchen door. There was a message on our answering machine. A Detective Schanzenbach. "*Nothing urgent, just need to clear up a few details.*" Breathe, I told myself. My finger slowly circled the old rotary dial.

"Yah?"

He was eating. I could practically smell the hamburger. He wanted to know whether we'd found a note or whether Father had been acting strangely of late. I laughed.

"He was the strangest man I knew."

"Nothing else you or your sister can tell us?"

I bit my lip. Where should I begin? The attic? The Peruvian shrunken head? "My father was never a good driver."

After hanging up I realized that Klara was crying. I heard it through the old metal ductwork. Clearly she wasn't wholly focused on her newfound wealth—or maybe she was, and it just reminded her how she'd gotten it. I left the kitchen. The crying only became louder. Our house has strange echoes. It was coming from all over, like the walls themselves were weeping. I was tempted to run away, to avoid a future of such sounds. Part of me knew Klara and I couldn't really care for each other, that too much lay between us and death wouldn't change a thing. But where could I go? Neither of us was suited for the modern world. Our parents had made sure of that. I had visions of freezing bus stops, distant impersonal cities where people rushed about doing jobs I could hardly comprehend. So in a moment of stubbornness—some might call it fear—I told myself that my place was here, by Klara's side, that we'd weather the postmortem storm together.

Marta was gone, so I marched back to the kitchen and prepared a can of Klara's favorite cream of mushroom soup. I took it to her on a tray. She was curled up in a ball, yet shot up when she saw me, her nightgown falling off one shoulder. She didn't put it back. "Milo? What are you…?" Then she saw the soup. Her eyes welled up. She patted the edge of her bed, and I sat and let her stroke my hair, and I even cried a little too. But mostly I kept watching her, waiting for her to say something else about the accident, about what might have happened.

She never did.

PERHAPS WE NEEDED A BLIND MAN. THAT'S WHAT FATHER WOULD have said. He loved telling the story of Oedipus—who pressed Teiresias, a blind seer, to reveal his father's killer. "*He is here,*" Teiresias says, referring to Oedipus himself, who doesn't know it yet. Father said you could learn a lot from the Greeks, who in their stilted way conveyed unspeakable horrors. It was unfortunate that what he learned most was how to distort them—to use them as vehicles for his mindless displays of slaughter. Father was adept at stealing from every source he could find: stealing and twisting them for his own terrible ends.

But the real tragedy of Oedipus wasn't that he'd unwittingly killed his father. It was that he'd ultimately learned the truth. So when the detective arrived the following day, I couldn't help feeling anxious, especially when I saw the eager-beaver look on his shiny face. Klara hardly said a word as she ushered him into the living room and laid out tea and an old tin of butter cookies. "This house is exactly how I imagined it," he said, chewing. He glanced at the spilling bookshelves and the swirling floral canvases that Mother had painted and the dusty curtains in front of our tall narrow windows. "A little spooky, like his books."

I had half a mind to show him the Peruvian shrunken head. But Klara beat me to it. She said what was on both our minds: "Have you found anything?" She was sitting upright, twisting her fingers in her lap. He swallowed and nodded, and I could see his chin: loose, on the way to fat. "An interesting development."

I leaned forward. Yet I should have known better. We were dealing with amateurs. "Your parents' car was going over 50 miles per hour when it crashed through the guardrail," he said.

"My God," said Klara.

"Your father seems to have been drunk."

Klara sighed, almost relieved, while I kept thinking: *Then why was he behind the wheel?* Even under the best of circumstances, he was a nervous, hesitant, turtle-slow driver.

"He *was* on his way to an important reading," Klara said, as if anticipating my objection. "His first one in years."

"That's the funny thing," the detective said. "We didn't find anything in the car. No notes, no speech, not even a book."

"They would have had a book at the store for him to use," Klara said.

"But the bookstore said he was going to read something new. Something about a sequel to *A Portrait of the Artist*?"

Everyone paused. His logic was impeccable. Only he didn't follow up. Not after Klara's eyes filled again with tears. "Sorry," he went on. "Just tying up loose ends. I suppose they're not that relevant anyway."

"I keep replaying that evening over and over in my mind," she said. "I wish I could be more helpful."

She got to her feet. They shook hands. "I'm sorry for your loss," the detective said. "I should've said that right away."

"Is there anything else we can tell you?" Klara asked.

"Unfortunately I've seen this too many times. Alcohol and bad weather. A terrible combination."

"I guess we're all left wondering why," Klara said.

The detective put a hand on her shoulder, a hairy hand with fat fingers like spider's legs, while I stared at him and didn't say a thing, too busy thinking about my own nagging *why—why* Father would have driven to a reading of his sequel with nothing whatsoever to read.

But these questions, like the shock itself, soon receded into the past, becoming like the old velvet wallpaper above the dining room's wainscoting: *muted* and *dulled*. The police report arrived with the verdict "accident." Then the insurance company called about the car. I overheard Klara say that we weren't interested in it, that they should sell it for scrap.

And then? Silence. Blissful, fragile, rural silence. The snow melted; trees sprouted leaves. Life seemed to become less complicated, with only occasional letters or visits from Father's fans. Every now and then Klara still became distraught, and the attic tantalized me, but we began to focus on other things, doing crossword puzzles on the patio and taking long walks in town. For the first time we really talked, now that it was quiet enough to hear our own voices. We talked about little things: the weather, the pattern on Klara's favorite china. Over meals Klara would read the newspaper aloud, grim articles about suicide bombers or deadly typhoons—news that insisted on its own importance and made our own tragedy seem small. She sent checks to every relief effort. This helped her feel better. I suppose it did the same for me.

Still something wasn't right—something in the air, in those shifty misty mornings or the late afternoon sun that kept throwing strange geometries of light across our floors. Occasionally I'd come across Klara on the living room sofa with her head thrown back, eyes far-away, book sprawled beside her. "Are you alright?" I'd rush over to ask, and she'd shudder as if woken from a trance; she'd claim she was just thinking of polishing the napkin rings or donating Mother's clothes to charity. At night I heard footsteps. I thought they were hers; I couldn't be sure. They whispered through the hallway, the guest rooms, up and down the stairs and across the attic—roaming, restless, searching sounds. Searching for what? Every time I looked there was no one, only the house with its gaping darkness. I began checking on her, hovering over the bed where she slept: on her back, arms folded across her chest. I put an ear to her mouth, fingers to her wrist and neck, not trusting her stillness after seeing Mother and Father on those slabs. Only once did she wake up, *shot* up like a resuscitated drowning victim—she had that same dazed panic. "What are you doing, Milo?" she gasped, and I just gazed at her and replied: "Making sure you're still here."

"Where else would I be?"

I didn't respond. This was precisely what I wanted to know. Where else was her mind? Once I saw her drift onto the patio to gaze at the trees. She spent nearly an hour in silent contemplation. Then it was the driveway, where she ran a hand across the half-empty garage. Did she need more time? For tranquility to take firm root? I imagined how it would happen, sitting on her bed, Mozart on the stereo, a light and airy tune—how she'd hold me like she used to do when I was small, and I'd close my eyes and hear the music and her breathing and the sympathetic beating of my heart. *"It's us against the world, just as it always should have been,"* she'd say, and that's how I'd know that nothing could ever hurt us or come between us again.

When did I first realize that she was waiting too? Harboring her own dark and secret hope, not for *us* but for *him*? Knowing is a gradual process, an accretion of detail that snaps into insight when you least expect it. I think of a bright early morning in June when she didn't descend for breakfast at the usual time. I was in the study. I'd just finished the Trojan Horse. Normally I'd pause after a complicated model like that and spend a few days watching television or burning ants under magnifying glasses. But when I saw that it was nearly thirty minutes past the appointed hour, I must have become especially ill-at-ease. I immediately began a 1/72 replica of an ancient Greek trireme, a wooden model a little over 20 inches long, with three banks of oars and two collapsible sails and a thin bronze ram. I quickly erected its support skeleton and began attaching hull planks using a powerful glue. In the process I managed to smear glue across my fingertips. I didn't panic—I'd used oceans of the stuff over the years—only this time I couldn't get it off. I rubbed and rubbed. It was like rubbing a magic lamp. The glue turned black and viscous. It was just like car grease. No—it *was* car grease. What was happening?

Suddenly I was lying on my back, the underbelly of the Volvo looming inches above. I reached up, one hand feeling for the brake wires—rubber casing, behind the shock absorbers—while the other held a pair of wire cutters with sand paper to stop them from slipping. *"It wasn't an accident, Milo. My killer is right here."*

No. This wasn't a memory, wasn't real. It was a conjured past, a *fiction*. I staggered into the living room. Father's novels lined the shelves. There it was, *Sleep Little Babe*, about a witch who snatched children and greased their hands so they couldn't fight or turn doorknobs to escape. I saw their lonely eyes, their helplessness, their tears. "*Mommy? Mommy?*" Their bodies were found buried beneath the witch's basement floor. Their skeletons looked like they'd died in prayer. The only one who'd survived had used wire cutters to escape, gripping them with sand paper as he snapped a basement window's lock.

I turned the book around to hide its spine. I heard the wind, clashing leaves. What could be keeping Klara? I raced back to the study and slammed the door. I tried to focus on the trireme, something historical and real, but Father used to say that if you could imagine it, it was real to you, so I closed my eyes and tried to bury my imagination, to shovel it over with great mounds of earth. Only I couldn't do it. The memories began cropping up like weeds, shoots everywhere, impervious to every poison, demanding *life*.

I'll begin with Mother, a glittering chrysalis. I see her painted lips, sunglasses, thick bejeweled fingers smoothing over the blazer and tie she made me wear to school. This seems like such a small thing in retrospect. Yet at the time it defined my existence. Beginning in second grade, every boy used me as the target of spitballs and charley-horses and wedgies and something I don't wish to describe called a "purple nurple." I refused to go outside for recess or to ride the bus. The cafeteria was like a shooting gallery. By fifth grade I'd developed kidney stones because I no longer dared use the bathroom. Why not? I'll simply say that no matter how much it's cleaned, toilet water still tastes like every defecation to ever pass through its porcelain receptacle.

I begged Mother to change my wardrobe to something flannel and denim—something that might fit in. She refused. She said no child of hers would dress like a lumberjack. No child of hers? You'd think she were European royalty. In truth she'd grown up on an Austrian commune, selling art on street corners and ingesting copious illegal drugs. She still put brush to canvas with hideous results, but most often spent her days driving around, trying to sell her "work"—sentimental landscapes and fruit and the like—or visiting people with their own artistic pretensions. One of them, a Roland something-or-other, made the big ugly

13

vases she kept in the entrance hall. She visited this Roland often. It was obvious what was going on. She was always coming home with hideous ceramic presents.

Every now and then she kept up the pretense of mothering by insisting we eat supper together. I've never understood this penchant for masticating as a social ritual. We don't make other bodily functions like defecation or nose blowing into elaborate occasions of forced togetherness. Mother would train her huge sunglasses on Klara and me and ask: "So how was your day? Did you enjoy school?" I'd mumble the most blatant lies, waiting for her to notice my bruises or soiled ties or the fact that I'd changed clothes. She never did.

"Now where's your father?" she'd say instead, as if he ever joined us—as if we were anything to him but distractions from his work. One night she claimed she was taking him to a reading at some Elks Lodge in town. "You know he'll never find it on his own," she said. "Of course he just has to follow the crowds. Everyone loves his latest book."

"They're stupid," I explained.

"Dear boy," she laughed, sending her silver pelican earrings tinkling against their hoops. "Whatever will we do with you?"

Klara looked miserable that night as she watched Mother slide on her fur coat and pucker into the mirror to check her lipstick. She was itching to leave as well—to leave me alone—something she'd started asking recently to do. "Can you drop me off at a diner?" she inquired. "It's on the way, and some friends are meeting for a soda."

These friends were always having sodas. God knows what they were really up to. Klara had just started high school and had fallen in with the drama crowd. Even then she was easily influenced.

Thankfully Mother ignored her, as she often did, just consulted her watch and primped her sprayed-stiff hair. "John!"

Most of the time he didn't come down, even for a reading he'd promised to do. Somehow the public didn't mind. They seemed to enjoy the suspense. But on that night, to our surprise, we saw his shuffling legs descend the stairs—the legs of a tramp, little sticks floating inside loose soiled pants. Then came eyes like a newly released hostage's and wildly disheveled hair. "Go clean yourself right now or we'll be late," insisted Mother with not the slightest recognition that he might be ill or out-of-sorts. Perhaps she knew something we didn't. He mumbled that he was trying to write a more literary and less bloody book for a change, a memoir describing his childhood in one of the rougher sections of London. "Only I can't do it," he moaned. "I'm a bloody failure."

"Don't be so self-aggrandizing," Mother responded as she pushed him back upstairs. "Not in front of the children."

"Milo?"

Why was he addressing me? I glanced around and spotted one of Klara's old hand-puppets in the alcove. I thought its dome-shaped eyes might replace missing hatch lids on a model U-Boat I was building. When assembling a model I thought of little else, just those pieces that by themselves are nothing, but together are sublime.

"Milo, I'm really trying . . ."

I pictured the U-Boat: periscope, conning tower, torpedo bay, ballast tanks, green-painted engine room.

"Enough," said Mother. "Get yourself in the shower, John. You stink."

"The words just die on the page," he said to no one in particular, to his pale hand sliding up the railing, "when they're only real."

"Go!"

Mother pushed him out of view. I didn't care. By then my mind was absorbed by images of the shiny pocket knife blade I'd use to extract those puppet's eyes.

Klara was livid when she found the puppet with only threads dangling from its sockets. She couldn't prove I'd done it—not after I painted the hatches a triple-coat of grey—but it didn't matter. Mother was venturing out more and more, leaving Klara in charge, and her frustration was boiling over—frustration at staying home with me, at being *mommy to little Milo*, as I overheard one of her so-called "friends" at school say.

"Milo? What did you do with Kermit?" Klara said breathlessly, holding up the frog.

I was sitting in bed reading an illustrated history of trench warfare. "I didn't touch him."

I hoped my terseness would make her realize the grave danger of indifference—what a double-edged sword it was. But she remained in the doorway, clenching her jaw and glaring. "Why do you make Father feel so bad?"

"What are you talking about?"

"You hate him. That's why he won't come down."

I squinted at the gruesome depiction of the first Battle of Ypres—bodies twisted in the mud. "Is that what he told you?"

"He didn't have to."

"He doesn't come down because he doesn't care about us, Klara. He only cares about his writing."

"You're wrong."

"No, I'm not."

She bashed Kermit into the wall and stormed off. But the next day, after school, she pulled out her conductor's baton—the one she used to conduct her stereo. She claimed I needed lessons in civility. I rolled my eyes. She whacked me across the forehead, then dragged me to the dining table. I was shocked; she'd never done that before, never dared *hurt* me. For a moment I wondered if Father was somehow making her do it, conducting her just as she was trying to conduct me. I wouldn't have been surprised— that was the sort of hold he had over her. Or perhaps the truth was more straightforward; perhaps this was how she'd answer my implicit charge of indifference, through the most cruel attention imaginable. I sat. Another whack. "Ladies first." This went on for nearly an hour, until I could hardly see. The following week she added lessons in grammar, Euclidean geometry, Earth Science—every conceivable subject, all enforced with the baton if I didn't get things right. Once I pissed the chair—I couldn't help it, she wouldn't allow me to get up—and she delivered such a vicious spanking that I almost fell over.

"I'm telling Mother," I managed.

She laughed. Over supper I showed Mother my bruises. She refused to look at them. "Your big sister only wants you to learn," she said, patting me on the head. Did she know what was happening? I suppose she did. She just couldn't face it. Those sunglasses were her way of dimming the world, keeping out not only light but darkness too. I could see the way her hands shook as she insisted on talking about school, the weather, politics—all the nonsense people use to stave off despair. Then she drove away, visiting friends who socialized at all hours. Klara watched her go before shutting me in my room. "I'm not tired!" I protested.

"I don't care."

I put an ear to the door. Sometimes in the evenings, when Mother was gone, I'd hear Klara sobbing, or talking listlessly on the phone, or calling Father's name. But on that night I heard nothing—the most frightening thing of all.

Then one day something odd happened. Klara missed an algebra lesson. By then I felt like a pincushion or voodoo doll, every inch of me subjected to that cruel baton. So when she locked herself in her room after school and didn't come out, I felt a wave of bittersweet relief. Only at suppertime did she emerge, and only after Mother began shouting Germanic obscenities up the stairs. What a transformation! My recent tormenter descended with the plodding of a death-row inmate, the delicate skin around her eyes splotched and raw. Even Mother noticed. "Is something wrong?" she asked.

Klara shook her head and sat. I put down my fork, imagining a day of cat fights or social ostracism or locker theft—hallmarks of my world, not hers. Despite everything I wanted to tell her I understood, that we were still more alike than she knew, but Mother was in one of her dominating moods again and I couldn't slip in a single word. "Well?" she insisted.

Klara sighed. "I got a B on an English test."

Was that all? Then I realized what it meant. She'd never gotten a B on anything, let alone an English test. "What was the test on?" Mother asked, but I already knew—I'd seen her reading it that morning, over breakfast. *Jane Eyre*. One of Father's favorites.

"It wasn't fair," Klara protested. "It was all about the social influences on Charlotte Brontë. There was nothing about the story itself."

The story that Father read to her every Christmas morning. It was his great present—his presence—and Klara loved it, perched

17

on his lap, entranced by his nasal drone. She could recite whole passages before she was six years old, causing Father to nod and half-close his eyes as if listening to his favorite Franz Liszt. He always said how smart and accomplished she was. So how would he react to news of this B? Would she tell him? I could see the struggle in her face, the determination never to disappoint him again. Would she waste any more time tormenting me or trying to impress her drama friends? *Surely not*, I thought, too caught up in this prospect of freedom to wonder how she'd spend her time instead.

I was right, at least. That test saved me. Did it do the same for Klara? While other girls began wearing tight jeans to show off their adolescent curves, she developed a lifelong fondness for Shetland wool. She studied until all hours and won every prize—the mathematics prize, the literature prize, even the science bridge-building prize. She became editor-in-chief of the high school newspaper, where she published a column on obscure New England writers and artists who'd attended that school. She went to the state Spelling Bee, only missing the final round when she bungled the last two letters of "espiegle."

Only later did I realize Klara was acting a role even then. This was her *play* at competence, maturity, worldliness—all the qualities she must have known she lacked. In reality she was just as scared as I was: scared and trapped. She might have been preparing herself for the wider world, but it was our own world that loomed over us always, a lost realm in the Vermont woods that Father oversaw, like any god worth his salt, from a terrible remove. Even in his absence he was everywhere—in the creaking floors, the grandfather clock, the footsteps and shadowy trees, in the books crowding the living room shelves and appearing, like not-so-subtle reminders, on end tables and our pillows before we lay down at night. Not just his own books but the ones he thought we ought to read—Dickens and Hawthorne and Charles Brockden Brown—books to *mold* our imaginations to some uncertain and terrifying end.

Still we did it. We read them all. I, at least, wasn't aware of having any choice. I also wasn't aware of the virus they contained, the virus of *fear*. This was the only world I knew, teeming with devils and damnation, creatures that would tear out your stomach and feed on your own last meal. It was a largely unspoken fear, immured in the walls of our loneliness. But I saw it in Klara's eyes, in the way she hurried past empty rooms and avoided shadows, even in the way she began to recoil in self-disgust whenever she was mean to me, afraid of what was coming over her. She read the same books as I.

"I'm scared," I admitted to her one night after Mother went out. I was standing outside my room. She'd just put me to bed and was in front of her own, a hazy figure in the sconce-light. I wasn't sure she'd heard, wasn't sure I'd actually expressed my fear aloud. But then she turned, her face shining like a wax figure's.

"Of what?"

"Everything he's making me read. I'm starting to see things."

"It's all in your mind, Milo."

It was the way she said it, so matter-of-factly, that made me want to scream, or to rush over and never let her go, tell her I knew she felt the same way and that we'd escape this place together. Instead I watched her turn the doorknob and disappear, and then I was conscious of how alone I was in the vast stone gullet of a hallway. It seemed to want to swallow me.

Occasionally, during the light of day, the fog of this oppression would lift and Klara and I would play—laugh and run and forget. Yet even then there was an intensity to her gaze, like she wasn't fully there. She loved mounting little costume dramas among the trees and grounds—anointing me Thomas Cromwell and herself Anne Boleyn. "I *am* the rightful Queen," she'd insist as she took off through the woods. She dared me to denounce her, but I couldn't, because her happiness seemed so desperate, so fleeting, as we breathed fast and ran even faster.

Of course, like Anne herself, these little plays were doomed; there were days when I might adopt my most Cromwellian pose—a harrumphing scowl, arms akimbo—only to be met with a sigh and a pat on the head. It wasn't just the increasing time she spent on her studies. The age difference (nearly six years) quickly became too great. I remember the final summer before Klara left for college, when Mother unexpectedly announced a trip to the New Jersey shore. It was there that I noticed what Klara had been keeping under wraps: a burgeoning womanhood. She seemed embarrassed by my staring, pulling a towel around herself as we built sandcastles amid the colorful umbrellas and people playing paddle ball and Frisbee and the seagulls squawking and hovering in clusters across the surf. It looked like something out of a 1960s Technicolor film; I half-expected Annette Funicello to leap at me with a song. Klara had a strange weakness for Annette Funicello and those silly go-go beach movies that kept appearing on TV.

"Isn't this wonderful?" Mother announced beneath her own umbrella. She was drunk almost the entire time we were there, lounging on a chaise and sipping champagne from a cooler. Father was curled up in a chair next to her. He looked out-of-place in the sunlight and blue waves and open sand, far from his usual hiding places. He never took off his shirt or pants or shoes, never did anything but stare at us and chew his fingernails. The only thing he ever said was: "nice castle."

Surfacing from memory is like coming up for air. There is that same exhausted relief, the wonder at being alive. Also the same moment of doubt, of whether *this* is really the dream and that *other* realm, the murky one of shifting shapes and swaying sunbeams, is the one you inhabit. But no. There was the trireme. I fixed my gaze on it, let it pull me back into the wider world: the glue pot, the desk and all my tools. I told myself: *I'm here. I'm fine.*

I tried to believe it.

A bird shrieked. It was a small thing, but it jarred me like a scream. I peered through the study's window, at the swaths of trees, hills, rolling clouds. A breeze sent up a great rustling warning from the leaves. I saw a hawk circling over the trees and a pair of squirrels hopping across the low patio wall. Were the squirrels afraid of the hawk? Did hawks eat squirrels? How would these squirrels know? I thought of nature as an all-consuming Passion Play in a language I had no hope of understanding.

At last I heard Klara on the stairs. I raced out of the study, eager to share my brake-wire hallucination and to inquire whether she'd been hearing false accusations too—if that was the source of her unease. Then I saw how she was dressed, in a bright plaid shirt with the collar slightly raised and dark new jeans that hugged her hips. She looked like one of those women who drove Range Rovers and descended on Vermont in the autumn to admire leaves. "You look different," I observed.

"I'll take that as a compliment."

She hardly touched her food, just cupped her tea and held her face to the morning sun. Finally she rose to her feet. That's when I saw them. Mother's earrings. Not the pelicans. The butterflies.

I should have known what this meant: transformation, flight, the spreading of fragile wings. "I have a few errands in town this morning," she said.

"Anything in particular?"

"Nothing interesting. Maybe visiting the cemetery."

"I've heard that Father's fans camp out there," I said. "Many of them still don't believe he's dead."

She sighed. "Listen, Milo, will you be alright for a few hours?"

That's when I realized she meant to go without me.

"Can we do another crossword puzzle?" I said, hastily picking up the newspaper. Yesterday's had been about famous literary heroines. We'd worked on it all morning. It had made Klara smile. "*My Mrs. Dalloway smile.*"

"Later, OK? I won't be long."

"But . . ."

She touched my shoulder. "I promise."

I brought our dishes into the kitchen. I never did this. I wanted to remind her how responsible I could be, what a good companion. But she didn't even remark upon it, not even to say thank you. I waited. There was a large knife on the countertop. I began chopping carrots. They were Klara's fingers. She couldn't run errands without fingers, could she?

"I won't be long," she repeated from the entrance hall.

She was already clattering to the door. I threw down the knife and followed, suddenly sorry I'd been chopping off her fingers. I tried to make amends. "I made you something."

"Really?" She was slipping on her shoes.

I began describing one of the trireme's galley slaves, a special figure I'd worked on for days. Special because he was no longer a slave—he'd led a slave mutiny and was now captain of the ship. I hadn't actually made such a figure, but I thought Klara would appreciate the notion because she was always talking about the evils of slavery and its lasting ill effects. I also began, with my foot, nudging a line of my own shoes across the front door—a line she couldn't cross.

"Listen Milo, that's wonderful, really, but could you show it to me when I return?"

Then she did it. She crossed the line.

After Harvard Klara had worked as an editorial assistant on some minor Boston literary magazine best known for typesetting nursery rhymes with surprising line-breaks: *Three Blind / Mice See How / They Run*. She lived in a cramped apartment on the North End and finally had friends and went to soirees and ate in middling restaurants with artistic pretensions. She even had a husband for a few brief months: a foreigner—Brazilian, I believe—who won her heart with his surprising knowledge of the poetry of John Donne. "*Oh my America, my new-found land.*" How apt that proved.

Mother drove us to the wedding in the Volvo, while Father fiddled with the car radio and I chafed under the requirements of forced cheer. "Can you believe our little Klara is all grown up?" she kept saying. "Making her own decisions?" She dabbed her eyes and distractedly jerked between lanes at fantastic speed. She must have imagined she was on the Autobahn. Even the notorious Boston drivers seemed terrified. She squealed into the parking garage and nearly ran over a man in a wheelchair. "He's got to learn to share the road," she muttered as he flapped his arms like a bird.

It was just us and a judge and the Brazilian in his baggy, borrowed tuxedo. He kept pushing up his sleeves as if challenging someone to a fight. He was shorter than I imagined. When he slipped the ring onto Klara's finger he looked like a tourist making love to the Statue of Liberty. Afterwards he shook Father's hand as if winding up a great big toy, saying in his smoky accent what "a yuge fin" he was. And that was it. They went on honeymoon to the Amazon, paid us a brief Christmas visit, and a year later, after securing his visa, he ran off with a woman nearly as swarthy as himself.

By the time Klara returned home she'd lost considerable weight: cheeks pale, hair flecked with gray. It was the first time I realized she'd loved that man. She couldn't bear to talk about him, though. Nor about the literary magazine which had folded, nor the friends who sent fat wedding invitations which she discarded with a bitter flourish. "Nobody in the world recognizes who we really are," she said to me once. "And nobody cares. Do you understand? All we can count on is family. Without family loyalty we're nothing, we're falling through the air without a parachute."

Family loyalty. It was a strange way to express our bond, but I let it go because I could see she wanted to cry. I moved close and a little to one side to offer a comforting shoulder. I was somewhat surprised when she took it. Her hair smelled like a cinnamon wax candle. Some of it hung across her cheek, and I curled it up over her ear and said: "I know exactly how you feel."

It was true. I'd just been to college.

It was a small liberal-arts institution in New Hampshire whose brochure was all Gothic serenity and leafy contemplation, but in truth it was more like Sodom. I watched young men crush beer cans into their mouths, light hair spray on fire, and gleefully terrorize farm animals. I'd requested a single room—I wouldn't have lasted a day with a roommate. Every open door seemed to reveal a half-naked man—they always dressed in full public view—or a woman clutching shards of clothing worn the night before.

I had no idea who first realized I was John Crane's son. Everyone looked at me with eyebrow-raised disbelief, snickering at my blazers and ties. By then I'd begun wearing them willingly, even enthusiastically, as a mark of intelligence—of my superiority to those low-class high school bullies in their hooded sweatshirts and football jerseys and backwoods plaid. I'd imagined that my fellow college students would feel the same way, that we'd enjoy an enlightened chuckle at the slovenly dolts now destined to pump our gas.

I could not have been more wrong.

One of them, a hollow-chested drug addict named Barry, approached me approximately a month after I arrived. I was returning from a lecture on differential calculus when he yanked a copy of *Hell's Fury* out of the back pocket of his ripped-up jeans. "You're Milo Crane," he said, a knowing gleam infecting his jaundiced eye.

I cringed and kept walking, hoping he was in one of his stupors and would soon forget what he'd just said.

"Dude, I'm like such a fan of your dad."

I fumbled with my room key. "His books are idiotic," I murmured. "Anyone who likes them is an idiot."

"Whoa." He chuckled. "You been to like therapy for that, man?"

I managed to get inside and press my back against the door as he called to a comrade: "Dude, you know who blazer-boy is?" Within days all sorts of people I didn't know began asking what Father was "really like." A few even wanted my autograph. "Go away," I said. "He wasn't my father. My mother slept with the mailman." They didn't believe me. It got worse and worse. I had to make it stop. But how? After trying various techniques, from pretending I was deaf to speaking in a gibberish language of my own invention, I hit upon something so beautifully simple that I wondered why I hadn't thought of it right off. Each morning I'd blacken several of my front teeth with a non-toxic magic marker. Whenever anyone asked about Father I hissed and gave a wide, carnivorous smile. They couldn't run away fast enough.

But there was a cost. I became an object of whispering wonder, a circus freak. I overheard some say that I must have been the inspiration for Father's work. When I gave Barry my black-toothed smile, he laughed and said: "Dude you are so like 'The Inspiration.'" That name stayed with me all year. One girl was about to pass out in our hallway when she spotted my blazer and asked: "Are you 'The Inspiration?'" I told her in no uncertain terms that she was intoxicated, and she rolled up her eyes and exclaimed "It's true!" and fell flat on her face at my feet.

There was only one person in college who took an interest in me apart from Father's work. But this person's interest turned out to be the only thing more distasteful. I am speaking of a student in the dormitory named Max, a blond, clear-eyed boy from Munich, Germany. He admired my ties, had a penchant for Parchisi, and also found life in the dormitory insufferable. "These Americans are like animals," he once whispered over a game. "They lack all dignity."

We always played Parchisi on his neatly made bed. What joy it was to have our existences narrowed to the clucking of plastic pieces as they hopped along colored circles and those exhilarating crackling rolls of dice. After a while I hardly remembered where I was. It didn't hurt that Max invariably let me win. "It must be my lucky day," I'd say with an irrepressible smile as I brought my last piece home. He'd just stare at the board for a moment as if confused, then slouch against the wall, letting his long thin hands fall palms-up on the bed, fingers curled as if in transcendental meditation. He wouldn't move until I took one of his hands and began to stroke the palms, the joints, each cold bony knuckle. It took me far too long to discern what all that stroking was about.

"You're too good for me, Milo," he said one afternoon as I rubbed the base of his curved, womanly thumb. "No," I replied. "You just have to concentrate. You try too hard to knock my pieces out when you should be focused on getting your own pieces home instead."

"You don't understand," he said.

"Trust me, I've won almost every time we've played and I know—"

"You don't know anything!"

His hand squeezed mine. When I looked up I saw the moist beginnings of tears. He'd always taken his losses badly, but never like this. I suspected something else, perhaps news from home—I knew his Mutti and Vatti were having financial trouble, their little stationary store near the Marienplatz suffering under the competition of a pen and paper conglomerate.

"Are Mutti and Vatti alright?" I ventured.

He shook his head. "They're fine. It's you. You are the matter."

"Me?"

"Argh!" He banged his head back against the wall with not inconsiderable force.

"Max?"

Before I knew it he'd hooked an arm around my neck and pushed me atop the board. "Max!" Plastic pieces gouged my back. But that wasn't all. I saw his thin lips seeking mine, felt a shuddering bulge against my leg. With a scream I twisted free, grabbed the Parchisi board and struck him repeatedly as he curled up in a ball. I didn't stop until the board was in tatters and Parchisi pieces lay everywhere and Max was a sobbing mess. Then I ran blindly to my room. I was numb; I needed to think. But my next-door neighbor, a beefy footballer, was hosting an all-night party: laughter and hooting and a wall-rattling stereophonic din that lasted until dawn. I spent hours banging my fists and kicking my feet to get him to stop.

I spent the entire summer in a stupefied recovery at home. Aside from a twice-daily bath I was incapable of doing anything other than watching television and staring at my bedroom walls. I remember little of what I watched. There was a popular news item that summer on the local CBS affiliate about a man outside of Brattleboro who was eating, bit by bit, over the course of several months, a bicycle, a motorcycle, and finally his own brand new jeep. This story kept appearing with updates on the man's progress and photos of his disappearing vehicles. It was supposed to be an inspiring portrayal of the human spirit, but I couldn't help thinking how the man must suffer the most excruciating trips to the toilet.

Mother suspected I'd become seriously ill or had a nervous breakdown. She kept asking, before going out each day, if I was well. "Of course I'm well," I always said. Only once did she question my truthfulness. She hadn't gone out for some reason, which made her sensitive to loneliness and failure. We were in the midst of supper, just the two of us, when she trained her sunglasses on me and said: "Milo, you would tell me if school has been too much of a strain on your nerves, wouldn't you?"

"I'm fine."

"There's nothing bothering you?"

I sighed. "There is one thing. It's the quality of my education. That school is for idiots. I could learn just as much through correspondence courses. And think of the money you'd save."

"But money is no problem," she said. "Father's books are doing quite well."

"Even so. Waste not, want not."

She was susceptible to sayings and clichés. She never knew how to respond. So she just nodded and said: "I see." And that was that. There was no further discussion. It helped that she was already beginning to suffer migraines. She spent the next three days in bed beneath cold compresses, and when the inevitable envelopes from the college arrived—invoices for tuition, class enrollment requests—I hid them in my closet and eventually cut them to shreds with her huge art scissors.

I began taking correspondence courses for my undergraduate degree. I only had trouble finding a suitable program. I wanted to study military history and was forced to apply to a so-called "war college" in Georgia. I had to pledge to purchase a uniform and send videotapes of myself parading around according to exacting drill procedures. I set Mother's old Panasonic video recorder on the low patio wall and marched into and out of the frame. It was like making my own history, my own recordings of battle. This helped me tremendously to get over that awful college. Occasionally I'd stage an epic clash, crouching behind the patio wall and lobbing rock grenades with a terribly wounded arm in order to save my beloved comrades. In my secret diary I penned stoic letters from the front lines—usually the trenches of France—to an imaginary girl named Mabel I'd met in the penny arcades of London: *Dearest Mabel, I'm awfully lonely in this ditch without you, but the lads and I are doing our best to keep up our fighting spirit. Yesterday I potted five Germans as they tried to sneak through our razor wire. They hang there like scarecrows . . .*

I tried to involve Klara. She'd just returned from Boston following her divorce. That must have been a terrible fight too—the war wounds lingered all summer in her listless eyes and hands. I suppose I hoped our mutual tragedies would bring us closer, that we'd compare tales of the terrible world and feel grateful to have each other. In my wilder moments I even thought we might strike out on our own, escape our house and our past. Once I turned the camera up to where she sat on her bedroom's balcony and asked if she spotted the enemy or if reinforcements were on their way. But she didn't acknowledge me, not even when I waved a white handkerchief at her, not even when I asked her to photograph the scene for posterity and write brief enthusiastic columns for the readers back home. Her own interest in writing and journalism had disappeared by then—her typewriter consigned to a box of expired medicines beneath her bed. I overheard her on the phone telling a friend that she didn't think anything was worth recording anymore, that *the world was too much with us* anyway.

I think she was quoting poetry.

IT WAS LATE AFTERNOON. KLARA STILL HADN'T RETURNED. HER promise had meant nothing—the promise, twice repeated, that: *I won't be long.* I watched the sun sink and turn blood-red, ushering the night—a night I feared I'd have to face alone, or not alone because the walls themselves were already beginning to whisper: "*Are you there, Milo?*" I whirled around, saw the crack of the study's door, the shadows shifting on the other side. "*You can't hide from me anymore than you can hide from yourself, my son.*"

At last came the MG's roar. By then I was in the dining room. The clock was ticking. On the table lay a platter of pork roast and potatoes and Brussels sprouts. Marta had prepared it in the morning and laid it out just so. I listened as Klara stamped her sensible shoes and flung off her coat and strode into the room like a Cossack. "I'm starving," she said as she slid into her seat and stabbed a piece of meat.

"You were gone," I managed, "all day."

"So many things to do."

"But you promised not to be . . ."

"What was that? You've got to speak up, Milo."

For a time after her marriage she'd thrown herself into various charitable efforts, letter-writing campaigns on behalf of foot-bound Chinese girls, that sort of thing. She'd even briefly taught literature to troubled youths at an academy in rural Ohio. She didn't last long among those thugs—not after a student masturbated into the pages of *The Catcher In The Rye* during class. Tonight I wondered if something similar had caught her fancy, if that light in her eye were the familiar flame of self-delusion.

I tried to be cheerful.

"I meant to ask whether you were petitioning to save the rabbits again," I said.

"Rabbits?"

"The ones they use to test cosmetics?"

"Ah. No."

I waited for her to say more. She didn't. "Or perhaps the local Red Cross was conducting a blood drive?" I ventured. "And you decided to volunteer?"

She shook her head and kept chewing. It was as if she hadn't had solid food in weeks. She paused only to ask about my day. I told her about my progress on the trireme. "Really? You've done that much already?" Her lips hardly moved in front of that working jaw.

"I would've done more if I hadn't been interrupted."

"Visitors?"

"More of Father's fans."

I closed my eyes and saw them: overweight, middle-aged, in their flannels and bomber hats. One especially large woman had stepped forward to read something off a sheet of notebook paper—a tributary sonnet of sorts. It was horrible; I tried to slam the door, but she lunged for my hand, pulled it toward her and pressed it against her tear-soaked face. I described this to Klara in gory detail—that woman's soft fat paw, moist cheek, flaring nostrils reticulated with capillaries. "She smelled like processed cheese," I said, "and she wouldn't let me go."

"So what did you do?"

"I kicked her."

"What?"

"It was self-defense. Our home is our castle, Klara. That's what the law says."

"My God, Milo. What did the poor woman do?"

"She hardly felt it under all that fat."

She looked at me sternly, and I recalled how after the funeral she'd been the one to handle visitors—Father's slick-haired dentist Dr. Farraday, his drunken wife Billy Jean, the muttering manager of the Barnes and Noble, and a woman calling herself Petal who claimed to be Mother's "holistic healer"—relishing the role of Keeper of Mother and Father's Flame. She'd even begun talking about conducting house tours and readings on the patio, perhaps converting the attic into a public museum.

"I'm sorry, Klara. I suppose I felt unsettled, being here by myself."

She paused, her fork half-raised, as she absorbed my suggestion that it was really her fault. "There was a garden show in town," she said. "I didn't expect to be so long."

"You spent all day at a garden show?"

"There is much to learn."

I imagined this to be another of her self-improvement programs, like the time she'd taken a course in Bonsai. "Well I hope it was enlightening," I said.

"Very."

But something gave me pause—the way she glanced down as if embarrassed by this answer, then quickly changed the subject to cleaning the linen tablecloth. She had that distant look in her eyes again—distant, watchful, and maybe a little afraid.

That night we watched a wildlife program on television—lions devouring zebras, monkeys pummeling other monkeys, the narrator intoning that this was nature at its starkest. We were in the two high-backed chairs with extending foot rests, sharing a bowl of popping corn. Klara had her feet up, the skirt draped halfway up her pale veined calf. I thought of shrimp, that satisfying snap when you bite into them.

"I'm sorry again about today," she said. "About being gone so long."

"Are you going out tomorrow, as well?"

"Not out, no." She shook her head, then pulled a woolen blanket around herself and said: "There are things I need to do here at home."

I looked at her as she continued staring at the screen, its images flickering across those blocky glasses she wore for television. "Do?"

"Improvements." She reached blindly for the corn, which she began feeding between her lips. "Getting the house and grounds into shape."

"What are you talking about? The roof?"

"Among other things."

"I'm sorry. I'm at a critical juncture with my trireme and even the thought of a repairman pounding—"

"We've got to have it fixed. Did you notice the stains down the kitchen walls after last week's rain?"

I had no idea what to say. I never noticed such mundane things as stains on the walls.

We watched an elephant raise its trunk and emit a haunting scream. "Well I suppose I can concentrate on some quieter things around the patio," she went on. "Would you like that?"

"Yes. Thank you."

My attention was then diverted by the elephants laying waste to a tree. As a result I didn't realize what had just happened. Sometimes I blame the television—an instrument of thoughtlessness. But not in a million years could I have known what she meant. I had only a hint, a vague suggestion. Behind the glasses I saw her eyes. They sparkled. With excitement. Looking back I try to give her the benefit of the doubt. I tell myself she must not have known what she was doing. Or who he really was. But in truth I'm not so sure. Because she was also nervous. Biting her lower lip. She must have been thinking about him. About the actuality of him. *Him? It?*

I'm not sure of the proper pronoun anymore.

A local gardening columnist is crucified on her trellis, her favorite flowers at her feet. A week later a middle-aged woman is decapitated, her body slung across a waterfall. How are these killings connected to the nearby town of Arlington, Vermont, former home of Norman Rockwell? It has become the epicenter of a terrifying new art form known as "Blood And Guts," whose practitioners include the elusive figure of The Master and his star pupil, Keith Sentelle, the Albert Bierstadt of murder, who stages bloodbaths among dramatic nature scenes. But even The Master is unprepared when Keith tries to break free of his influence, to become a modern master of death. A Portrait of the Artist as a Young Psychopath *is John Crane's most complex, chilling creation—an exploration of the cold indifference at the heart of murder, nature, and artistic creation alike. It is an instant classic that will haunt well after the last breathless page.*

HE ARRIVED THE FOLLOWING AFTERNOON WHILE I WAS IN THE MIDST of a delicate operation requiring a smock and surgical gloves and a wire contraption I'd designed myself—an oversized gyroscope with tiny clips added to the ring. The clips held a galley slave suspended like Da Vinci's Vitruvian Man. I was painting his upper body—muscles, wounds, tattered clothes—spinning him to get all sides. Could I capture the grimacing agony of a life in chains? A life spent rowing the giant triremes? I was using my thinnest horsehair brush—perfect for a ruffian. Time became a distant historical concept measured in ages, not hours. Pericles' funeral oration seemed far more immediate than my measly lunch.

Still there were signs if I'd been attentive enough: leaves on the patio stirred into a vortex by the breeze, or the robin that banged angrily against the study window, nearly causing me to smear the galley slave's face. But it was an eerie silence in the lambent afternoon that finally gave me pause—a silence that was false, because even then he was making his way up the driveway and around to the back of the house. I didn't hear him; I heard what he caused, the hush that came over our world. I laid down my brush and listened. Through the never-ending howl of my tinnitus I heard the ineluctable *tick-tock, tick-tock*. I exchanged my smock for a blazer and ventured into the living room. It was the pendulum clock—the only thing that moved. That and the dust glittering in the light of a tall brittle window.

"Klara?"

I drifted to the French doors. She'd been on the patio, reading one of her interminable Victorian novels and making occasional flourishes of a pencil in a sketchpad. Now I saw the novel and sketchpad abandoned in the empty depression of her chaise.

Still I hesitated. I was on the precipice of something—even then I knew. Could I ignore the signs and turn back? The patio stones, the insects, the beating sun—everything waited for me to decide. In the end I just did it, held my breath and swatted my way to the end of the patio like the outdoorsman I never was. I remembered Klara earlier that day adjusting her hair in the entrance hall mirror, twisting the premature strands of grey beneath their darker counterparts. "Just freshening up," she'd said to my questioning stare.

"What for?"

"Do I need a reason?"

I descended the mossy steps. To my right lay the crumbling remains of an old stone banister. Its base was topped with the head of a stern, garlanded Roman that Mother had purchased in Italy many years before. Beyond the banister stood a line of overgrown bushes. I peered through them and spied a flash of blue. I leaned across the Roman's face where his proud nose used to be until I saw it: the eggshell blue of Klara's blouse. She was bent over, stabbing a small metal spade into the earth.

And she was not alone.

I spied blond hair and a weathered face that appeared hazy in the broken light. He was behind her, guiding her with sharp jabs of a finger—a snake's tongue shooting at the ground.

"Hello?" I called out.

Klara jerked. The spade fell from her hand. She didn't pick it up, just slowly raised her eyes. "Oh Milo, it's you."

I moved forward. "Is everything alright?"

The figure behind her remained hidden in the shrubbery. She whispered to him before saying: "Milo, I'd like you to meet Henri Blanc. He's a gardener. Henri, my brother Milo."

He stepped out from behind her. The first thing I noticed was his shirt: blindingly white and open at the neck, blond chest hair emerging like weeds through a cracked sidewalk. "A true pleasure," he said, holding out a hand. He smiled—confident, at ease—his face well-lined from the sun and his hair held in a ponytail meant to look more casual than it was. I recalled an image from one of Klara's magazines—a famous actor (Brad Pitt?) on vacation in Cannes—and I thought Henri resembled this man.

His eyes were a pale green and his voice low and serpentine—the vowels accented with a Western drawl and the consonants with a French trill that created the simultaneous impression of a cowboy and a fairy. Ple-*ZHURE*.

He came toward me. That's when I noticed more: how shallow and dead his eyes were, how waxy and fake his skin. Before I knew it his hand had enveloped mine—an iron-cold embrace that gave me chills despite the balmy weather. "How fortunate that you could come for such a quick consultation," I said, trying to free myself. But he wouldn't let go; his grip was like a cage, drawing me closer until I smelled his breath—earthy, like rotting mushrooms. He grinned: "I am a lucky man."

Finally I managed to writhe free, recoiling until I'd nearly backed into the old Roman. "I hope we won't impose upon your time too long," I breathed.

"It's no imposition at all," said Klara, oblivious to what had just happened. She smiled in a prim, proud way—a parent introducing a child to the neighbors. "He's been working for Elizabeth Silfer, whom I had over for tea recently?"

The image of that shambling mound of ruined womanhood rose like a spot of bile in my mind and momentarily blotted out the gardener. She was an old friend of Klara's, one she'd met again by chance in the local china shop. Time wreaks havoc, I know, but that kind of transformation—from bony pig-tailed girl to a walking jelly—was like the crushing sadness of a child's death. You always wonder what might have been.

"Anyway," Klara continued. "Elizabeth has graciously freed-up Henri for much of the summer."

"For the rose garden," Henri added with a smile, as if sharing a delicious secret.

"The what?" I managed.

Klara ignored me, waving the spade across the bushes like a wand.

"Over here we could put several ramblers. Albertines perhaps? Or Canterburys?"

Henri raised an eyebrow. "Perhaps Bonicas and Carefree Wonders?"

Her mouth became a whorl of pleasure. "Such profuse blooms."

They began talking as if I wasn't there, about floribundas and hybrid teas and something called lady's mantle. Wittgenstein once claimed that private language was impossible. He'd never heard this.

"We can under-plant them with some fragrant old-fashioned pinks," Henri began, ambling closer to Klara now and touching her elbow, caressing it almost. "So the colors will balance. And the scent. Yes, we can achieve a perfect harmony among all the senses. Perhaps Gran's Favourite, which has the scent of cloves?"

"Oh and Henri is willing to do landscaping, too," Klara beamed at me.

"The setting is just as important as the flower," he said. "There is no beauty without context."

Beauty without context. I saw how Klara hung on his every word, how her breath fluttered like an excited bird's. Was she blinded by his cheap charm? Or by a misguided sense of beauty: the prospect of transforming our grounds into some hideous floral theme park? That wasn't beauty, I wanted to tell her. It was manipulation. True beauty comes from leaving things alone, from watching nature at a distance and wondering what untouched treasures it contains. That's what Father once said, why he'd always resisted Mother's desire to landscape. It would have ruined the mystery.

"What's that rose with decorative hips?" Klara asked him.

"Ah, the Burnet."

"Yes!" She nodded—an eager child—and he smiled as if he despised her already—as if winning her over was proving too easy. "You wish to have Burnets?"

"Please, many."

He paused.

"What's wrong?" she asked. "Is there another one that's better?"

He tilted his head, gazing past her, studying the landscape. "There is. Only a little more expensive."

"I don't care. I want the garden to be sublime."

Their conversation soon turned to sun angles and prevailing winds. Klara led him away, walking along the shadow lines, keeping him close. I watched the way the sun bounced off Klara's straw hat to create an aura of light, yet was absorbed into Henri as if he wasn't really there. Then he bent to examine the soil. He took a pinch of it and rubbed it between his fingers. That's when I saw the scar. Up his left thumb, jutting into the hollow of his wrist. I was sure I'd seen it before. But where?

I drifted back to the study—to its dust-mote stillness, congealing paints, galley slave that hung half-formed, not quite a man but not quite anything else just yet. I took it all in: the desk, the bookshelves, the warships bristling across the shelves—all those hours I'd spent on every last detail. Only through the fog of memory did I eventually hear them: the patio doors, creaking steps, Klara's laughter and the tinkling of icy summer drinks. The fog of memory that had heard it all before: Klara and Father's languorous afternoons, their epic *discussions* about politics, theater, art. I put my ear to the door, expecting to hear more of the same, but then came something new: a click of a pen and that serpent's voice: "My accountants, they insist: please make it out to cash."

A chuckle. "I feel like I'm signing my life away."

I opened the door.

They were on the sofa, side by side, leaning slightly toward each other, their heads only inches apart as their thighs casually grazed. He had one arm folded like a bat's as he tucked the check into his loose shirt pocket. It was a protective, menacing gesture—the fingers beaking down, the eyes alight. I actually found myself searching Klara's neck for a bite mark—the neck she held open to him, pale and enticing. It was almost to break that spell that I said: "Hate to interrupt."

She turned to me—turned only her head as if she hoped I'd prove a temporary interruption. "Yes, Milo?"

"Have you seen Father's pipes? I was wondering if Henri might like one of them. Since we have no more obvious use for them."

"Pipes?" She laughed, a fluttering sound that suggested a courteous, exuberant politeness—nothing like real mirth but often as close as she came.

"I thought perhaps because he was French . . ."

"Do all Frenchmen smoke?" This was Klara, dabbing her eyes, turning that rigid smile on Henri.

"I'm afraid not."

"Of course not. How ridiculous. Milo, you are being ridiculous."

"They're very nice pipes."

"Yes, but if Henri doesn't smoke . . ."

"He might want to learn."

"He works outside, with his hands, in the sun. He doesn't want to smoke a pipe."

"Perhaps I might simply look at them?" Henri offered.

We hunted around the living room because neither Klara nor I really knew where Father kept them—he'd pull them out of crevices in the bookshelves or from the windowsill whenever he needed one. Eventually we found one in the cabinet below the television, with a few morsels of Father's tobacco, Balkan Sobranie, still lining the bowl.

"It is a very nice pipe," Henri said, holding it the way Father always did, his forefinger knotted around the stem.

"You can have it," I said.

He shook his head. "Not for me."

He handed it back. I took it by the lip, careful not to touch the stem, where his fingers had smeared dirt. I remembered Father's own big hands as he puffed away on those occasional Sunday afternoons, how he'd grin as I crawled to escape the smoke.

"I'm sorry about all this nonsense with the pipe," Klara whispered to him.

She led him back to the sofa, determined to *carry on*, which meant opening a rose book and ogling its abundant and sharply photographed varieties. Henri ran a hand across the page. He didn't seem to care that he was smearing dirt there, too. Or perhaps that just made everything more *real*. He murmured approvingly as she turned the page, as if the roses were trusted friends he wanted to introduce and they wouldn't mind his liberties. His fingers traced little circles around the pictures as he talked about *nestling a garden into nature* and *preserving the 'wild' in wilderness*.

"Yes," replied Klara, shrinking a little as she struggled to agree. "Yes."

Then he paused as if assessing whether this was the right time to press further, whether she'd been sufficiently wowed. He kept one dirt-streaked hand on the book in her lap. She tried to avoid looking at that hand—so dangerously near, separated from her *essence* by only a few thin layers of paper and cloth—or at anything else. "I hope it is not too soon to ask a favor," he said.

She shook her head.

"You know I've been working for Elizabeth Silfer for months," he went on.

"She's been so generous to let you come here."

"She hosts occasional dinner parties for my gardening clients. Only this summer, because I am here with you, she is having her dining room remodeled."

It took Klara a moment to catch on. When she did she nearly jumped up and toppled the book, which might have spoiled the moment and saved us all a lot of trouble. "It would be an honor. Truly. Wouldn't it be an honor, Milo?"

"Wouldn't *what* be an honor?" I asked.

"To host the next dinner party."

I held up the pipe. I meant it to seem like I was considering the offer. But he was already touching her shoulder, saying: "It is an honor for me, really—to build my dream garden here. A dinner party will be the perfect occasion to show it off when we have finished, don't you think?"

She nodded. It was settled then. I lowered the pipe and watched the muscles above his nose. They kept tightening and loosening as he smiled, as if someone else was inhabiting that ruddy skin, pushing and pulling to make it work.

Klara was always reminding me NOT TO RUN OFF WHEN WE HAD GUESTS. But on that day I was sure she wouldn't mind. I marched upstairs to my room. I switched on my bedside lamp—a gooseneck—and angled it down for better study. The pipe wasn't one of Father's favorites. It was too straight and plain for his taste. He preferred the elaborately curved ones that he could hold below his chin. He'd smoke this one mostly in the car, I recalled, or when he was in a hurry. I looked at the smear of dirt, the lines and swirls from Henri's fingers. Then I had a moment of inspiration. I opened the closet. Behind my winter boots lay a fingerprinting kit. I took out its brush, a tin of aluminum powder and acetate film. Carefully I brushed the powder across the dirt and pressed the film on top.

Nothing.

I tried again. Same result. Not even a smudge on the film. That's when I heard the faint sound of Henri's laughter from downstairs. *No*, I told myself. There was no gardener, no dinner party, none of this was real. I closed my eyes. I was dreaming again. I'd fallen asleep while working on the trireme. Any moment now I'd wake and there would be the squirrels and the hawk.

I opened my eyes.

The pipe was still there.

I threw it in the wastebasket and hurried to the window. In the driveway glimmered a silver Peugeot. How odd. I'd always thought gardeners drove pickup trucks or bicycles. Then I saw the man himself, *meandering* across the driveway, admiring the trees, the scrubby grass, the bushes around the fence, as if they were all his own, or would be soon. He paused at the garage door. It was a double-garage, and he stood on the right, exactly where the Volvo had been parked.

Would he have opened it if Klara hadn't flitted toward him, her skirt undulating like a jellyfish? I was sure he would have. But she got to him first. She was breathless, excited. I couldn't hear what she said. She pressed something shiny into his palm. He smiled as he dropped it into his shirt pocket, where he'd put the check, then began caressing her bony fingers. I couldn't believe it, yet I could, as he turned them over and pressed his lips against the pale inside of her wrist. Klara froze, her mouth open, before giving a quaint curtsey, an odd thing to do even for her. She kept standing there as he drove off in a cloud of dust—as the breeze rustled her skirt and the dark hair that hung haphazardly at her shoulders. I thought of her outing yesterday. Had she met him then, too? I also recalled previous errands—not as long, but long enough.

Eventually she trudged upstairs, looking as if she'd spent the day digging ditches or plowing rocky fields by hand.

I was waiting for her at the top of the stairs.

"Pipes?" she said wearily when she saw me.

"Father always loved them."

"I suppose you were trying to be nice. Were you trying to be nice, Milo?"

"No."

She strode past me, shoulders lowered, face impassive, as if she hadn't heard me, hadn't *wanted* to hear. But I refused to be deterred. She sat at her dressing table full of Lladro figurines—half-clad angels and unicorns—all this childish old-fashioned stuff she couldn't bear to throw away. She had her elbows on the table, palms pressed against her eyes. "I wanted to see if he smoked," I explained.

She picked up a comb, then set it back down. "He doesn't. Believe it or not, most gardeners don't."

"I know."

She sighed, uncertain what I was implying. "Anyway, it doesn't matter. He'll begin next weekend. Can you be on your best behavior by then?"

"But . . . "

"Yes, Milo?"

"Father loved these woods."

"He's not here anymore."

"They were his inspiration. And now you're going to . . . "

"Maybe we need a change."

"If only you'd talked to me first."

"I'm sorry, Milo. Everything's happened so fast."

"Like giving Henri a key?"

She picked up the comb again. This time she pulled it furiously through her hair. "You were watching."

"We're all alone out here, miles from anyone. Have you thought about our safety?"

"He may need to use the bathroom. Or someone on his team . . . "

I gripped the doorframe. "Team?" I felt my voice rising. I couldn't help it. "How much do you know about these people?"

She stared at the blank wall in front of her. "You're being ridiculous again. Just like that nonsense with the pipes. Henri is a well-known gardener. He's worked for Elizabeth Silfer for months."

"And before that?"

"He came from upstate."

I lowered my hand, trying to appear calm, having seen that my direct questions were having no effect. "What about our peace and quiet?" I offered. "We've just begun to . . . "

"To what?" she snapped, turning to me.

"To understand each other."

She threw up her hands. "You spend all day working on your models. Whole afternoons go by when hardly a word passes between us. Is that understanding?"

"Yes," I said, my voice suddenly small.

"Don't delude yourself."

I bit my lip, tasted blood. "How can you say that?"

"I'm sorry, Milo. It's just . . . " Her face softened. "I know you don't want a gardener, or guests, or a dinner party. You'd rather we lived here alone. But do you remember after the accident, when you begged me to stay and not go back to teaching? I told you I would but said we needed to make an effort to get to know people in the area. Do you remember what you said? That you'd always wanted to feel part of a community too? Well that's all I'm trying to do. That's all."

I had no idea what to say. I'd never *begged* for anything after the accident, only suggested that it would be good for her *own* peace of mind to remain at home. And when I'd said I wanted to feel part of a community I'd simply meant the two of us, Klara and I, because no one else had ever understood us anyway. So why was she saying such mean things?

I walked away without another word. I was far too upset to face my galley slaves—or even to read Thucydides. I went to the patio and its Roman, my one true and steady friend. His nose had been hacked off and his ears looked like a boxer's, yet he still bore the rugged handsomeness of a youthful Rocky Balboa. *Rocky*—the only film Mother ever took us to, her not-so-subtle warning against the ills of poverty. "*Do you see why school is important? Do you want to end up like him?*" she'd whispered as Rocky was mercilessly pummeled, and it was all I could do to laugh, desperate to stand and shout: "*At least Rocky can fight back!*"

I approached the Roman and put a hand on his forehead and explained everything as best I could. *Is it just my imagination that's making me wary of the gardener?*

Tu es miser, he said. You're unhappy.

But why?

Cum Caesar venisset, Pompeius miser erat.

He often spoke in parables. "When Caesar came, Pompey was miserable."

What can I do?

He said nothing at first, then I saw him nod, narrowing those sage and stony eyes. *Scruta illa frutices.*

Examine those bushes?

I turned. I thought this was another parable. Then something caught my eye. A gleam of metal. The spade. I glanced back at the Roman, wondering what I ought to do with it, but he'd said what he had to say—the rest was up to me. I removed a silk handkerchief from my blazer pocket and stepped carefully across the dirt. I reached down and lifted it by its rubberized red plastic handle. It was about eight inches long and came to a sharp point, with "Made in China" stamped across the back. It looked new, hardly used. I regarded its heft, its size, then it suddenly came to me, where I'd seen a spade like this before. The same place I'd seen Henri's scar.

I dropped the thing as if it were a hot potato. I stared at it. Then I picked it up again. Surely this must be a coincidence, I told myself. Every gardener must have a red-handled spade and scars. I thrust it into my blazer pocket and drifted back inside. Yes, I told myself, just a coincidence, because what I'd imagined wasn't possible—was a violation of the fundamental divide between fiction and life. Still I remembered the odd feeling I'd had when first meeting Henri. And then . . . It came back to me suddenly. Something he'd said when describing the importance of landscaping. I could swear he'd given a sly smile before the words had left his mouth. He must have known I'd recognize them. And I had. I hadn't wanted to, but I had.

"There is no beauty without context."

No horror, either.

Excerpts from *A Portrait of the Artist as a Young Psychopath*

(Dedication): "To Milo, who knows why."

> "Now listen, Keith, you can't have beauty without context.
> It's like a killing without pretext,
> Like everything you hate: all artifice and little art,
> An empty flourish of technique, no heart."

> But Keith had doubts. Was this another rule?
> Another boundary that was just a tool
> For bold transgression? It was hard to always shock,
> To make it new, to pick the lock
> Of ordinary life. But isn't that the role of art?
> To take what's normal and show its true and terrifying heart?

> He thought all this as he sat down to work,
> His toolbox and his spade, scarred hands so full of dirt
> That he could hardly grip the needle or the string.
> Behind him was the waterfall, the trees, the ring
> Of boulders he had made. The camera on its tripod
> All set to show the truth behind the great façade
> Of skin. He looked up at the sky and saw the crows
> And said: be patient! Then he smiled, bestowed
> On Alice all his comfort and his charm.
> Here, he said. Let's start with your arm.

I AWOKE THE NEXT MORNING TO THE SOUND OF RAIN LASHING THE windows and beating the roof. The house felt under siege. I curled beneath my blanket and squeezed my eyes, but it went on and on, with crashes of thunder like cannon shots and rustling leaves like advancing men. I heard Klara shuffling in the hallway, closing windows. She'd recently begun leaving them open at night. Then she dashed downstairs. I imagined water sliding down our kitchen walls and dripping from the low warped ceiling, leaking through the old casement windows and the heavy front door, seeping into the dank basement, filling the patio, flooding the grounds until our house became an island in a roiling sea. And Klara moving through the rooms clutching her nightgown, her face lit green by every lightening flash as she chose whether to do battle or succumb.

I missed breakfast. By the time I trudged downstairs Klara had buckets in the kitchen and rags wedged beneath the old French patio doors. Something brooding and dim was on the stereo—probably Chopin—and she stood in the living room, near Father's vast library shelves, with her nightgown loosely buckled and her face puffed from the morning's exertions. The storm still raged. But she was absorbed in reading. She didn't even notice me until I cleared my throat. I tried to smile with my usual pleasantness, but everything suddenly weighed on me: my irrational yet inescapable fears about Henri. I recognized the book.

"Father used to read this to you, didn't he?" she said.

I shook my head, refusing to be drawn into the memory, even as she intoned the words: "*I remembered, shuddering, the mad enthusiasm that hurried me on to the creation of my hideous enemy . . .*"

"No," I said. "Please."

"He was always fascinated by these old horror stories."

Why was she doing this? Why pick out *Frankenstein*, of all things, on a morning like this? "Are the leaks very bad?" I asked, glancing around.

"Not as bad as I'd feared."

She returned to volume to the shelf. "I received a letter from Father's literary agent," she said.

I struggled to recall the man's name. He'd only ever come to the house once, from New York, in his Audi and pressed khakis. "When was this?"

"Yesterday, I think. I didn't open it until this morning."

"What does he say?"

"He asks about unpublished manuscripts. Especially the sequel Father was working on. I know there must be something in the attic, but . . ."

I glanced at the rain-streaked window. There was a face. Hovering just outside. It looked melted, smeared by the water's refraction and its own glistening wetness. It saw me and smiled—not a white-toothed smile but something horrible and maggoty. I knew it must be an illusion, a warped rendering of the swaying trees beyond, but for the moment this knowledge did me no good. I heard Father's gravelly voice in the wind: "*Don't let them destroy the woods.*"

"Did you get it?" I asked Klara, determined to snap out of this. "The manuscript, I mean?"

"I don't have the heart to. It's still too soon. I'm thinking of your peace and quiet too, don't you see?"

All that day and the next it came down, sheets and sheets of rain. This was the way of Vermont summers. Every now and then a spell of winter's gloom breaks up the monotony of sun, sun, sun. I took advantage of the weather to work. I holed up in the study, trying to forget, to wash away everything from that dripping face to Henri's scar to Father's increasing agitation in the days and weeks leading up to the accident. I pushed it all out of my mind: Father's sleepless eyes, his irritability, the way he began to avoid me, even the time he tripped down the stairs and nearly broke his leg, yet seemed oddly *disappointed* that the injury wasn't worse. Yes, I washed it away, away, and soon the universe was no bigger than the miniature spear-points I sharpened, the chains I tautened, the support skeleton I laid down in preparation for the upper decks. I vaguely heard Klara drift around the house checking for leaks. But it meant nothing. I didn't even know who she was anymore. A workman? She might as well have been. I succeeded in this until the following evening, over supper, when we sat together at our usual places in the dining room. She'd lit a pair of candles. It was the storms. She was afraid of the lights going out. Their flickering flames shone against the wallpaper. "How is your model boat coming along?" she asked.

She was wearing a high-necked blouse with an ivory brooch— one of those carved ovals with a woman's profile. She'd occasionally dressed this way after her divorce. She called it "retro" but really it was like Emily Dickinson in her Sunday best. It was as if she rejected not just her ex-husband, but the entire era in which he lived. "Fine," I said.

"Isn't it good to work with your hands?"

I took a bite of sausage. She'd boiled wieners and sauerkraut because she didn't want Marta driving in the rain. "It takes my mind off things," I said with caution, wary of a trap.

"Exactly." She sipped white wine, eyes glittering behind her upraised glass. "Now do you see why gardening is so appealing?"

No, I didn't. If she wanted to work with her hands, why not knit? Or weave? Or do *papier mâché*? "I still fear it will take attention away from your charitable efforts," I offered.

She took another sip. "It's hard doing things that only have benefits you can't see."

"Think of everything you might do. Endow starving artists. Bring children's literature to Africa. AIDS research."

"I never knew you were interested in those things."

"Think of the impact. All those starving children…"

"There will always be starving children."

Since when had she become so hard-hearted? She set down the glass. "This is what I want, Milo. To start doing something here, at home."

"*Because of him? The man who has our key?*"

Had I said this aloud? I wasn't sure. She didn't move, didn't respond, just gazed at her fingers snaked around the wine glass' stem. "I've made up my mind," she finally said. "I only wanted to tell you . . ."

Lightening struck the nearby woods. It made a damp sullen whump. I leaned forward. "See? You've made the heavens angry."

She raised her eyebrows as if I'd just blasphemed something.

"You don't remember?" I said incredulously.

She shook her head. I had to spell it out. "You told me exactly those words when I was in the third grade. During one of your lessons about cumulus, cumulonimbus, and altocumulus clouds. You told me I wasn't concentrating on the differences between them. Then it thundered. You said I'd made the heavens angry and you hit me right here"—I pointed at the top of my ear—"and I still have a scar."

She took a deep breath. "Those were difficult times with Mother always gone."

"Well these are difficult times, too," I said. "Now that both of them are."

She sat back, shoulders drooping—all the resolution drained out of her. I picked up my fork and continued eating. I wouldn't let good sausage go to waste. Still the silence was oppressive—every raindrop like a finger's impatient tap.

That night we watched television. *Some Like It Hot*. Klara burst into frantic giggles every time Tony Curtis adjusted his wig or push-up bra. I pretended to laugh too, but it was difficult. Nothing in this film was funny. Cross-dressing? Girl bands? I suffered every minute. It was no wonder our country had to invade weakling states like Granada and Panama and Iraq to prove its national manhood.

But this movie did get me thinking about what makes something humorous and whether I could make Klara smile, even laugh. I suppose I hoped that if I did, I could take it as a sign—that the plot forming in my mind was wrong. Almost desperately I cast about for a laugh-worthy topic. The idiocy of our President? The mangled grammar of billboards? Homosexual marriage? All seemed too obvious and contrived. The following day I picked up a copy of the newspaper's Living section and remarked that I'd never understood its title. "Are the other sections not about living?" I asked. "Are they about dying?" I tried to move my face in a humorous way like I'd once seen Johnny Carson do, but she just looked at me and said: "Oh Milo, you're trying to be funny."

The Mormon boy came that afternoon, during a brief break in the weather. He had horrible acne and unblinking eyes, and every month he trekked up our winding driveway to insist we let Jesus in. They're making inroads in Vermont, these Mormons. They're like Postmen—neither rain nor sleet nor snow can stop them. I told the boy what I always told him: that Jesus and those other prophets were welcome but that he himself was trespassing. Then I pulled my old trick, reaching behind the door where many local residents store firearms. The boy turned and ran, and I laughed and laughed. Was this the sort of thing Klara would find amusing? Somehow I knew it wasn't.

Afterwards I finished installing the trireme's bottom deck. This was where the *thalamioi*, or lower rowers, were stationed. These were the ones who suffered—from the dank close quarters, from frequent seawater intrusions, and from the worst torture of all: the foreknowledge that if the ship were rammed, they'd be doomed.

Klara went to bed early, complaining of a headache. Mother had suffered terrible migraines too, losing entire days twisted like a mummy in her bed sheets with dark patches across her eyes. I made Klara another cream of mushroom soup. I stood in front of her door, waiting for the proper words to come: soothing sympathetic ones that spoke of *brotherly love*. Then I heard a sound. I put my ear to the door. She was whispering. Whispering so I wouldn't hear. I hurried downstairs. By the time I lifted the receiver in the kitchen she'd already hung up. I held the soup until it turned cold and filmy, then dumped it into the sink and scoured the bowl so she'd never know.

The rain stopped the following morning, leaving behind puddles and worms on the patio and fingers of fog in the distant trees. I didn't bother with breakfast. I wasn't hungry. I went to the entrance hall and reached for my shoes. To my surprise I saw that they were caked in mud. Had I left them outside? Or fetched the mail or spare modeling tools from the garage without remembering? I didn't know, and this disturbed me, so I tried to forget it; I kept my slippers on and began my morning's work. Soon I was preoccupied with sealing moisture cracks in the trireme's lower deck. But then came something else—a movement beyond the patio. It was Klara. She was in the bushes, sweeping aside branches and peering at the ground. I saw her perturbed expression, her London Fog's hood flat against her bony cheeks. I hurried to the French doors and removed the rags, cracked open the doors just enough to feel the damp on my face. "Taking a stroll?" I called out. "When it's still so wet?"

She stopped and shielded her eyes. The grooves of her cheeks were cut deeply by perspiration, giving her the appearance of a pale moist pumpkin. "Have you seen Henri's spade?" she asked.

I cocked my head. "Spade?"

"He left it here. To take soil samples after the rains."

"Whatever for?"

"It's how we decide on a fertilizer, Milo."

I paused, noting the plural, turning it over in my mind as I realized it wasn't meant to include me. "I'm sorry, I thought that after the past couple of days you'd decided . . ."

"Never mind," she said. "Don't trouble yourself about it."

She turned and continued on. I closed the doors. I returned to my desk, yet it was impossible to concentrate with all that stomping and bushwhacking outside the window. I glanced at the bottom drawer of my rolling cabinet, at the worn steel handle and crude lock. Should I say something? No. Let her discover the truth for herself.

At last I heard her slip back inside, her boots in the entrance hall and slippers in the kitchen. Then came a click, a whisper, and the hushed tones of another telephone conversation. I knew whom she was calling, but I didn't care—she was distracted, and that was enough. I fumbled with the key and pulled open the drawer.

It wasn't there.

I looked in all the others. I pawed over the desk, the bookshelves, even patted down my blazer. Had Klara taken it? No, she would have confronted me right away. Then who? I thought of my muddy shoes. Had I walked off with it myself, in a kind of *film noir* stupor? Then I remembered the face in the window.

Every sweat-moistened molecule of me screamed *don't do this*, yet I did—I slipped on my spare loafers and strode out the French doors, across the patio, past the Roman, the bushes, the little skirt of grass. Beyond the grass rose a hill. Atop the hill began a path—a path into the woods with their needles and looming shade, tangled oaks and ghostly beeches and dead undergrowth humid beneath my feet. I thought of Father's midnight walks, how these woods were a refuge for him, and I was certain that if the face in the window had been his—if he'd returned somehow to warn me, and perhaps taken the spade as a sign—I'd find the answer here.

I stood for a time atop that rise, the trees swaying in an almost ritualistic beckoning. *Why?* it was like they were saying. *Why do Klara and Henri want to destroy us?*

Exactly what I asked myself as I ventured forth.

I used to know these woods like my own pale knees—every crevice and stump and knoll—but now I found myself groping, led by instinct and half-memories down a path that was hardly a path anymore, just a gap between the trees marginally wider than all the other gaps. I fought through every branch—every greedy limb desiring a touch, a scratch, a raking *caress*—fighting through my own rising panic as I scanned the ground, strobe-lit by a leaf-pierced sun, for a white stone marker I'd made when I was small. "*This is for you, Klara. So you won't get lost.*" Could I really expect to find it now, after all these years? Something told me I would. After a few twists and turns I noticed a fallen branch. *Underneath.* I pulled it away.

There it was. The white stone. And on it a childish arrow perfectly drawn, eerily visible. As if I'd done it only yesterday.

It pointed to the right. I knew I was close. Here was even less of a path. I had to push through the trees with both arms high—through wet leaves and branches and, once, a spider web

I hacked away with a stick—until everything began to thin and I found myself stumbling into a sun-lit realm, a circle of vibrant grass between the trees.

"Momma had a baby and her head popped off!"

It was a magical place, one of endless possibility where I lay on the grass snapping heads off dandelions while Klara shrieked and ran around, arms outstretched, legs a bony blur. She was chasing pigeons. She hoped to train them to carry messages to distant shores. "We can have Pen Pals," she said. "And no one will ever know."

Laughter, forts made of fallen branches, endless wars against savages in the woods. We were pioneers living off the land—this was our country. In early spring, when sap began to flow, we marched about with hammers and spikes and buckets, harvesting maple syrup to sell to a local dealer. He'd give us a dollar per bucket—extravagant riches in those days—which we'd use to buy provisions for our rustic outposts: canteens and freeze-dried ice cream, pocket knives and signal mirrors. We were a rough-and-ready family, Klara and I, combing each other's hair, sucking the venom out of each other's snakebites, huddling together for warmth under scratchy Indian blankets. *How long can we last out here?* we kept wondering, leaving unsaid our deepest private hopes:

Forever.

But no. It couldn't be. No walls were high enough, no pocket knives sharp enough to protect our childish fantasies.

At first the savages infiltrated under cover of darkness, stealing food and spears, leaving behind huge footprints and the occasional crumb. It felt like a game to heighten our suspense, and each of us secretly suspected the other of playing it. Then one day, in the center of the clearing, we stumbled across ashes from a fire and scattered pigeon feathers. We were stunned. "What do you think happened here?" Klara asked almost indignantly, hands on slender hips. I shook my head. The whole forest felt on edge—the birds gone, the animals strangely silent. I'd noticed this on my way in, but had dismissed it as the product of my imagination, and now I struggled to keep this same imagination in check as I spotted one of the trees behind her. It was staring at me. How could that be? Gradually it came into focus. Still I didn't believe it. In the center of the trunk, nailed to it, was the oozing gelatin of a bird's dead eye.

I must have screamed. The next thing I knew we were running, breathless and frantic and more than a little excited by our find. For days we talked about it, in private whispers, while playing board games and hopscotch on the patio. Eventually the woods called us back, spoke to us in the language of children. We tiptoed into the clearing again. Everything was still there—the ashes, the nail, the eaten-away eye—shrouded with a reality that smothered any attempt at fantasy. We huddled beneath trees with sharpened spears, watching for what the woods would bring us next.

I saw him the following afternoon—a middle-aged man. I didn't get a clear look at him—just a face between the leaves— but I saw him scribble something in a notebook, a gesture that I knew with an intimacy that frightened me. "Milo?" My sister called to me as if from far away. I didn't respond, couldn't—I was too busy trying to trick my eye into *not* seeing him. Suddenly her hand gripped my shoulder and her uncertain smile hovered in front of me. "Is it another . . . ?"

I nodded. He'd dissolved into a cluster of maples. Still I recognized Father all the same. Then everything became clear, but no less terrifying. "Let's go," I said. "We're not safe here."

"What did you see?"

She looked at me, and that's when something came over her, because she gripped my shoulders hard and continued in a shaky dramatic whisper: "The devil?"

And now, as I stepped across the ant-eaten logs, I half-expected to see him again—older, leaner, but with the same savage gleam. The grass was overgrown and weedy, and everything looked smaller—the forts gone, the arsenal of spears and rocks weeded over. Still the sense of magic remained. I glanced at the trees. Many of the maples still bore crusted-over wounds. I picked a dandelion and popped off its head. It fell.

That's when I heard footsteps.

I whirled around. There, behind the trees. A shadow. In dark clothing. It melted away into the woods. Klara? Henri? Or was it. . . ? No, it was nothing. Just a breeze rustling branches. Or a nosy deer. Or maybe one of the 2,500 black bears, or *Ursus americanus*, still living in Vermont.

Or so I hoped.

It was on the way back that I spotted, buried in the trunk of a maple, a metallic glint that I first took to be an old spike. I blinked several times until I saw it, then wished I hadn't. I stumbled on, faster now, not looking at anything, the image burned into my mind of a slender pale trunk, cuts in the bark, and the spade's red handle sticking out of a gaping, sap-filled wound.

There is a feeling when first waking up in the morning, before dusting off the cobwebs of the mind, of being locked in a fiction—of *knowing* you're locked in a fiction yet being unable to do anything about it. This was the feeling I had as I stumbled into the entrance hall. I heard myself in words: *Milo stumbles into the entrance hall.* I began removing my shoes when . . . *Klara strides out of the kitchen, wondering where he's been.* I wanted to embrace her, to feel her corporeal existence, but it seemed, as in a dream, that too much lay between us: the black-and-white checkered tiles, the wooden bench, one of Mother's fuzzy fruit paintings and the chandelier with its crooked flame-shaped bulbs. And Klara's own implacable face, hovering before her like a slightly detached mask.

"Where were you?"

Her apron flapped with accusation. Beneath it she wore a white cotton blouse with puffy sleeves that gave her a vaguely piratical air. Her face, too, was slightly puffed, as if she'd awoken from a long but not restful slumber.

"Gathering supplies," I offered, stumbling through an implausible story about using real tree-pitch for the trireme's hull.

"In the woods?" she asked, narrowing her eyes.

"Is that a problem?"

"I'm just surprised, that's all. That you'd go traipsing around there on a day like this."

I shrugged. I knew I had to get away before I'd be tempted to blurt out the truth. So I started walking in the direction of the study. "Listen, Milo," she called after me. "There's a television program at six o'clock that I'd like to watch. If you'd care to join me for supper, I'll be at the table at five."

Klara spent most of the meal gazing at Mother's antique china cabinet, the one with the glass doors and interior lights. I stared at the opposite wall, at one of her paintings—a red rose in full bloom, its petals swirling toward a turgid center. I felt the ineluctable pull of falling, of invisible forces taking me into the dark heart of something.

"Marta is coming in the morning, now that the rains have stopped."

I blinked. Klara was looking at me, her knife and fork upon a smeared-empty plate. I had no memory of her eating.

"Good," I said.

"And Henri, too. I've asked him to come in the afternoon, after Marta leaves. I thought it might make things easier for you, not having so many people here at once."

I nodded. I didn't know what else to say. Finally I asked, "Do you think Father would approve of your garden?"

She pushed aside her plate and sighed. "Isn't it time we became our own people? And stopped doing what Father and Mother always wanted us to do?"

She didn't say a word during the television program—some interminable costume drama—and afterwards went straight to bed. I stayed up, unable to sleep, staring out the window at the trees, their leaves rippling like an ocean's waves. I kept thinking of an early Hawthorne tale, *Young Goodman Brown*, where the pious townsfolk reveal their true natures only in the woods, as "rampant hags" and "polluted wretches" in communion with the devil. It was the first story Father ever read to me, the first time he ever told me how *perceptive* I was, when I pointed out that Goodman Brown ought *not* to have seen his fellow townsfolk's true natures because it only made him unhappy.

But how perceptive was I now? I had only the vaguest notion of what was going on. A notion as implausible as a John Crane plot. And what was Klara's role? How much was she herself involved? All I *did* know was that our lives were about to change for good—that any hope I'd had, in those rainy days, that Henri wasn't coming back or wasn't what I feared him to be, was a Great False Hope akin to alchemy or world peace.

Wild nature tamed is nature lost, Keith thought,
It's sacrificed to our ideals, our hopes, our bought
And paid-for Disney-sense of peace, tranquility.
But it's a bald-faced lie!
The beast is always there, just buried far
Beneath our cultivated souls, machined and razed and tarred
So we can't see it. Here, Keith said, I'll rip it out
And show you: wilderness and savagery. I'll flout
Your laws, your norms, your sense of common decency,
Your feeling that the world has gone to shambles only recently.
And here's the thing: you'll love to hate. You can't ever have enough
Of feeling righteous outrage and disgust.
But that's your mask, your veil
Convincing you you might prevail
Against your own dark devil,
Your own requited love of evil.

CHIRPING BIRDS. SUNLIGHT. CRUNCHING TIRES AND THAT GREAT wheezing engine I knew to be Marta's station wagon. It was like a dream, except it wasn't—the sun flashed through my window and the digital clock read 10:03. Normally I woke precisely at 7:35 (all primes, hence my little joke: PRIME TIME). My alarm must have failed, or for once hadn't penetrated my sleep. Why not? I realized that I had no memory of going to bed. Between watching the trees at the window and this moment lay a chasm of forgotten hours.

I shot to my feet. I saw Marta in her faded blue uniform hobbling toward the house. She was carrying a sack of groceries, her left foot encased in a giant blue boot. It was such a relief to see her—this great matronly hope of normalcy—that I failed at first to register the oddity of the boot. I gave a little wave. She didn't see me. The smile fell from my face. I ran a finger across the windowsill, across the chipping brown paint and dusty glass, the little edges where decades of weather had blown in despite every effort to keep them out. I ground the dirt into my skin and made a soiled question mark in the pane, then one in mirror-image to form a heart . . .

When I looked up again Marta was gone. I panicked, ran to the bathroom to splash water on my face, then back to throw on clothes. By the time I arrived downstairs she was in the kitchen, unpacking the grocery bag. I saw how she winced with the effort of all those cans of my favorite peaches. "Here, allow me," I said, stepping forward. She looked surprised, flashing her heavy-lidded eyes as I plucked a can and slid it into the cupboard.

"You OK, Milo?" she asked.

"I should ask you that," I said, wiping my damp forehead. "Whatever happened to your foot?"

She shrugged her dumb old peasant's shrug. "Oh, it's nothing." Then she made the sign of the cross. In a way I envied her blind faith. Only after the accident did she ever doubt it, when I noticed in her a void, a listlessness, an occasional shuffling gloom—when she left feather dusters on the furniture and the toilets half-cleaned. But like a kayak she soon righted herself and carried on. She had responsibilities that gave her weight, while I—I always felt on the verge of floating away.

She told a story about her cat tripping her while she carried a box of food to send to her native Philippines. How many times had I told her to get rid of that beast? I explained how cats can transmit plague by a single bite, but then, because I didn't want to seem overly harsh, I softened my face and added: "Of course I can feel your pain."

Her thick lips trembled. It looked like she was going to cry. I was reminded that empathy seems to be what everyone—even Marta—desires these days. Not advice or moral guidance, only an empty recitation of the most obvious lie: *you are not alone.*

"Thank you, Milo," she said.

I finished putting away the peaches and slouched against the kitchen sink. "They had beautiful lamb chops at the market," she smiled as she began ripping lettuce into a colander with those meaty hands. I nodded and turned to a small potted cactus on the windowsill—a green lump of a thing with spikes like hair—and thought: *here's my chance.*

"Did you happen to buy this?" I asked.

She stopped. "The cactus?"

"That's right."

"You want another one?"

"No, no, I was just wondering"—I gave a short laugh—"whether you happened to buy it or whether Klara did."

She pushed out her lower lip as if giving the question considerable thought. "Both of us. At one of those fairs in the town. That was two, three years ago."

"Ah," I said. "Did my sister ever talk to you about a garden, or a gardener, or any of that sort of thing?"

"Just that she wanted things around the house to be beautiful."

"Did she ever mention that to Father?"

She shook her head. But I could see a hesitancy come over. I pressed on: "Did they ever argue about a garden? They seemed to be arguing all the time before the accident."

She shrugged, but otherwise kept her eyes fixed on the lettuce.

Klara was sitting on a chaise in her loose white summer dress, the one I'd never liked because it billowed over her breasts and accentuated the slackness of her upper arms. She was gazing out over the grounds and sketching in that rose book, biting her lower lip like a girl trying hard to please. Through the study's window I watched as Marta limped onto the patio with a glass of ice water. Klara drank several glasses of ice water per day, believing, as she'd read in a woman's magazine, that they helped the wrinkles around her eyes.

Klara shot to her feet and made all sorts of concerned motions as she ushered Marta into a chair. Marta sat heavily, her back to me, while Klara bared her teeth to the incisors like a mad tribeswoman. This is what often passes in her for laughter, this carnivorous expression. Gradually her face sank back into its normal controlled tightness as her lips quivered with speech.

I put my ear to the glass. I couldn't hear a thing. I didn't dare open the window. Then a solution hit me. I dashed upstairs, through the museum-like dimness of Klara's room. Quietly I slid open her balcony door. It was excruciating to be perched out there with nothing between me and certain death but six inches of uncertain masonry. Still I persevered, closing my eyes to blind myself, to hear their voices better.

"Please, Marta. You must have an X-ray. Should I bring you there myself? I have an appointment with the gardener, but I can try—"

"No, no. I will go tomorrow."

"You need to take care of yourself."

"Everybody is so worried about me! When I should be worrying about you! This gardener—he the one Milo talked about?"

"Oh dear, I can only imagine what he must have said. Milo hates what we're doing. He thinks it will interfere with his toy-making. Let me tell you, Henri is very famous, a distinguished member of the American and French Rose Societies and the International Gardener's Guild. He'll breathe new life into our home, which we've desperately needed for ages."

"Because of the sadness."

"The sadness, yes, I suppose that's it. Oh, I'm under no illusion that a garden by itself will make us happy. I just don't know what to *do* with myself anymore. I'm stuck here, you see."

"You're family."

"Yes, that's part of it. Milo is all the family I have left in the world. It's also . . . I've always had to take care of him. I have no choice."

There was a pause, during which I ran my fingers across the balcony floor, distractedly gathering pebbles and other lapidary fragments.

"I'm sorry, Marta. This is all obviously pent-up inside me. You know Father never let Milo go anywhere. He claimed he was being protective, but really it was terrible. Do you know why he kept Milo here?"

"Ooh."

"What's that?"

"A stone?"

I must have twitched. It didn't matter. I beat a hasty retreat and opened my Moleskin notebook. I always keep one in my inner blazer pocket because inspiration can never wait. With my tiny spy pen I wrote: "American and French Rose Societies. International Gardener's Guild."

Then I strode into the kitchen. The telephone book. I called a local florist. Annie's Flowers. A grouchy-sounding man answered, and I nearly hung up, but I forced myself to remember what Klara had said: "Do you have the telephone number for the American Rose Society?"

"What?"

"The American Rose Society."

"American Roadside?"

"Rose Society."

"Wrong number, mister. Try Triple-A."

I punched the plastic knob to hang up on this imbecile, then tried another florist in more metropolitan Manchester. Finally

I found a woman who gave me exactly what I required, and I dialed again, long-distance, to Shreveport, Louisiana. There was a faintly swamp-like ring before a woman's southern drawl informed me that I'd reached the American Rose Society. After a raspy smoker's cough that shook my earpiece, she asked how she might direct my most important call. I thought of rhinestones and trailer parks, fake eyelashes and gleaming motorcycles and toenails painted with the American flag.

"I wish to inquire about a membership."

"I can help you with that myself, sweetie. Is it for one or two years?"

"Actually it's about a membership that's already active. You see, I lost my card."

"Totally understand, hon. Now what's the name?"

"Henri Blanc." I gave a hopeful spelling.

"Well we've got two here in the computer. I'm guessing you're the one who's still alive?" She chuckled, slow and honey-sweet.

"It's funny," she continued. "Both have the same membership number. Did you die and come back to life? We'll have to straighten that out. Anyway, I've got good news. You're all set through the end of the year. Do you need a replacement card?"

"My Vermont address," I managed. "I assume you have it?"

"Sure do."

"Could you verify it for me please?"

"You'll have to give it to *me*, for security purposes."

"Of course."

I hung up. If only I had a cigarette. I wanted one, not physically but metaphorically. Something to pull into my lungs, to spark that little frisson of death that is supposed to lead to contemplation, insight, smoky divination.

I heard them before I saw them—Henri's Peugeot and a white Ford "Super Duty" truck—grinding to a halt below my bedroom window. I watched a tall hippie with tattoos on his forearms climb out of the truck holding a shovel. The implement looked brand-new, like the spade—even from a distance it had that gleam. Henri muttered a few words to the man before the man disappeared, the shovel over his shoulder like a bat. Still Henri kept standing there, surveying the driveway, the garage, taking it all in like he had on that very first day. At one point he reached up to stroke his neck, *leaned* into his hand in an almost sensual, feline way. Again I saw Keith in that gesture; again I had the feeling I was witnessing an impossibility. Then Klara emerged, waving and gesticulating. She kissed him twice, once on each cheek, something I'd never seen her do. She did it awkwardly, as if unsure which side to kiss first. Afterwards Henri brushed a stray hair out of his face and said something out of the side of his mouth—something that must have been amusing, because she leaned forward and gave one of her polite twittering laughs. This pleased him; he smiled; he took her hand and led her around the house so fast that she had to skip to keep up.

I waited until they were gone. Then I fumbled for my spy glass. I trained it on the Peugeot's license plate. Carefully I copied it down. I hurried to the kitchen and called the Department of Motor Vehicles. The woman sighed when I asked who owned the plate. "You know I can't give you that information, sir."

"Can you at least tell me if he's real?"

"Excuse me?"

I hung up and called the police. I pretended I'd lost my car registration. They referred me to an automated line where I could enter the license plate into the keypad to check for outstanding warrants. Our old phone didn't have a keypad, just a rotary dial, so I had to wait for a live person to help. It was one of the few times I've ever longed to speak to a machine. I had to read back the number three times before the gruff old man got it. "Sorry, son," he said. "There's nothing. That license was only issued a few months ago."

I drifted into the living room. They were outside. Talking. Henri was describing something with one hand while the other hung close behind my sister. How much did she know about him? Could she really suspect the impossible? Meanwhile the workman was digging up our old bushes. Klara clearly wanted to replace those ugly things. That's when it occurred to me that she might want to replace *me*—that *I* might be the real weed here. That she might be planning to pull me out and discard me like those old bushes—like Keith's hapless victims.

And install someone prettier in my place.

He'd heard it many times: the eye of the beholder
Determined beauty, truth, and all the bolder
And finer feelings men might have. The eye!
The eye! He laughed and with a wry
Small twist of that red-handled spade,
He dug it out of Mary Megan McCade's
Dead face. And dropped it in a clear and plastic ball
So it could see. Then tied the ball to a small
Army of balloons and let them go. Should he write a note?
To say how ugly she had been? But no. Too late.
At last she saw herself the way she really was,
A sack of skin, the beholder now beholden to his cause.

WHO VANQUISHED GOTHIC HORROR? THE VICTORIAN DETECTIVE. Take *The Hound of the Baskervilles*. It's stuffed full of Gothic elements—a fiendish hellhound, craggy moors, a crenellated old estate and eerie noises like sobbing women in the night. But Sherlock Holmes isn't afraid. He cuts through it all with science and deductive logic, revealing the cheap machinations behind the terror, and the jealousy and greed driving it. It's a simple story, really. A man is trying to kill a gentleman who has romantic designs on his sister. All the rest is puffery.

Science, deduction, logic—these were my touchstones now, my antidotes to the horror novel developing all around me. I would have worn a deerstalker cap and injected cocaine except that the cap isn't actually featured in the Holmes stories—it was an invention of the illustrator Sidney Paget—and I was too frightened of losing my mind (not to mention needles) to inject anything psychotropic. So I became Holmes on the inside, imagining myself in that "large airy sitting-room" on Baker Street, wreathed in pipe smoke as my mind worked over the problem of *whether a fictional character could actually come to life*. There was also something else buried deep within my fears, the nagging question of *how much of this plot Klara herself was responsible for*. Despite all signs to the contrary I convinced myself that she was just as innocent as I was—that she must know nothing of any darker story here.

Then I went down for breakfast.

She was sitting at her usual place, behind her usual newspaper, but I knew at once it wouldn't be a usual day—that we wouldn't have one of those again for ages. She was wearing a blouse I'd never seen—red, silky, dangling from thin straps. I stared at her like I would at an ancient frieze if one of its stone figures had popped to life and was lounging in short-shorts and a low-slung half-ripped tee-shirt. And there was more. With two lazy fingers Klara cradled a burning cigarette. She took a puff. Smoke shot out of her mouth. Suddenly I was in a fog; I could hardly see; I began to cough, my eyes to water, I got down on my knees and . . . No. Wait. She didn't smoke. There was no cigarette, no smoke, I never did those things at all. My memory is playing tricks. Yet there *was* something smoky-white about her, in her hair—a line of white along the fringe. It looked like a flare of sunlight or a bird dropping. But when I peered more closely I saw it was a deliberately colored white streak, a Bride-of-Frankenstein bolt of lightening shooting down one side of her face.

"Oh please, Milo, don't look at me like that."

"What are you doing to yourself?"

"You make it sound so serious."

"Since when are you not a serious person?"

"Can't I do something different for a change? Something a little rash?"

"When did you do this? Last night? This morning?"

"It doesn't matter. It's nothing," she said, flipping it back with a come-what-may jerk. "It's just fashion."

It is the mark of any civilization's decline when a long swoon into decadence takes on the trappings of fashion. That much is clear from even a cursory reading of Gibbon. But there is a private debasement as well, which Klara displayed with a half-twist of her bare shoulders, a defiant little shrug so garish in a woman of her age. It was like an impersonation of a younger, briefly fashionable version of herself—a self that scared me more than any other memory yet to surface in my mind.

She'd been a high school senior. The occasion was a school play. This play was directed by her English teacher, Mr. Mann—a greasy old bug-bear with his striped cardigans and his habit of watching girls' gymnastics competitions using opera glasses. That year he was staging a sultry adaptation of *The Iceman Cometh*. Klara obtained a part as a barmaid. I thought it was a joke until Father made a surprise appearance at supper to congratulate her. He stood in the doorway, hands in his pockets, his lop-sided smile showing-off those yellow British teeth. "You know I once dabbled in the theater myself," he murmured.

"Really?" Klara looked up from her soup. Her barmaid persona—which she'd been flashing all evening long—fell away in an instant.

"A vampire show. I think I still have the make-up."

"Could I see?"

Father shrugged. He never talked about himself, never revealed anything that would make us confuse him with an actual human being. I wondered if any of this was even true. "Well . . . "

"Don't be silly," Mother said, putting down her spoon. "Klara's playing a serving girl, not a vampire."

"But I'm interested," Klara pleaded.

Mother picked up her spoon again. "Another time."

Father was on the verge of saying something else when he stopped. He must have known he had no authority here, in the house's lower realms. "Anyway I think it's wonderful, Klara," he simply added. "O'Neill has always been my favorite American playwright."

She stared at the table. "I know."

She began never taking off her make-up. I believe this is called Method Acting. Really it's just forgetting who you are. She also started mixing Mother's drinks (Long Island Iced Teas in tall glasses) and chewing gum and talking like a New Jersey whore. I wish I could say the actual performance was any better—that seeing her in context made everything comprehensible. But it was an endless cavalcade of over-acting—bright young high schoolers putting on despair the way they'd put on a new shirt, constantly checking themselves in the mirror to see how it fit.

Then there was Father. He said he wouldn't miss it, and for once he kept his word. He sat perched at the edge of the folding chair like a bird, a black-clad parrot mouthing her words and echoing, in haunting miniature, her every grimace and smile and fake-drunken lunge. At first I thought he was just playing along. Then I realized it was far more sinister than that. He wasn't mouthing her words *after* the fact, wasn't *imitating* her at all. No, what I realized was that he was actually *controlling* her, *manipulating* her like he did me, night after night. I began to sweat. My fists balled up. Yet I couldn't simply punch him—that would accomplish nothing. He probably wouldn't feel it, or my fist would go right through him. So during the third act I excused myself and hurried to the bathroom. I hovered over the line of institutional sinks and mirrors until I was alone. That's when I took the dime from my pocket. Roosevelt was a strong President and the year it was minted, 1971, was an auspicious one—all odd numbers with a symmetry of first and last digits. With its rough edge I etched a large X in the mirror. I centered my reflection over it, cross atop my nose. I'd never done this before, but somehow I knew it would work. Though my resemblance to him wasn't as pronounced as Klara's, he was right there staring back at me—the small bloodshot eyes, the heavy brow.

When I returned he was gone.

I felt powerful that night as I turned off the light—more powerful than ever. The wind rustled through the trees and an owl hooted as if to congratulate me for what I'd done. Still I couldn't help being uneasy. For the first time I felt myself in a fiction. One where truly anything was possible. Looking back, I realize that even then I knew it wouldn't be the last.

After breakfast Klara strolled onto the patio. She stood with her hands on her hips, letting the breeze tease her hair. Meanwhile I hovered behind the patio doors, playing out various conversations in my mind: how I might tell her what I suspected and gauge how much she knew. I practiced such talks nearly every day, in steamy bathtub whispers or across the unlined pages of my diary. But I hadn't yet found a way to do it for real.

At one point she took up her sketchbook from the chaise. She cradled it in one arm and began to draw. I could tell she was distracted. I decided it was now or never. I propelled myself onto the patio. "Oh, hello," she said without turning. "What do you think of a little bower over there?"

She was gesturing vaguely into the distance. I didn't care. I was focused solely on my own careful words. "There's something wrong, Klara."

"Really? Is it too near the woods?"

"With Henri, I mean."

"Is he ill? Did he call?"

"He's—he's not what he seems."

She sighed. "You're still upset about my hair."

Then we both heard the car.

"I am so happy to see you both," he said as he climbed the steps. He wore a weathered beige shirt and faded jeans. His hair in its ponytail was as glassy and shifting as a springtime flood.

"I was just showing Milo where I wanted to put the bower."

He glanced at the sketchbook, then at her. He was too polite to say anything directly about her dress or the white streak. "Perfect," he said.

"Milo thinks it's too close to the woods."

"Not after we cut them back."

He glanced at me, and again I was struck by his eyes, how they shimmered with such clinical dispassion.

He turned back to Klara. "Come, let me show you." They descended the steps. I didn't follow. I just stood there watching. He held his hands behind his back as they walked. "You mentioned the garden as a tribute to your parents," he began, "but mostly I see it as a tribute to you. Please forgive me if I am overstepping . . . "

"No, please," she said, touching his broad shoulder. "It's true. For the first time in years I can see the possibilities. Of what *I* want."

He stopped and glanced around. He seemed to be judging distances. Klara handed him the sketchpad. "Do not mistake me," he said as he began roughly drawing. "Your father was a great man. In many ways he made me what I am. But we all need to become our own people in the end."

Klara paused. "Whatever can you mean?"

"In his books one senses the dark mystery of wilderness. But we can tame this. You see, he has inspired me."

He held up the sketchbook. I could just make out what it showed. The woods cut back, the land plowed into rows, its *dark mystery* expunged.

I'd hardly moved when, around noon, a pair of workmen arrived with great bags of fertilizer across their shoulders. Henri and Klara were still traipsing about. He was talking about *Gaia, Rebirth, Nature's endless recurrence*—obvious manipulation-words—and I could see how they affected her. And me, too. I actually got the feeling he was saying these things for my benefit, in a sort of coded language—telling me *he* knew that *I* knew exactly who he was.

Then he saw his men. Suddenly I sensed a different act, a different audience. He whistled at them to stop. They looked at him with more annoyance than fear, as if they'd rehearsed this moment many times against their will. "Take those bags back," he said. "I told you *not* to use sodium nitrate. It will only ruin these clay soils. How many times must I remind you to use my natural alternative? Is it in the truck?"

One of the workmen nodded.

"Come," he said to Klara. "Let me show you my secret formula."

I watched them go. Yet their effect lingered on. The gusty, unpredictable breezes, the harassing flies, the shrieking birds—everything around me seemed agitated somehow, in flux. Even the recent rains could be interpreted as a sign of divine displeasure, of the heavens out of sorts. That's what Klara used to tell me when it stormed. Also how Father himself once wrote it, in one of his darkest, grimmest tales:

> *The thunder crashed, the waves welled up and down,*
> *And Martin should have known 'twas time to turn around,*
> *To listen to the signs and portents,*
> *The weather-churned and evil torments*
> *That plagued his mind, that fed his rage,*
> *That made him keen to set the stage*
> *For his own ruin. But in the end he didn't care.*
> *He knew himself; he measured what he'd done,*
> *Still saw the child, a neighbor boy, so curious about his gun,*
> *And pointing it at his own head, was playing with the trigger*
> *When Martin interceded, saved him. Hero to the neighbors, yes!*
> *And to himself? He'd placed the gun right by the bed,*
> *   then got undressed,*

Said: "Here, young man, you owe me." He saw the look
  in that boy's eye,
Betrayal, sure, but more. Respect for Martin's honesty?
More like expectation.
For Martin, like the ancient gods of Greece, had quite a
  reputation.
(From *Fair Weather Fiends*)

Yes, I knew something was coming—knew it in my bones—
yet it wasn't until mid-afternoon that I saw what it was, what
our own *signs* and *portents* amounted to. I was in Klara's room.
Occasionally I do this, sit on her four-poster bed and smooth a
hand over the crinkly pink cover she's had for years, an innocent
girlish thing she could never let go. Would she now? I wondered.
I was already becoming nostalgic. I picked over the items on her
nightstand—a fat novel (*Middlemarch*), lip balm, hot water bottle for her back, an old *Cosmopolitan* magazine (devoid of white
streaks). Really I was breathing in the scent from her pillow and
thinking of childhood—the smell of her dresses and knees, her
laughter, her teasing—before everything had become so complicated, so adult, between us. I was in a kind of reverie, lost in
those lost years, when it all came crashing down—when I heard
a great crash at the bottom of the stairs.

I jerked upright, suddenly alert to the *here and now*, half-ex-
pecting the door to fly open at any moment and for Klara to
stand there aghast, accusing, *agape*. But all was silent. I crept
across the room. I opened the door.

"Hello?"

"It's nothing, I'm OK," came Marta's voice—a plangent cry.

I bounded down and found her there, at the foot of the banister, her dark arms and heavily stockinged legs clawing the air like
an overturned beetle's. I gripped her crepe-paper arms. They were
cool and spongy. I helped her up. "What happened?" I asked.

She hobbled into the kitchen and fell into a chair at the wood-
en table where she ate. "The floor must have been wet. I didn't
pay attention."

"Had you been washing it?"

"No."

I went back into the hallway. Only then did I notice the dirt tracked everywhere. Not just dirt—also pine needles and leaves. I marched out the patio doors. There was a workman raking a hoe. It wasn't the tall hippie but a skinny young man with hair greased to a point like some drug-addled rock star soon to die from a heady dose of heroin and fame.

"Have you seen my sister?" I asked him.

He stopped work and glanced into the distance, at the birds circling over the woods. That's when it occurred to me that Henri had taken her out *there*, into Father's realm, and without waiting for an answer I hiked past the workman, hiked straight up the now-barren rise. The trees loomed impassively in front of me, giving nothing away—no broken branches, no footprints, nothing to confirm my fears. Still I knew they could have entered at a different path—there were several leading in. I strode along the latticework of branches. The ground became muddy and damp.

At the next path I saw it, the fresh stamp of a boot heel.

Before I'd made a conscious decision I'd plunged back inside, stumbling over fallen branches, trying to ignore the creatures chirping all around—that excited, *eager* sound. I crossed a shallow ravine. On the other side lay a mound of stones—an Indian grave, as we'd once called it. I hiked up to the intersection of the path that led to the clearing. I stopped and glanced every which way. Something was missing. The spade in the tree. I could have sworn it was right here.

There rose a mocking clash of leaves.

I panicked and hurried on, telling myself it must have been there, that I must have missed it or gotten the wrong intersection, the wrong path. Up ahead I saw sunbeams. A promise of happiness, warmth. I picked up my pace until the leaves had thinned and I spied, in the clearing, the telltale flash of clothes, different-colored clothes close together. *Huddled.* Huddled and bent over. I lunged behind a bush. Did I really want to see?

I couldn't resist.

Darkness. That's what it felt like—a great darkness clouding my mind, a vision of Satanic rituals and all the lascivious acts New Englanders used to imagine occurring in the woods. Klara and Henri were standing over the ruins of one of our forts. Her hair was disheveled. She was holding a Chilton's Auto Repair Guide and wire-cutters.

"I can't believe this," she said.

She was flipping through the book. Henri thrust his hands deep into his pockets, a gesture of seeming innocence. "It was hidden beneath that log. I do not know what made me look there. What does it mean?"

"The pages are all wet and stuck together. It's very hard to read."

A terrible memory came to me: the shadow I'd seen when I was last in the woods.

"Here," she went on. "Diagrams of brake wires, with handwritten instructions for accessing them."

"The handwriting. Is it Milo's?"

"It's very smudged. I can only make out a couple of words. Oh God."

"What is it?"

She pointed. "Volvo."

He touched the small of her back as she lowered herself down, her hand groping until it found a log to sit on. Henri sat next to her. "We should call the police, no?" he said.

She shook her head.

"You said you had doubts about your parents' deaths," he went on.

"No, no."

"We have a duty. The police could investigate. Inspect the car."

"It's gone. Totaled."

"We can't simply ignore what we've found."

She paused. "Maybe this was just Milo's way of understanding what happened."

"You give him great benefit of the doubt."

"He's the only family I have left." She leaned against his shoulder. "Maybe I should have warned you. As a child he could be so quiet and innocent, then do something terrible, pretending it was a game . . ." She closed her eyes. "He had a hard time with our father. We both did."

"A lot of people have had hard times with their fathers," Henri said. He looked at his hands. "Did I ever tell you of mine? He insisted my brother and I join the Army. He whipped us with his belt to get us used to the discipline."

"I'm so sorry. I had no idea . . ."

"What I am saying, Klara, is that I have changed. I grew up. I escaped him. So your brother . . . If he did this, it can be no excuse, what happened years ago."

What was he saying? That history didn't matter? That we were all born yesterday?

She glanced down. "There's something I ought to tell you. About me. It's not just Milo—"

"Shh." He touched her chin. "What is past is past, Klara. You don't have to tell me anything." He reached down to pluck a dandelion. "How perfect these are," he said, pushing it into the hair above her ear. It hung there, drooping. "You deserve to be happy."

I barely heard her voice through a tear-choked smile. "I don't even remember what that means."

I had no idea how long I sat there. At one point I noticed insects buzzing against my face and moisture on the seat of my trousers. When I looked up again Klara and Henri were gone, the clearing empty, and I wondered if I'd been dreaming again—if this had been a trick of light and sound. Then I realized what I hadn't heard. She hadn't told him it was impossible—that I'd never sabotage the Volvo because *I did nothing all day except build models out of wood and plastic* and was a *harmless house-bound boy*. She would have said such things in my dreams.

The young workman was gone when I returned—his hoe abandoned in the soil, the patio doors open, sounds of commotion emanating from within. Then he appeared in the doorway, smirking as if eager to see what would happen next. "Your sister is asking about you," he said.

She was in the entrance hall, hair disheveled, face clenched in a grimace that would have been appropriate in charades to express divine wrath. "I can't believe you abandoned Marta," she hissed.

I opened my mouth. I was still a little dazed. I wanted to rewind history's clock, to put our relationship on firmer footing for this moment. But I was compelled to speak the simple truth—that Marta had slipped on the dirt *her* workers had brought in, no doubt using the key *she'd* given them, and that I'd only left Marta to find her.

"Me?" Klara said. "Why?"

"I needed to talk to you."

"About what?"

"The difference between happiness and delusion."

She threw up her hands and stormed out the front door, leaving me alone on the entrance hall's sea of chessboard tiles. *Pawn on Queen Four.* I heard a car engine hum to life. I went to the door. The workmen were helping Marta into the Peugeot. Henri was making a great show of inspecting the engine as Klara circled to the passenger door. "Get back inside, Milo," she commanded. "We're taking her to the hospital."

"Wait."

I moved forward. But I didn't get very far. Klara intercepted me, holding up a hand. "We'll talk later," she said, her voice soft, almost pleading. She was breathing heavily through her nose. Beads of perspiration hung across her upper lip, bringing into relief a thin line of hair. All around us was silence—the workmen had stopped moving—and her breathing was the only sound, her face the only object with any life. She pushed the white streak off her forehead. "Just go back and wait."

"Don't do this," I said.

"We have no choice. Marta is hurt."

"That's not what I mean. Don't think you can write this story however you want."

"Come quickly," called Henri. "She's in pain."

Klara turned and walked away, choosing *him.* They drove off—averted faces, crunching tires—while the workmen vanished around the side of the house and the dust settled all around me. What would she say if I just walked off into the woods? I wondered. Lay down beneath a tree and never moved, becoming a mossy mound that someone found years later and wrote sad poetry about?

Ode to a Forgotten Corpse.

I wandered back inside. I stopped at the line of hooks in the entrance hall. The MG's key dangled there like a half-forgotten talisman. Father used to rub it—for good fortune, he said—before traveling the countryside looking for old houses to inspire the settings for his books. This was when I was very young, before he was satisfied with just having me.

I took the key and rubbed it with my thumb.

The garage door opened with a sound like cars rushing over a metal bridge. I saw the blank spot on the wall where the wire cutters used to be and an old workbench where I'd last seen the Chilton's Guide. Henri could have easily stolen them, but... when did he have the opportunity? That's when I remembered the footprints on the morning after the rains, muddy and filled with water, leading right up to this door. From where? I closed my eyes. From the house. That was why I'd ignored them, assuming they were Klara's. But if Henri had parked further down the driveway, where his car wouldn't be seen, and walked the rest of the way, he'd emerge from a hedge on the side of the house and approach the garage from there.

I leaned against the MG—sleek and blue like a fish—as I pondered this possibility, knowing I wouldn't be able to prove it, wondering how much that even mattered now. I climbed inside. The car was cramped and smelled like Father—a musty, feral scent emanating from the cracked leather seats. I held my breath and turned the key. *Chigger chigger*—a clown's evil laugh. Was the car itself mocking me? I tried again.

It coughed to life.

I didn't have a license. But Klara had taught me to drive like she'd taught me everything else. I focused on the delicate dance of clutch and brake pedal and gas, swerving down the driveway and nearly running into a wretched elm. At the bottom I turned left. I managed to keep to the road. The trees gathered overhead, curious and dark. They were like all native Vermonters—rigid, ill-spoken, menacing in crowds.

I lowered the window. Wind felt good. Soon I reached a bullet-riddled sign that read "M14." A swath of cracked pavement led toward town—an outpost of illusory civilization where the mountain folk went when they wanted to practice standing in line and tucking in their shirts. But at least it wasn't a "cosmopolitan center" like Burlington or Brattleboro. One didn't encounter transient students or "civilly united" lesbians or fur-clad New Yorkers doing "outlet shopping" or "après ski."

I suppose I should say its name. Battenkill. *Kill* from the Old Dutch *killa*, meaning a riverbed or channel. Battenkill is where Klara's favorite china shop is located and where there's a medical clinic with more than a single doctor. Actually it's the medical clinic with virtually all the doctors, having absorbed or driven out of business eleven other medical offices in the surrounding region. This has caused some people, including Klara, to refer to it grandiosely as a "hospital" even though it consists of a single brick building and performs only the most rudimentary surgeries.

I sped toward Battenkill, the town, along Battenkill, the river, crossing the water several times over covered wooden bridges—the sort tourists love but locals hate because they have only a single track, so whenever a car comes from the opposite direction there is endless maneuvering over who will cross first. But on that day I didn't care, didn't slow down at all. I felt an accident would be preordained or not, and there was nothing I could do. I passed an old green road sign that read "Battenkill" and "Pop. 3888" and "Elev. 3525 ft." Then came a few slumping shacks and prefabricated monstrosities with aluminum siding and backyard trailers. The town's center was a row of dilapidated red-brick storefronts built during some long-forgotten industrial age, flanked on one side by a concrete municipal structure and on the other by the post office. The clinic was a good mile or two beyond.

In town I was impeded by an old woman in a powder-blue Buick who drove like an old woman in a powder-blue Buick. Finally she veered up onto the sidewalk, as I knew she eventually would. Within seconds the post office was behind me. Then the clinic's ever-illuminated sign appeared between clusters of bushes on my right: *A Service of the United Healthcare Network, The Nation's Healthcare Provider.* This sign was the only new or refurbished thing about the place, other than a façade painted to look like windows and a corporate banner fluttering above the entryway that depicted little silhouettes of people in different colors holding hands.

The parking lot was behind a screen of bushes. I stopped some distance away and approached on foot, not trusting my ability to circle back. The Peugeot gleamed in the sun. I cupped a hand over my eyes and peered through its tinted windows. I saw no

Chilton's guide or wire-cutters. I slipped my fingers beneath the door's handle, but it was locked. Then I remembered what was in the MG's trunk. I hurried back and fetched it—an old wire hanger. I slipped it below the Peugeot's window, fished it around. I'd seen this done in police shows and read about it in Father's books. Still I was amazed when it snagged. I lifted, heard a click, and opened the door.

The button for the trunk was beneath the seat. I pressed it. The book and wire cutters were in the wheel well, where everybody in novels conceals everything. I slid them inside my blazer. Then I glanced around. Nobody was near. I returned to the driver's door and squeezed into the seat, nearly overwhelmed by the new car scent, that odor of volatile organic compounds clearly in excess of EPA guidelines. It reminded me how new Henri's car was, just like his spade and shovel—how everything about the man seemed to be of recent manufacture.

I opened the glove compartment. A sheaf of papers. I flipped through them: receipts for soil, seeds, various chemicals. I tucked one of them inside my blazer pocket, but the true prize—a car registration with Henri's name and address—was nowhere to be found. Was this itself revealing? I began poking my hands into any other plausible place—lifting the plastic armrest, pulling out the cup holder, peering into the thin recess beneath the radio. The man was a blank.

I was just bending beneath the imitation leather seat when I saw, out of the corner of my eye, a shimmer at the clinic's door. I didn't move. I remained half-crouched, my tie hanging down, a sheen of perspiration erupting across my skin. Slowly I raised my head. A bird was watching me—an old blackbird with jaundiced eyes. When it turned to peck at a weed I grabbed the charm hanging from the rear-view mirror, a plastic rabbit's foot, and flung it into the nearby shrubbery. The bird didn't move. I took out the MG's key and gouged a tiny question mark into the car's sleek outer skin.

The bird flew away.

I hurried back to the MG and stashed the Chilton's guide and wire-cutters beneath the seat. Then I approached the clinic door. It was not automatic, so I had to go to the side and punch a blue shield with an outline of a wheelchair. The lobby was bathed in a fluorescent light that reflected harshly off the speckled linoleum floor. Soporific music seeped out of ceiling speakers. A couple of formless hags leaned on canes and an old man couldn't keep his jaw from clicking up and down. Only a young Hispanic boy appeared sentient, holding his hand and whimpering into his father's shoulder. There was also a hanging television on which an earnest newscaster intoned: "We're United Healthcare, here to serve you better."

There was no sign of Henri or Klara or Marta. I approached the counter. "Excuse me?" I said to the nurse behind it. She was a young woman with long red hair like they used to burn witches for having. Her cheeks were chubby on their way to being fat and her dimpled chin receded. She reminded me not just of witches but also of a girl I once knew in middle school, Veronica Stimmel, a ponderous bookish lass who thought I might share her interest in silly novels about gnomes and warlocks and impossible journeys through icy realms. "*You remind me of—*" she'd said one day, uttering some unpronounceable name, *Etihadilough* or *Letihoulituff*, a name supposed to sound noble and brave, not like the stupid *kerfuffle* it was. I'd laughed. There was nothing else to do. She stared at her blocky feet, which had drifted close to mine, and when my laughter died I said: "I'll tell my sister. She'll find it hilarious, too." And that was the end of Veronica Stimmel.

This one, though, seemed less reticent, less easy to dispatch. She was scrutinizing her fingernails and talking rapidly into the telephone. "You've got to tell him to open up to you. I mean how were you supposed to know what that old radio-controlled speedboat meant to him?" She smiled at me, a quick sideways stab of lips, and pushed a clipboard across the countertop. It held a sheet of paper with "Patient Information" printed across the top and several blank spaces to be filled in.

"I'm not sick," I said.

She held up a finger. "He also needs to learn to admit he can't fix everything. Just tell him to buy a new one already and get over it."

"My sister, Klara Crane, and a gardener who goes by the name 'Henri' just brought our housekeeper Marta in a few minutes ago."

She frowned and thrust the finger forward more intently, like showing off a paper cut. Her fingernail tapered to a perfectly oval point. "Listen, I got to call you back." She slammed down the receiver. "What is it you want, sir?"

I cleared my throat, recalling other girls, haughty vixenish things trying to maximize their few precious years of youthful bloom. It was satisfying to see this one already past her prime— the skin falling slack beneath her eyes and her hair hanging limp across her shoulders. But the way she clung to her attitude told me she didn't know it yet.

"My sister, Klara Crane and a gardener named Henri brought our housekeeper Marta in here, and I wanted to know whether they had to fill out forms with—"

"Marta? Marta what?" she snapped.

I sighed. "Surely there can't have been more than one person named Marta who just arrived."

"Doesn't matter. We've got rules, sir. I can't let you in if you don't—"

"I'm sorry. There seems to be a slight misunderstanding. I don't wish to go in. I merely wish to see whether this gardener has filled out one of these forms."

"Everybody has to fill out a form. Those are the rules."

"Yes, good, I see we both appreciate rules, now if I might just be able to see this form?"

She gave a pert little smirk. "You must be kidding."

"I can assure you I am not, generally speaking, a kidder."

"Then who the hell do you think you are, mister?"

I cleared my throat. It was always so tedious speaking with members of the public. I found I had to constantly explain myself as if to a child. "As I just said, I'm Marta's employer, and it was my sister Klara, Klara Crane, who came in here with the gardener."

She blinked and looked at me.

"You probably haven't filed their forms yet," I continued. "Look, what's that on your desk?"

I pointed to a filled-in Patient Information sheet, which she quickly covered with her freckled elbow. "Rules are rules, sir. Now don't make me call security."

I smiled, half turning to the others in the room, who remained stupefied by their ailments, and then, finally understanding her, pulled out of my wallet a pair of twenty dollar bills. "I trust this should suffice," I said in a low voice.

She rolled backwards on her swivel chair. "Hey! Ralph! Can you help me out here a second?"

I could see she was serious. There was no use continuing. I turned and walked away, past the gauntlet of infirm limbs. I didn't wait to punch the blue shield on the inside of the doorway. I thrust my shoulder against the glass, thinking: *what am I running from? I haven't done anything wrong.* But I knew I had. I'd botched the interrogation. Sherlock Holmes would have done it much better—would have disguised himself as an inspector and demanded to see the hospital's paperwork. I pushed my hands into my pockets and told myself there was a good reason I hardly ventured into town. I couldn't navigate it; I was not welcome here.

This time it was easier to start the car. I drove to the Battenkill river and stopped in the middle of the bridge. I reached beneath the seat. The Chilton's guide and wire-cutters were still there. I flung them into the water and watched them bubble away, the wire-cutters disappearing instantly, the Chilton's guide holding out a little longer, swirling and scrabbling to stay afloat. Then I pulled out the receipt. It was dated some months ago. It was for five fifty-pound sacks of organic fertilizer and something called "pH balancer." The letterhead was from a "Girardi & Sons"—the logo printed inside a silhouette of a greenhouse—with an address on "J" street, only a few blocks from the center of town.

I held the receipt as I drove, turning left at the post office, then right down another tree-lined street. "Girardi & Sons Gardening and Nursery Supply, Since 1946," was painted on a swinging sign. Behind the sign lay an old ramshackle building with aluminum siding and a greenhouse with several broken windows. The driveway was lined with potted plants, which I had trouble avoiding as I parked, crunching one beneath my tire, toppling another when I swung open the door.

I began in the greenhouse. Almost instantly I was struck by its moisture, the physical sensation on my skin and the dank metallic stench. There were plants everywhere—small buds, blooming flowers, half-sized trees—lined up in rows like slumbering troops. But otherwise I could tell right away that I was alone. I've spent enough time in solitude to recognize the stillness, to know the signs.

There was a door at the far end. I passed through it. I found myself in the main house. In an office.

"Hello?" I called out.

The room was small, with a heavy wooden desk in the center and wood-paneled walls. On the walls hung pictures of oarsmen and flowers and lions emblazoned with the words TEAMWORK and QUALITY and SUCCESS. There was also a rifle hanging behind the desk. I walked up to it and leaned forward. I could hardly believe my eyes. An authentic World War II M1 Garand.

"It was my dad's. He started this business after the war."

I whirled around. Behind me stood a rock of a man—his short sleeves taut around his biceps, his forearms webbed with veins. Beneath a loose silk shirt moved tectonic plates of pectoralis muscles. He thrust out a hand. "Phil Girardi," he said.

"Oh, yes, Milo Crane," I replied. His hand was hot and dry and callused and so large that it nearly enveloped mine.

"You a World War II buff?"

I nodded. He smiled, then walked to another door at the far end of the room, one I hadn't noticed because it was cut into the wood-paneled wall like a trap door in novels. For a moment I wondered if I *was* in a novel, and I pinched my earlobe—an old trick.

"My dad was in the war. Brought back loads of stuff."

The door opened on a spring. It was a small annex—really more of a shrine—and on the walls hung black-and-white photos of a young man whose chiseled features bore a striking resemblance to Phil's. Only his physique was much thinner—his pale Army uniform hung loosely over his frame. It was the uniform of the Pacific Army Group, and in the more formal photos I spied the double-bar insignia of a Second Lieutenant. But in the combat photos he looked like a plain infantryman squinting nervously at the surrounding palms, or wading through chest-high water holding a rifle like a trapeze bar over his head. There were other memorabilia—medals, newspaper clippings, a bullet-riddled helmet and dilapidated combat boots. On the far wall hung a rusted bayonet, an officer's .45 caliber pistol, a few mortar casings, .50 caliber machine-gun bullets, the shell of a hand grenade, the nozzle end of a flamethrower, and a slightly unsheathed Japanese officer's sword near whose hilt I could just see the rusted flecks of blood.

"This is incredible," I breathed, noticing that none of the weapons had been defused—the bullets' powder not removed nor the pistol's barrel spiked. This gave me a thrill beyond any normal museum display.

"That sword belonged to a Japanese officer they trapped in one of the caves on Guadalcanal," said Phil, rubbing his goatee. "Poor bugger killed himself instead of being taken prisoner."

"They did do that," I agreed, recalling my picture books of the battle—the rotting corpses, emaciated Japanese defenders, one American officer with the top of his head blasted off and a stump of cigar still clinging to his chin.

"Crazy bastards."

"They took dishonor even more seriously than death," I said.

"Boy, has the world changed." He closed the door again. Then he rubbed his massive hands together. "You looking for perennials? I think I've got some delphiniums back at the greenhouse."

"No, no, I'm just—"

"Sorry. Everybody seems to want perennials lately."

"Ah yes." I took a deep breath. "I'm afraid I'm not much of a gardener. I'm a journalist, you see." I pulled out my notebook and spy pen.

"What can I do for you?" Phil said warily.

I smiled, explaining that I was researching several of the more prominent gardeners in the area and that Phil's name had arisen as a source for many of their soil and fertilizer needs. "For example, I've already spoken with a Mr. Henri Blanc. He comes to you regularly, does he not?"

Phil nodded.

"I understand he's got some sort of"—I flipped a few pages in my notebook for effect—"secret fertilizer or something?"

"He calls it that, but everyone who works around here makes something like it. You got to, with these soils."

"Do you think he's not an especially forthright gardener, then?"

He cocked his head. "He's a good guy. Just interesting."

"Do you know where he's from?"

"He's French, right? I don't know much else. He kind of came out of nowhere."

"What do you mean?"

"He showed up suddenly a few months ago. Then it was like he was always here."

"A few months ago?" *I've worked with Elizabeth for months.*

"That's right. Hey, what did you say your name was again?"

I hesitated. "Milo Crane."

"Your father was that writer, wasn't he?"

I nodded, bracing myself for the inevitable barrage of questions: *What was he like? How did he come up with those books?*

"Because Mr. Blanc said he knew him," Phil went on. "Your father. Said that's why he moved here. This was right after, well, that terrible accident. I'm so sorry, you know, for your loss."

But I wasn't thinking of *my loss.* There were too many questions, too many strange coincidences. "He moved here in the winter? From where?"

"Said he was working upstate. Near Burlington."

"Why would he move here for my father after my father's death?"

Phil shrugged those huge shoulders. "You mean you don't know?"

"He's a stranger to me."

"Oh." Phil looked perturbed, like he was trying to solve a difficult sum.

"Do you know anything else about him?" I asked.

"I heard he was pretty popular."

I snapped closed the notebook. "One last question. When Henri orders supplies, where do you deliver them?"

"He picks up everything here."

"I suppose he always pays cash?"

"Listen, I can't . . ." He looked away, fingering a couple of papers on his desk. "I really can't get into that. Sorry."

I bit my lip, knowing I'd bungled things again. It seemed so easy in stories to question witnesses. They either answered the detective or had something to hide. Either way they gave useful information.

"Is there anything else I can get you before you go?" Phil asked.

I paused, wondering if I could salvage something yet—an *insurance policy*, so to speak. "Actually . . ." I smiled meekly. "You wouldn't have any sodium nitrate fertilizer, would you?"

It was simple enough to find information at the local library concerning the impact of sodium nitrate on ornamental plants. In a monograph entitled "Soil Fundamentals," Dr. Willis Greene writes that "sodium ions increase the density of clay and can lead clayey soils to assume a cement-like hardness." Mrs. Meg Mc-Donald, in her seminal work *Your Perfect Rose Garden*, suggests that "to keep from burning the rose, apply inorganic fertilizers to moist soil and avoid spilling fertilizer on the bud union. If this occurs, wipe off fertilizer at once!" Both sources agreed that over-use was harmful because sodium nitrate was concentrated and fast-acting. "No more than a light dusting of nitrates, followed by a good watering," says Mrs. McDonald. "Or else you'll quickly drown your roses in nutrients. You *can* have too much of a good thing!"

I returned home and parked the MG in the garage just as it had been before. I left the fertilizer in the trunk. I was taking no chances. The workmen's truck was gone, as was the Peugeot, but Henri may have dropped-off Klara and Marta—they might be watching through the windows. I walked into the entrance hall. "Hello?" Nothing. Still I didn't move. The emptiness weighed on me. Because no place was truly empty. There was history, memory, and I began to see them—the ghosts of Mother and Father flitting across the tiles. They were getting ready for that last reading at the Barnes & Noble in Manchester. "Don't forget your coat," Mother said. Father didn't reply. He was more distant and self-absorbed than usual. Maybe he was drunk. Music from Klara's bedroom trickled down the stairs—brooding, low, romantic—Beethoven's Moonlight Sonata, as I knew from her long-ago lessons. Father was listening to it intently, like it was some kind of code. Klara had been anxious all day, knocking at his attic door, yelling that she'd steal a key. Did Mother have a clue what was going on? Did she even care? She planted a kiss on my forehead and said: "Be a good boy." Father nodded as if he agreed with her, then turned to me, his mouth open, eyes bleary, some painful pretense to profundity shambling across his lips. But in the end not a sound emerged. He couldn't seem to muster it. Then they were gone. I watched them march across the driveway, watched the Volvo pull away and their footprints fill with snow and the silence as the whole world slumbered. That's when I retreated to my study and my tiny Greek.

Finally they came.

Tires squealed across the driveway. I'd drifted into the kitchen and was consuming a tall glass of water to flush away the memories. The front door burst open. I heard Klara and Henri conversing in urgent whispers and Marta's protesting moans. Heavy footsteps on the stairs. Henri's insistence on medicine. "It will help you sleep." Then the kitchen door swung open and there he stood, bottle in hand, his thin red lips an O of surprise.

"Milo?"

I closed my eyes. I needed to be strong, I told myself, to not succumb to his charms as easily as Klara had, for I was fighting for my—our—future, the future that had been so achingly close before he arrived. "I can see you're disappointed," I said, looking at him straight on, studying that chiseled, suntanned face.

He smoothed a hand over his ponytail. "Nothing could be further from the truth. I am only sorry we've not had a chance to talk. Perhaps after I've given Marta her medicine?"

He moved past me to the sink, his rough veined hands pulling a glass from the drying rack and filling it with water. I watched him, how carefully he moved, how conscious of being watched, and while he was preoccupied I sent a whisper across his sweat-damp back, an insinuated magical word:

"*Malevolent.*"

I told myself it was a powerful word, one that Father always loved, with its shades of *reverent* and *violent* and *malignant*. Yet as soon as I'd uttered it, I realized my mistake. Because suddenly it was more than a word. More than a *spoken* one, I mean. I saw it hanging in the air like an invisible word cloud. What was happening? Henri turned and flashed his yellow teeth. Then the word was gone, bits of its dismembered letters dribbling down his chin. I saw a footless *a*, severed *m*, decapitated *e*. I backed up, moved a chair between us, a flimsy barrier that I was sure would do no good. Yet I clung to it for something tangible to hold onto.

Is this how a fictional character reveals himself?

"Are you alright?" he asked. He'd become absolutely still, a rough hard trunk of a man with branch-like hands, the scar oozing sap across the knotted base of his thumb. His body was all sinews and crooked angles, a tree growing in poor soil.

"I . . ." No, I wouldn't give him more words to chew and spit out, so I just shook my head and watched him bend toward the door, keeping an eye on me as if I might hurl the chair at him at any moment. "I am sorry if the garden feels like—an imposition," he said, before smiling and flicking his tongue.

It took only a moment. Afterwards I wondered if it had happened. If any of this was real. I rubbed my eyes and squinted. Still I couldn't tell. It was like those times when I see a familiar word and fail to recognize it, when the letters themselves can't coalesce.

"Have you considered a vacation?" he said, a hand already on the door. "Going someplace to relax? I know of a place outside of Burlington where they are very kind. A wonderful facility. If you like, I can place a call."

Go away. Leave us.

He gave a sly smile, a slight shift of his mobile mouth as if he'd heard my thoughts.

"I am only trying to help," he went on. "To make things easier for you."

He turned to leave, and that's when I decided to risk more speech: "You mean until you have me arrested? Or killed?"

This time the words swirled around him too fast for his snatching jaws. He smiled again, which I didn't expect—the eager expression of a boy with a slingshot who's finally spotted his elusive squirrel. He must have been relieved to finally know what he was up against, to have the battle lines so unambiguously drawn. But was *I*? The man remained a cipher, and that was the trouble. I thought of what he'd told Klara earlier—that Father had inspired him. *Inspired* as in breathed life into? That would be just the joke Father would make, a *double-entendre* to hide the truth in plain sight.

"I understand you had a difficult relationship with your father," he replied with a hint of wary tease.

He shifted shapes again, leaning against the countertop with his shoulders hunched to make himself appear like a rattlesnake about to strike. "You cannot escape him, am I right?" he said. "He influences you still? Yes, I can see that. You have a powerful imagination, just like him. In fact both you and your sister have a touch of the artist about you."

"What are you making her do?"

"No one can make anyone else do anything."

"Are you saying she's . . . ?"

I closed my eyes. I remembered marching off to look for them. That workman dialing his cell phone. "You knew I was coming," I said. "In the woods."

But when I opened my eyes again, he was gone.

The next thing I knew I was in my room, writing the whole strange scene in my secret diary. Again I wondered if any of it had been real. Still I kept thinking about what he'd said at the end: *No one can make anyone else do anything.* Klara's sympathy for me in the woods had given me a glimmer of hope. Only now I realized it wasn't that simple. The fact that they knew I was coming meant the entire thing could have been staged—to make me *think* Klara was an ally.

Yes, the more I thought about it, the more I realized this might be a classic John Crane plot, where nothing was what it seemed. After all, it was Klara herself who'd always insisted the car crash had been an accident. She'd refused to admit that Father might have been afraid of something at the end. Was that because he'd been afraid of her? Or of Henri? Or of them both? Had Father finally realized the power of his fiction—the power to literally create a life that *leapt off the page* and *crossed over* into the so-called *real world*?

The questions wouldn't stop. I had to do something. They'd overwhelm me if I didn't. So I peered into the hallway. It was empty. My mind screamed to stay inside my room where it was safe, but no place was truly safe anymore. Cautiously I crept out. Past Klara's room, past oil paintings of Father's literary heroes looming from shadowy nooks—Mary Shelley, Shirley Jackson, Bram Stoker, Edgar Allan Poe—between guest rooms that I had no memory of ever being used. I opened the first one. A single band of sunlight leaked through its wooden shutters. I imagined dead moths trapped between the slats, crumbling if you breathed on them. Otherwise it was empty, a pile of unused furniture covered in sheets. The others were the same—all except Mother and Father's at the end of the hall. That's where I finally found her, sprawled atop their bed, uniform disheveled, skirt riding up her bare puffy legs. Marta had once lived with us in the servant's quarters off the kitchen, and a memory came back to me of watching her sleep, trying to decide if she was dead. Why had she moved away? Had she been running from something too? It was impossible to know. She never talked about herself—about anything, really—but I hoped she'd talk now to me.

"Milo? Is it you?" she whispered.

I went to her side. One foot was still in the boot and there were bandages on her arm from drawing blood. "Are you alright?"

"Don't worry about me."

Her eyes were heavy. I knew I didn't have much time. I bent low, nearly overwhelmed by her animal scent of sweat and fear. "Did you notice the gardener's real name at the clinic? On one of those forms he had to fill out?"

"He was so nice. The doctor was his friend."

"What's his name, Marta?"

"One time the doctor called him . . ." She moved her mouth. A long sibilance emerged: "tthhhhh." She smiled. Not at me, at something beyond. I turned. There was the ladder. I had another idea. "This doctor . . ." I began.

Too late. She was already gone, her mouth open, her chest barely moving. I could only imagine what Henri had given her—what he'd conspired with his doctor-friend to do. I draped a dusty blanket loosely over her. Then something drew me to the balcony. I opened the door. Night was rapidly descending. Trees were becoming silhouettes. Nature itself was turning dark and inward.

I tried to sleep that night. But I should have realized I couldn't, that my dreams would conspire against me. In my mind I saw Klara enter my room, her face like a wooden mask in a museum: *Helmet Mask, Kingdom of Bamum, 19th Cent., Cameroon.* "Would you like supper?" she asked. Then Henri pushed past her and sat on the edge of my bed. "It pains me to see you so unhappy."

"You're a fraud," I told him in the dream. "A fiction."

He untied his hair, shaking it loose like a girl. His neck was thin and red, his skin blotched from the sun. "Do you think that only those things in your history books are true? What about belief? Faith?"

"You're making Klara think the most terrible things about me."

"It doesn't have to be this way, Milo."

He smiled like the daguerreotype of a snake-oil salesman holding up a flask of "Peterson's Copper Canyon Snakeroot Cure-All" in George Lyon's *Illustrated History of How The West Was Won.* The figure in the daguerreotype had a thick moustache and more muted expression, but one that contained the same *promising* quality, in all senses of the word.

"You can choose to be happy with us, or unhappy without us. It's up to you."

"And what if I want nothing to do with you?"

He leaned close, his smile becoming lopsided as if he were daring me to recognize him, as if to say *that's impossible now.* "I've seen your models," he said. "You are precise, with a flair for the dramatic. I think you'd be a natural gardener, just like her. Why not join us?"

"Because you don't really want me. This is all a lie."

"What's your favorite color?"

"My favorite—?"

"Color."

I paused, uncertain where this was going. "Blue."

His eyes sparkled beneath those sleepy lids. "I've always said that blue is the most underrated color in the garden. Red, pink, yellow, everybody uses these colors. But blue? Now there's a challenge. There are beautiful blue hyacinths and irises and crocuses and daffodils, but did you know that no one has yet been able to breed a blue rose? It is the holy grail in roses. The first to breed a blue rose, he will be someone who is remembered. Our garden is already ground-breaking for so many reasons, why not try for the blue rose too? We could have a corner of the garden devoted to nothing except that. Think about it, Milo. Think about it."

He reached up and placed a hand on the side of my neck. His skin was cool. Mine, by contrast, burned.

It took me a moment to realize I'd been dreaming. I could still see Henri's face hovering close, still smell his musky incense-laden scent and hear his unspoken challenge: *impossible.* Yes, that's what my dream was telling me, that there was something impossible about *him*—that *he* was the blue rose. I pushed back the covers and got to my feet. I peered through the curtains. A sliver of moon had risen high in the night sky; it suffused everything—the driveway, garage, woods—in a dim blue light. The Peugeot was gone. I crept down the hallway and listened, first at Klara's door, then at Marta's. I heard nothing. Both were fast asleep.

I put on a black cotton turtleneck and trousers, then floated down the murky stairs into the kitchen. I opened a drawer and removed the heavy scissors that Mother had once used for her artistic projects. From another drawer I took a thick rubber flashlight and a garbage bag, and from the cupboard an old plastic cup I knew no one would miss.

I stole across the entrance hall and crept out the front door, into a cricket-filled night whose constellations hung low outside the soft aura of the moon. I recognized these from Klara's drills: Draco and Cepheus and Leo Minor. I also saw what's commonly known as the Big and Little Dippers, which were of course not constellations but rather parts of Ursa Major and Ursa Minor—the big and little bears. I could only hope there'd be no bears tonight.

The flashlight's beam extended forward like a lance. I picked out the garage. The crickets went silent as I approached, their bug-eyes and quivering antennae alert behind every tree. I lifted the door. The MG's trunk was barely visible. I slipped in the key, creaked it open with the hushed deliberation of a priest. My light washed over the fertilizer sack with its picture of a jaunty mustachioed farmer in overalls. I raised the scissors. He didn't flinch. I stabbed him in the face—again, again. Then I thrust the cup into the gaping wound, scooped out fertilizer and added it to the garbage bag. I took only half the sack—that was all I could carry. I found one of those funnels for changing oil and a pair of old work gloves. I slipped on the gloves and carried the bag and funnel to the rear of the house. The old Roman glowed a cadaverous green, moon-shadows falling across his eyes. It lent him the same haunting surprise one sees in photos of dead troops. And here I was, about to add corpses to the heap.

I began with a cluster of yellow roses near the patio wall. They were in full bloom. Henri must have planted them that way. I wasn't surprised. I dug out the soil near its roots and with the funnel carefully replaced it with sodium nitrate. Then I doused the buds. I could practically hear the flowers scream. I repeated this procedure with the others—the pinks, whites, purples, reds—replacing their soils with this binding agent, choking them with "too much of a good thing." I worked for almost three hours until my back ached and I could hardly breathe through all the dust. Still I was careful to cover up the sodium nitrate with a thin layer of soil to conceal my handiwork. I felt sure no one could tell what I'd done, how I'd break Henri's spell. Yes, Klara would *have* to doubt Henri now—she'd see the failure of their garden to thrive as symbolic. We'd both been immersed in novels long enough to feel the heavy weight of symbolism.

Suddenly I heard something. A footfall.

I froze. The night felt alive. Like the trees were aware of my presence. But I couldn't see a thing. I glanced at the house. For a moment I thought I saw Marta in the window—saw her eyes trained on me with the same hovering inscrutability she'd displayed when I was a child. But when I shined my flashlight, no one was there.

Keith breathed it in: the trees, the rocks, the humid earth,
The perfect place for nature's sweet rebirth
As "Devil's Garden." So he dragged her body by the hair,
A body he had touched and loved and dared
To tell the truth to. Truth: the cold indifference of the stars
To us, our hopes and dreams and fears, our feelings we're on par
With God, not dust, recycled dirt, and food for worms.
She couldn't hear it, couldn't come to terms,
Her shrunken face, protective hands across her belly,
"Think of the future," she had said. He had to tell her:
It wasn't real. So now, her flesh excised in steaming piles,
Her belly packed with dirt and face a mild
Reproach, he could relax, and smoke, and run his blade
Across his left (or sinister) thumb, not green! But red, with blood,
A hallowed nothingness that gave aborted birth
To his profoundest work: MOTHER / EARTH.

IN A NEARBY PARK STANDS A WOODEN SIGN COMMEMORATING THE massacre of Baylor's Dragoons. Hardly anyone knows this history. During the Revolutionary War a band of British soldiers detached from Cornwallis' main army and stumbled upon several Americans on their way to join Ethan Allen's Green Mountain Boys. The Americans were under the command of a local blacksmith named George Bellows Baylor—an enterprising fellow who thought the future of weaponry lay in hand-manufactured swords. He'd outfitted a motley crew of farmers with his own shining cutlasses, training them to parry and thrust in high officer style. Not surprisingly the British made quick work of these fools and collected their fancy weapons as prizes, one of which still hangs against a blue velvet board in an obscure corner of the historical museum in Bennington.

I drove to the massacre site at dawn. In our age of interactive displays the single wooden sign and commemorative plaque generated little interest. To most people it was just a grassy field and a bunch of trees. I knew I'd be alone. I heaved the fertilizer sack out of the trunk and dragged it like a dead body to a green trash receptacle. Somehow I managed to pitch it inside. Then came my tools and clothes—anything that might link me to what had happened.

Aside from this single outing I endeavored to adopt my typical routine. I returned to bed and set my alarm clock at maximum volume. I shot up like a cannonball. After some quick ablutions and a change of clothes I appeared, smiling with my usual pleasantness, at breakfast. Marta was already up and about the kitchen. She seemed much improved—or was skilled at hiding pain. I slid into my place just as she brought me a cup of cocoa on a saucer.

"How are you feeling today?" I asked.

"Fine, thank you."

But there was a shiftiness to her eyes. She seemed to be avoiding my gaze. It was like when I was a child and I'd done something naughty—something only she'd noticed. "Did you sleep well?" I asked.

"Oh yes."

"Any dreams?"

"I never remember them."

Klara descended for breakfast with her usual quietness, sipping her morning tea and scanning a day-old newspaper. She looked tired. Her eyes were puffy and dark. Everything was taking its toll. She was wearing a bright red dress with three-quarter length sleeves tied in knots, hardly the sort of thing for gardening. But did I dare hope?

"Henri sends his regards," Klara said to Marta.

"He's not coming?"

"He said he needs to look after Mrs. Silfer's geraniums today."

I blew on the cocoa's steam, sending it into spasmodic, lucky waves. Not only would I be free of the man, but my raid upon the roses could hardly have been more perfectly timed. Now the sodium nitrate would have all day to burn and bind, to destroy the garden and Henri's false pretenses along with it.

"It looks like a beautiful day," I said to Klara with a sigh.

"I suppose it is."

She turned the pages and paused at the headline "Ancient Rituals, Modern Oppressions." There was a photograph of a dour African girl with a red cloth around her head—no doubt more grist for her charitable mill. I picked up the financial pages. I've always taken comfort in the stock market's rational precision: *Mattson, + 1/32; MaxEr, - 1 1/2*. I had no idea what these companies did—I imagined men in starched shirts pouring over spreadsheets while uttering words like "efficiency" and "gross production" and "value added"—the words themselves evoking skyscrapers and airport lounges and computerized cars, the engineering of anodyne calm.

"Anything interesting in the paper?" I asked.

She didn't look up. "In Africa they still practice genital mutilation on girls as young as five or six."

I shook my head. "Barbaric."

Marta returned with a tray of soft-boiled eggs in decorative ceramic cups. That's when Klara finally put down the paper. "It's important that you rest," she said, carefully taking the tray. Marta tried to protest, but Klara would have none of it. "Go. We'll be fine." She watched Marta hobble into the entrance hall. I could swear Marta was putting it on for Klara's benefit—she hadn't been limping a few minutes ago. When she'd gone Klara sighed and turned to me. I stared at my egg, knowing what was coming. I'd known it since yesterday.

"We need to talk," she said. "About what happened to Mother and Father."

I gave my egg a whack, cracking its delicate cap, so like an old man's skull. I saw them at the police station on those slabs, their coffins descending into frozen ground. I remembered even then having a moment of doubt, wondering if those coffins were empty. "We know what happened."

"Everybody assumed it was an accident because of the icy roads. But what if they couldn't stop? What if their brake lines had been cut?"

"Why are you asking me this?"

I could see the struggle in her face. "Henri found things in the woods."

"Things?"

"Hidden in our old clearing. An auto guide and wire-cutters. You know that. You followed us."

"I came to tell you about Marta."

"So you don't know anything about them?"

I looked at my egg, dribbling yolk.

"I'm sorry, Milo, I have to ask."

"Why?"

"Only you and I knew about that clearing. It was our special place."

"So why did you take Henri there?"

She paused with her little spoon in the air, a bit of egg white on her lip. I could swear I saw it trembling—whether out of anger at my insinuation or embarrassment at what she'd been doing, I couldn't tell. "He was the one who . . . He wanted to show me wild nature. It's a quality he wants to capture in the garden."

I nodded, looking into her eyes, so skeptical yet so trusting—the eyes of a broken bird: vulnerable, wide, yet still imbued with that reptilian gleam. *Do you see what this means?* I told those eyes. *Do I have to spell it out for you?* "He led you there."

"We started walking down the path and he noticed the stone marker."

"I suppose he also found the wire cutters and auto guide?"

"He'd run ahead and gotten to the clearing first."

She said this in an almost dreamlike fugue, as if starting to piece it together, how Henri was the sole source of everything against me. Here was another pinprick of doubt, another hole in that man's conspicuously constructed image. If I could make enough such holes, I knew the entire edifice would fall under the weight of Klara's own self-doubt, the self-doubt that must already be wondering *why am I attractive to that man? Why is he here?* And then, out of the dust and ruin of her fantasy, would come the truth as only I could reveal.

"I see," I said, taking a spoonful of creamy yolk.

She pinched her lips and sat a little straighter, gathering herself in long-habitual opposition to me, unwilling to let the fantasy die. "I'm sorry, Milo. This is not one of Father's novels."

"'*My dear fellow*,'" I quoted Sherlock Holmes, "'*life is infinitely stranger than anything which the mind of man could invent*.'"

"Nor is it one of your games."

"I know," I said. I was about to say more, but I decided to be cautious, to avoid revealing my evidence. "I'm following up on a few things and should have more to tell you soon."

"What exactly are you doing?"

"Everything I can to protect you."

"From what?"

"Yourself."

I shot the word straight at her, seeing the hesitation in her eyes, the slight flinch that told me I was onto something. "You knew him," I ventured. "Before the accident."

"Who?"

"Henri."

"Don't be ridiculous. He was living in Burlington."

"You went there several times last autumn."

"That was for a fiction writing class with Jason Patrick."

Jason Patrick was Father's great rival in the realm of *reclusive literary horror novelists*, one who taught at the University of Vermont. Father called him the *"vanilla thriller miller"* for how he ground-out bland plot after bland plot. "I thought you'd given up writing," I pointed out.

"It's not something you ever really *give up*, is it?" She took a spoonful of egg, then put down the spoon and wiped her lips with a cloth napkin. "Anyway you know how things were then, with Father working on his long-awaited sequel. I had to get away."

It's always the smallest things that transport my mind. Take spiders. There's a web below our roofline that I can just see from the corner of my bedroom window. One minute I'll be observing its creator sidle toward a trapped fly and then an entire hour will have passed. The same is true for a dripping faucet. Have you ever observed how long a drop of water can cling, distended, to the edge? I've read about viscosity and fluid dynamics, but it still thrills me to watch a little water bubble hang there and slowly, slowly succumb to the pull of gravity. There is something poignant in the moment of breaking that reminds me of films like *Casablanca* or *Star Trek II*—films in which Humphrey Bogart or Mr. Spock say to their lover or comrade to go on without them, and the lover or comrade hesitates, and then does. I watch the water fall helplessly into the sink, and I want to cry.

I concentrate intently on the minutia of modeling. I can spend an entire morning hollowing out the insides of a tiny ship's cannon with an even tinier bit of wire. It's an escape into another time—an escape from time itself. I feel detached from my surroundings and at the same time most alive. It frees my mind to work through difficult problems, to mull things over from every angle. Sherlock Holmes has his violin and his pipes, while I have my models and my Greeks.

After breakfast I painted Athenian colors on the trireme's oars. I applied the pale blue and white paint with my second-most exacting brush—a Spanish Escoda Tajmir. Its long bristles hold plenty of paint, and its thin tip applies it precisely. I also smoothed down the oar handles with sandpaper until they fit neatly within the slaves' pre-formed grips. Then I added a rare touch of verisimilitude. I washed one of Marta's sewing needles and sterilized it with a match flame. I held my breath and jabbed it into the end of my thumb. I squeezed, pooling the blood atop the skin before dipping in the needle. I carefully dabbed it across each oar handle.

Klara spent the day on the chaise, writing a letter—no doubt to the State Department or Amnesty International or some other organization that might help those poor African girls. That evening we watched the first part of a televised adaptation of *Great Expectations*. She was distracted, picking at the collar of her blouse. I sensed all the things she wanted to say to me—all the things locked up inside. But I was the one who asked the questions that night.

"Do you have a formal contract with Henri?"

"Hmm?"

"A legal document? Executed by a lawyer? Notarized with his legal name and social security number and everything?"

"Don't be silly. He's a gardener, not a bank trustee."

In the morning I was in the study carving the Athena's head at the tip of the trireme's ram when I saw Klara dash across the patio, one hand on her straw hat and the other waving in frantic little clutches of air. Henri was in the garden. He had his hands on his hips. He didn't move. He said something cutting—I could see the bitter curl of his mouth. She stopped short, a hand still on the hat, the other frozen in mid-wave until it joined its counterpart atop her head in an almost childishly protective gesture. Henri turned away. He was standing over a rose's bleached and spotted leaves. He plucked one of them and tossed it aside. Then he slipped out a gardening knife. His thumb rubbed the top of the blade. It was a pent-up, angry motion, yet a strangely intimate one—of a man who loved his steel. In a flash he swung it. I saw a glint, a blur, the top of a ruined flower slowly toppling, then another and another, scythed away by his quick and expert violence. Nobody moved after that: not him, not Klara, not I. I got the sense he was embarrassed by what he'd revealed, while I kept thinking: *I've seen this before. Exactly this.* I watched Klara inch toward him and put a hand on his shoulder. She whispered something. He nodded. Then she turned and caught my face in the little study window, while hers remained hidden in the angled shadow of her hat.

I bent low and took up my Exacto knife again. My hand was shaking. I was conscious of how alone I was. I stared at Athena's hair, each line of it swept over the hull as if wind-blown. Then time passed and I calmed, I began to carve once more, focusing on the triangular blade, the wood shavings falling like dry snow.

Eventually I looked up. By then everyone—Klara, Henri, the workmen—had moved to the garden, working in furious silence to shovel up the top layer of soil and upend it into wheelbarrows. This was my chance. I exchanged the smock for a blazer and hurried through the entrance hall. The driveway was empty except for those crickets that sing on humid mornings—that never want the night to end. The Peugeot gleamed between a pair of pickup trucks. I ran a finger over the question-mark I'd gouged. I wondered if he'd noticed it—if part of his anger stemmed from the fact that he knew that I knew him. I pulled out my notebook and peered through the windshield and copied down the VIN number. Then I went into the kitchen and pulled the telephone book from its drawer. I located the company I'd seen in a recent television commercial.

"CarInfo," said the man on the phone.

"Yes, hello," I said, relieved not to be talking to a machine. I claimed I was buying a used car and needed a full report on the owner and vehicle. "I have the VIN."

"Perfect," he replied, drawing out the "r" like those drug addicts in college. "We can mail you a report for $49.99, OK?"

"Just hurry."

"I only need your info and a credit card."

A credit card. "Hold on." Klara's purse was in the alcove off the entrance hall—a slim black leather thing with stiff loop handles. The clasp opened with a snap, and I pulled out her wallet with its MasterCard. Just then I noticed something at my feet—a shiny plastic square. It must have fallen out. I picked it up. It crinkled between my fingers. It took several moments before I recognized it from my college dorm.

Trojan.

Klara said nothing to me all afternoon, hurrying past the study when she was inside and never again glancing at my window. Supper was painfully silent. Her face was waxy from congealed sweat and a little sunburned; she kept fingering the low neck of her blouse where it met her ruddy skin. How many condoms did she have? I closed my eyes and saw them bursting from her pockets, spilling out her brassiere, piled atop her nightstand and covering the MG's floor. Where did she use them? And how often? Did it give her pleasure or was it just something she suffered to alleviate her loneliness?

Later we watched Part Two of *Great Expectations*. That's when she finally turned to me, scrutinizing me above the rims of her television glasses, lowering her head an inch or two while raising her eyebrows the same distance as if they were held in place by invisible strings. "Is there nothing you don't hate?" she said, her voice sour from being bottled up so long.

"I don't hate you."

"You have a funny way of showing it."

I turned back to the television, on which a particularly spooky scene in Miss Havisham's dining room was playing. The room was illuminated by a dim gas lamp and curtained with cobwebs. Our hero, young Pip, stood at the entrance, his mouth an amazed little O.

"You never appreciate what I do for you," I said.

"Like trying to ruin the garden?"

"Is that Henri's latest accusation?" I said, my voice slipping a little. "When will he stop?"

"You added sodium nitrate."

I tried to laugh, but the sound stuck in my throat like a pollen-induced tickle. "Where would I get sodium nitrate? And how would I even know what it's supposed to do?" She held me in a steady gaze. I refused to twitch or turn away. "You've always been vulnerable to the suggestions of men who flatter you," I went on. "Men who are trying to take advantage."

"Excuse me?"

"Like your ex-husband. And Father."

It was an inspired afterthought, but I saw how she perked up, ruffled and alarmed—saw I'd hit a nerve. "Why do you mention Father?"

"He used to praise you for everything. It affected you. You played to him. You thought he could do no wrong. Henri is doing the same thing."

"That's ridiculous."

"A dashing French gardener? Interested only in your gardening technique? That, my dear sister, is ridiculous."

I turned back to the television, where Miss Havisham was laughing at a stream of spiders pouring from a rotten banquet table. Even this was not as revolting as what poured out of Klara's mouth next: "Is it because I'm finally happy? Can you not stand to see me happy?"

Poor Pip's blanched face suddenly filled the screen.

"Listen, I'm sorry about what happened in the past, Milo—how I treated you, how Mother and Father treated you. But there's nothing I can do about that now. We have to live our lives. And that means taking responsibility for our actions, not always blaming someone else."

"What was that?"

"Taking responsibility for our actions," she repeated in a slow voice, spacing out the words so their import was impossible to escape.

I've always admired the ability of small animals to cheat death by playing dead. It is the ultimate example of gaining freedom through abject submission. I looked at her straight on, without blinking, and said: "What do you imagine I'm doing?"

"You really have no idea how sodium nitrate got in the soil?"

I shook my head. "Maybe Henri isn't quite the gardener he makes himself out to be. Or maybe he's deliberately trying to blame me in every way he can. Either way you should be very careful. There is more to that man than meets the eye."

"What do you mean?"

I wasn't sure how much to say, so I said nothing at all. Klara didn't say anything either. She just turned back to the television, and for the remainder of the film we did little more than stare in parallel at the screen. At one point I inquired whether she wanted a chocolate from the kitchen (she always kept several boxes of them with her favorite marzipan centers), but she raised a hand and motioned me to be silent as if even the hint of continued conversation were too painful to bear.

Keith wondered sometimes whether he'd been made,
An emanation from the Master's head,
Sprung forth at that man's words?
The notion seemed absurd . . .

And yet he couldn't shake it.

At times he also felt, when gazing in the mirror, naked,
That he wasn't of this world, as if his flesh itself were plastic,
Illusory, a pantomime of nature, some fantastic
Shroud to hide the monster deep inside.
Was that what made him keen to peel it all aside
In others? To check if he was different or unique
Or if their core, their being, was equally as bleak?

THE FOLLOWING MORNING I THOUGHT ABOUT HENRI'S MOVE TO southern Vermont after the accident and the difficulty of finding any identifying information with his name. It was a puzzle that Sherlock Holmes would have spent many grueling hours pouring over, piecing it together with all the other clues, arranging them until they formed a coherent and satisfying tale. And what would such a tale be in Henri's case? Again I wondered if I'd been wrong to fear in him some profounder threat. Perhaps the truth was simple, even mundane. Perhaps he was just a confidence man—one who'd read about the accident and decided to take a chance, who'd discovered in Klara an easy and suddenly wealthy mark.

I turned this possibility over in my mind as the sun brightened my bedroom window and the walls began to creak with the day's first warmth. In many ways it offered hope, a way to rid myself of deeper fears, yet it was precisely for this reason that I distrusted it—it was too convenient a solution, one that required me to be blind to what I knew. Yes, I knew something darker and more sinister was at work, knew it the way one knows lightening is about to strike or snow to fall—by the smell and feel of the air. I had only to close my eyes to sense that he was already at our house that morning and plying Klara with his lies, that these lies were taking hold of her like a coil of rapacious vines.

The breakfast table was empty. This was the first thing I noticed when I descended—the sense of abandonment that had come over the dining room, its long thick table hosting only a single place setting: mine. I put a hand on my chair's high back, tempted to enact the normalcy I craved, knowing Marta was in the kitchen waiting until the chair scraped back before bringing out my eggs. That was her little trick. Only I wasn't hungry suddenly.

They were sitting on the patio, Klara in a low-cut blouse that revealed the reptilian ridges of her spine, while Henri talked in rapid whispers, mouth stuffed with croissant. I opened the French doors. It was like stepping onto a stage without any lines, just the dim realization that something momentous was about to happen. Klara whirled around and said "Look, it's Milo," as if I were a dangerous zoo animal.

"What are you doing?" I asked.

"Having breakfast in the fresh air. Won't you join us?" Her voice was like a shiny new penny, and just as cheap. "Henri was saying he wanted to talk to you. About our plans, our vision for the garden. He was also hoping to clear up any misunderstandings. We're both sorry, Milo, that everything has been so hard for you."

I moved forward. Klara was pointing at a chair. It had all the expectancy of an electric chair. I sat in it anyway.

"Klara is right," Henri said in the miserable tone of a child forced to be polite. "I want to show you our plans." But his eyes weren't polite at all. He knew Klara was in his power. My heart beat faster. "I fear you have the wrong impression of what we are trying to do here," he went on.

"I don't think so."

"I understand why you love these woods." He leaned toward me. His lips were moist from the croissant's buttery sheen. "Such a sense of mystery. Of things *hidden*."

He began to roll up his sleeves. I watched the muscles in his arms bulge like little animals trying to break free. "Then why not leave it the way it is," I said.

"Ah," he replied. "That is the question. Why disturb things now?"

I reached forward to the little table and poured myself some orange juice. Thankfully there was a third glass. Just in case? Or was this planned? "Exactly," I said after I'd gulped it down.

"The answer will have to wait until we're finished," he said. "Then you can be the judge."

He leaned back. That's when I noticed something on his arm. On the smooth veined inner skin just below the elbow. Even now I wonder how this story might have turned out if I'd never seen it—if I really *had* stayed in my room—whether it was possible to have avoided the terrible spell he was about to cast.

"Henri was in the military once," Klara said. "He was a *soldier*, Milo."

"Actually I spent most of my years as a military police officer. We investigated everything from murders to war crimes in the areas we controlled."

"Did you hear that?" she smiled. "He was a soldier *and* a detective."

This was her eager-to-please morning voice—a voice both naïve and false. It was like she wasn't the one talking, like another voice was coming *through* her, and she was just an empty shell, a ventriloquist's dummy.

I turned to Henri. He was holding up his arms, hands locked behind his head and his mouth held in a sly grin as if to say: *Can you doubt who I am now?*

"I think you'd find you have a lot in common, actually," Klara was saying.

But her voice had become a distant memory, a scratchy gramophone recording of another, simpler era—one that didn't include atomic bombs or sarin gas or suicide vests, nor the dark blue tattoo on Henri's arm: a horseshoe with a flame-like fleur-de-lis in the center and the number 2 at bottom.

"I was for two years in Chad," Henri said. "In '79 and '80. Brutal. We could hardly count the bodies. You cannot imagine how it was, trying to sort out the truth under such conditions. Afterwards I dedicated myself to creating life, not killing it. Loving, not hating."

Klara raised her eyebrows at me. "Did you hear that?"

I turned to her. Was it possible she hadn't seen it? Or recognized it? She, who read all of Father's books at least once a year?

> *Keith did the Foreign Legion tat himself, by copying an art book.*
> *But what it meant? He didn't know; he liked the look*
> *And all the searing pain that came*
> *From holding that sharp needle under hot blue flame.*

"We were based in Atti and in N'djamena, the former Fort Lamy area," Henri was saying.

"You were a Legionnaire," I said.

"I was young."

"Is that how you got your tattoo?"

His eyes widened. *Ah, you recognize it.* Yes, I recognized all the signs. There was no doubting anymore. This was preceisely what Keith would do before his killings: display the tattoo and invent stories about his past. Draw his victim close with a slow tease and then . . . Bam! True, Keith was pale and bald and dark-eyed, but this could be a minor obfuscation—a way to keep us off-guard while he worked his way into our lives. I thought of the names. They were so obvious now. *Henri, Keith.* Both were five letters. Both shared an H, E, and I. And what did those three letters spell? *"He"* and *"I."*

"He could tell you lots of stories," Klara said to me. "But they're not always the sorts of adventures you read in your books. Isn't that right, Henri?"

"War brings out the worst in people. And war in Africa? It makes savages of us all."

"I'm so sorry," said Klara. She leaned over and touched the tattoo, rubbing a forefinger gently across it—a gesture that made me want to scream.

"It was a long time ago," Henri told her. "Still you never forget these things. Gardening has been good therapy, as you say."

"You see?" Klara said to me. Then she whispered, too loudly, into Henri's ear: "For me, too. It's been that for me, too."

I felt I ought to say something, *do* something, but my old helplessness seized me suddenly. Even my raid upon the roses seemed like an impotent gesture now. "I always heard that the Foreign Legion's military police were notoriously corrupt," I managed.

"We did the best we could under difficult circumstances."

"Did you ever plant evidence? Arrest someone you knew was innocent? Or torture people into false confessions?"

Klara gave me a sharp look. "Milo!"

Henri put a hand on her arm. "It is a fair question."

"It's insensitive," she insisted.

"I cannot say I was perfect, but I always thought I was just," he said to me. "Perhaps we all have things to atone for, no?"

I looked at Klara. I wanted to shout at the top of my lungs: *Why can't you see it?* Yes, it was brilliant, I had to admit it, because Keith had also once worked for the police—as a crime scene photographer. Not an investigator, true, but close enough. *"He'd learned to see a body, bloody clothes, and limbs in binds / As elements of composition, the aesthetics of the crime."* Still a part of me resisted. I hung on to reality as if for dear life. I told myself, more forcefully this time, that there must be another explanation—that fictional characters didn't step off the page, didn't come to life. Or did they?

I shot to my feet.

"Please sit down, Milo."

"Excuse me."

Back in my room, I pulled my secret diary out of the lockbox beneath my bed. Part of me didn't want to revisit these old scenes, but I had to be sure, because I no longer trusted fickle memory. I turned to a passage from shortly before Father's death: *"He's been dressing like his characters. Today he's Lumber-Jack, The Ripper."* I remembered the red plaid shirt, the axe he carried around, his gruff manner of speaking without moving his newly bearded lips. At the time I thought he'd been gathering fictional material: *"getting to know his characters."* Then came Keith. I could see him even now: paint-spattered pants, shaved head, Bowie knife with its thick handle wrapped in electrical tape and the gleaming half-serrated blade. He'd been at the edge of the woods, on one of his midnight walks, when he'd pulled that blade out of a sheath strapped to his belt and marched toward a tree—a tree where, I suddenly noticed, lay a cage, and inside the cage something snorted and squirmed, an animal wracked with fear. I felt for this poor beast—I knew the feeling intimately myself, the small death that comes from helplessness, but I wasn't prepared for the larger death, for what Father had obviously planned. He lifted the top of the cage. Down plunged the blade. Suddenly the night, the woods, were filled with a horrible baby-like scream. I could hardly move as Father bent over and got to work, wiping his brow on his sleeve as he sawed off the poor thing's head. He raised it. I saw a band of white fur, glittering eyes. A raccoon. "*Now he's talking to it,*" I'd written at the time, in my shaky hand, "*just like Keith talks to the severed head of Beatrice.*"

I closed the diary, tempted to believe this had been fantasy, because that's what I sometimes wrote in my secret diary: the world as it ought to be. But I'd never wish for what had happened that night, and I never embellished when it came to Father. I wrote only the facts about him—no matter how strange—to provide a record, to prove to myself and perhaps ultimately to others what kind of man he was.

So what did it all mean?

I crept onto Klara's balcony. They were directly below, Klara rubbing her forehead while Henri stroked her shoulder. With the rustling leaves and chirping birds I could barely make out their words, but on that day I wished I hadn't—wished for once I could be satisfied with ignorance.

"You see how he reacted?" Henri was saying.

"He's all I have."

"My dear, what if that is his own doing?"

She waved a hand uncertainly.

"Listen to me, Klara. He followed us to the hospital and stole the evidence. Why else would he do that?"

"For fun? Milo can be like that."

"Don't you want to know the truth?"

"The car is gone."

"Are you sure? All the insurance companies in Vermont use the same scrap dealer outside of Brattleboro. One of my workers has told me of this." He took a deep breath. "I know it is none of my business. I only want you to be happy. Maybe a phone call to see if the car is still . . . ?"

I couldn't deny it any longer. This was Keith exactly. He'd always taken a shrewd measure of his victims. It would be just like him to realize Klara's secret longing to be taken advantage of, to enslave her desires to those of a stronger man. Even a man bent on destroying us? Yes. It would make his victory that much sweeter, knowing that she knew what he was up to, but couldn't help herself. He could take everything—my freedom, her wealth, her self-respect—and still she'd beg for more.

I staggered back through Klara's room, wondering whether Father himself was doing this somehow, grasping at us from beyond the grave. But why? Unfortunately the question answered itself: to punish us for daring to move past him, to remind us we could never forget.

"I am always with you, Milo. Never forget that. I am part of you, and you are part of me."

I drifted into the hallway, where his voice suddenly emanated from every stone, every shadowy corner: *"'Close your eyes, Milo, and let it come to you.' 'I'm scared.' 'Move closer to me and you'll see everything.'"* I found myself beneath the Bram Stoker portrait. Dracula had always been one of his favorites. Only I'd never realized its significance before: how it was full of unholy creatures, dead yet granted eternal life: *"Lucy's eyes in form and colour; but Lucy's eyes unclean and full of hell-fire, instead of the pure, gentle orbs we knew."* And what could be more dead—yet more eternally alive—than a fictional character?

I managed to reach my bed. It was like a ship floating through space, a place of safety even though it never was—even though Father always sat on its edge and watched me fake sleep, his face looming close, his sulphurous breath washing over me. *"'You know the secret to creating fear, my son?' 'Please, Father, no.' 'Planting belief.'"*

No. I buried my face in the pillow, resisting even now. *If only I can break this spell . . .* I reached into my night stand's drawer. My photo album. This is what I do when situations seem overwhelming—I turn to my baseball photos. Not reminders of a happier time but just the opposite: proof of my ability to endure when things seem most impossible. I studied the washed-out images of my childhood like a desperate archivist: the blur of a ball, my maroon uniform and cavernous helmet and high white socks. I remembered what a nightmare it had been—how I couldn't hit or catch, how even the coaches made snide remarks. At the time I saw no escape, because Mother believed that all American boys were required to play baseball, and nothing could dissuade her.

"What if I were in a wheelchair or retarded?" I'd pleaded with her once. "Then I wouldn't have to play."

"But you're not," she'd replied, folding the Little League's liability waiver into an envelope. "You're a healthy boy. Healthy boys play baseball."

"Not every healthy boy. Not Eric Chin."

"He's Chinese. That's different. He can't help being un-American. You, on the other hand, are an American boy."

I tried explaining that baseball actually derived from the English game of rounders, so it wasn't really "American" at all. Or that I rarely played, relegated to the bench or far right field. But it didn't work. She mailed in the form. It was up to me to end this charade. How? It took patience, waiting for an opportunity, and ultimately an act of grit and bodily sacrifice—letting my worst fears materialize and pushing straight *through* them. A lesson that wasn't lost on me now.

It happened when our team's catcher, Davey Moor, fell ill with chickenpox. His usual replacement was undergoing an orthodontic procedure, so the coach, some beer-swollen imbecile, pulled me aside and pointed to the pads and plastic guards behind the bench. I hesitated. I'd never played catcher before. I just stared at the equipment—remains of a vanquished knight—before realizing what I had to do. I picked them up. My teammates grumbled. "So much for our chance of making the playoffs," I heard.

Just you wait, I wanted to say.

I never made it through warm-ups. The first pitch hit me squarely in the shoulder. The second bashed my shin. The third crashed into my face guard and sent me reeling in a cloud of dust.

"You OK?" the coach asked.

"I've almost got the hang of it."

By the end I could hardly walk. The coach had to peel the equipment off me. "Jesus Christ," he said when he looked at my swollen, useless arm. The other boys all turned away, but I just smiled as Klara picked me up and fussed over me the entire way home. "What did they do to you?" she asked. Even Mother noticed what awful shape I was in.

"My God, did you ride your bicycle into a tree?"

She was hurrying across the living room with a painting of sunflowers under her arm and a gold speckled scarf around her head. She looked like a glittering pirate. She pushed her sunglasses to the tip of her nose. "Or were the boys at school—?"

"Baseball," I said as I heaved myself onto the sofa.

"But you can hardly walk, and why are you holding your arm so funny?"

"I was trying out for catcher and kept getting hit by the ball."

"Why do they allow you boys to do such things?" she said as she put the painting down and examined me more closely. "I'm going to call the school principal."

"This is Little League. It has nothing to do with school."

"All we have is our health. Without our health we have nothing. Always remember that, Milo."

"Yes, Mother."

"I don't want you playing this baseball anymore," she said, holding the painting against the dying light. "I'm sorry if you're disappointed."

That night I doused my baseball uniform with nail polish remover and brought it to a ditch by the side of the house. A single match was enough. I wished Mother could see the flames, the smoke, the crackling of burning nylon. This was a much more American activity than baseball—as American as smoke-signals, really.

It was early afternoon when Klara pounded on my door.

The pounding—loud, insistent—shocked me out of my reveries, and another dark thought occurred to me: that Henri had already turned her into his accomplice, that she'd come with a poisoned needle or a fat little Derringer to murder me. Or that she'd called the scrap dealer. Perhaps she had *news*. Perhaps there'd been a *development*.

I opened the door.

"What is it?" I asked.

"Come."

She turned and descended the stairs, her footsteps echoing on the cold hard stone. She led me into the living room. The television was on, the screen a solid blue. She sat in one of the high-backed chairs and took up a pair of remote controls, arranged just so. I sat beside her. The screen popped to life. The picture was shaky at first, then colorful flowers came into view, set to warbled Vivaldi-like music.

"What is this?"

"Watch."

The title "America's Best Gardeners Speak Out" flashed across the screen. Then a dowdy woman appeared on a garden path. It was like watching a distant member of the British royal family—an old revered Duchess or something—touring the grounds of Buckingham Palace. She began describing various flowers she remembered from childhood ("*and on the trellises hung the sweetest wisteria*") when the image froze and disappeared into static.

"I have no idea what . . ." I began.

"Wait."

It flickered back to life, and there was Henri walking through a greenhouse in a loose tan shirt with rolled-up sleeves. I gripped the chair's leather arm. But I couldn't look away—my curiosity was aroused. I found myself searching for stitches, scars, rivets— signs that he'd been *made*—or the unholy aura of a creature *summoned from another world.*

The dowdy woman's voice came in disembodied narration again: "*It all begins for Henri Blanc with finding the right seedlings for the harsh Vermont winters, which he does by working closely with local greenhouses.*"

He began strolling through a garden with the old woman, proclaiming the virtues of "controlled wilderness" and speculating about whether having a garden might help "us all" to "reconnect with nature" in a more "symbiotic" way. "*In America, just like in Europe,*" he said, "*it has always been fashionable to dominate nature. To bulldoze it and make it safe and comforting. What I like to do is to bring back a little of the danger, to set my gardens in remote places, to have the threat of the wilderness encroaching on all sides. I think it helps people appreciate the garden more, to see it as the remarkable thing it is, but also temporary, fragile. It's really a sense of humility I want to bring out.*"

"*Humility,*" said the old woman. "*That's not a word one often hears from an award-winning gardener.*"

"*It's an approach to life, not just to gardening. I see the two as very connected.*"

"*This sense of connectedness comes across in most all your work. The gardens you design—I've always thought—are more like extensions of their surroundings than separate little domains.*"

"*They are both separate and connected. The feeling I want people to have is, at first, not even to know they've entered a garden, and then, when they realize it, to say: 'Of course!' I want it to be more a gradual seduction than an overwhelming display.*"

"*How very French.*"

[Laughter].

Then the dowdy woman said: "*And here's Yvonne, our lucky garden owner.*" The screen suddenly filled with a middle-aged woman with dark hair cropped short like a medieval knight's.

"*Isn't Henri wonderful?*" said the old woman.

"*It's really incredible what he can do.*"

"*What's your favorite part of the garden?*"

Yvonne turned to Henri, and I could see it in her eyes, the same thrall he held Klara in. "*It's all so magnificent, it's hard to say which particular— The colors, for example—your use of colors, the way you contrast them? It's like an artist.*" Henri thrust his hands into his pockets and flashed a modest smile. Yvonne turned to the old woman: "*There's also, you have to see this. His attention to detail is just amazing. Right over here. Do you see these tulips? When you walk down this path, the tulips get closer and closer—the path narrows until it's gone, and you're, like, standing in the middle of tulips, tulips all around. Or sitting, I guess, because he's put a bench there—do you see? And to get out again, you literally have to tip-toe so you don't step on them. Tip-toe through the tulips!*"

"*Oh that is just precious,*" said the old woman. "*I didn't know you had such a whimsical streak in you, Henri.*"

"*Well—*"

"*I'll have to try that. Can we get the camera in there? OK. Here I go!*"

We had to watch the old woman walk to the end of the path and sit gingerly on the little bench. She raised her chin, straightened her arms, and placed her hands on her knees like a preening girl. Then she tip-toed out, squealing with delight.

"Do you see?" Klara said. "What we're trying to do?"

I stared at the screen. "What about his other clients? Were they also single women of a certain age?"

"That isn't the point, Milo."

I almost laughed. "He's using you. And you don't even know who he is."

She slammed down the remote. "This isn't one of Father's novels."

"You really have no idea?"

"Stop it."

"Believe me, you'll wish you'd written this one yourself."

"Written what?"

"How he's trying to get rid of me. Maybe in the same way he got rid of Father. By making me afraid. And then . . . "

"Nobody is getting rid of anybody. You're here to stay, and so is he. Frankly I don't care what happened in the past. We're a family."

"All three of us?"

"You know what I mean. This garden is important to me. We might even film it for a television show if everything turns out, if we can recover from the sodium nitrate. And we will. We'll make it even better than before."

The video had paused, freezing an image of the old woman's quivering, constipated lips. She was staring at Henri, who was bent over, sleeves rolled up. He did look like a typical gardener, and I began to wonder, despite everything, if I was wrong about him—if he really was a gardener, perhaps one who hoped to take advantage of my sister but not one who was Father's fictional character come to life.

Then I saw his arm.

"Are you OK, Milo?"

"My God."

"What is it?"

"You have no idea who this man is. He could be a psychopath."

"What are you talking about? If you have something to say, just say it."

"How old is this video?"

"From last year. Why?"

"Look at his arm, Klara."

"Yes?"

"Do you see a tattoo?"

She fumbled for the remote and snapped off the video player. She must have seen its absence too, but she just sat there letting the television's chaotic light play across her face, letting it bathe her in frantic nonsense, while I wondered: had the gardener been *transformed* into Keith? Did that explain the mystery of the two Henris? "That doesn't prove anything," she eventually told me. "A lot of men might get a military tattoo only later in life, after they've left the army."

"Even men who claim they're dedicating themselves to the very opposite of what the army stands for?"

"Maybe it's a symbol of what he's left behind."

"Or a symbol of something else?" I waited to see if she'd respond. When she didn't, I said, in a thin voice: "Don't you recognize it?"

"Why should I? I've never known anyone in the Foreign Legion."

"Think about Father's work."

"His fiction?"

"Keith Sentelle has the exact same tattoo."

Klara turned to me, and for a moment I saw it—the same fear that was coursing through me. "No, no, Keith's is, was—I don't remember a horse. I remember a snake."

I closed my eyes. "True, it was from a different Foreign Legion regiment. Still, could that be a coincidence? And what about the scar on his thumb? The obsession with nature's dark side? The way he wielded that knife?"

"Henri feels inspired by Father's novels, by his dangerous vision of the woods. And every gardener has scars and is good with knives."

"What about his background as a police officer?" I pressed. "Surely you can't ignore that."

"Keith wasn't a cop, Milo."

"He was a crime scene photographer. It's a passing reference only, but it's there."

"It probably also says Keith likes hamburgers. Do you want me to see if Henri likes hamburgers, too?"

I remained silent, because I could tell her sarcasm was forced— that she wasn't nearly as confident as she made herself seem.

"He's just a gardener, Milo," she insisted, a little too loudly.

"He's trying to break up our home. Accuse me of terrible things. And then what will he do to you?"

She threw up her hands, her fear replaced by exasperation. "I refuse to be afraid of ghosts or coincidences or unsolved mysteries or anything like that anymore. I don't care about the past. Not yours, not his. I want to put it all behind us."

"But it's not so easy, is it? It has a way of insinuating itself into everything."

"You're trying to make me afraid of him."

"No, I'm trying to make you *see*. Perhaps that's why Father was so afraid. Because he'd come face-to-face with the true power of his fiction."

"This is lunacy."

"Henri keeps talking about rebirth, rejuvenation. Don't you get it? He's not just talking about you or the garden, he's talking about *himself*."

"Please, Milo."

"Can't you at least acknowledge the risk? We have everything to lose. The question for you is: is it really worth it? Just so you can look at some pretty flowers?"

Her mouth tightened in a bitter little spasm; I knew I'd gone too far. "The garden isn't just pretty flowers," she said. "It's not even about me anymore. It's something larger. I've decided to dedicate it to Mother and Father's memory. It's going to be a memorial garden. A place where people might come to honor them and have readings and the like. I won't let the accident be the end of them."

I sat perfectly still, not saying anything. I don't know why *this*, of all things, sent my mind reeling. Perhaps it was the sudden notion that I was suffering for the sake of Father's fans, so Klara could lead them on tours and make witty remarks and never, ever allow us to forget the past. And why was she pretending it was not about her? It was always about her.

121

"Was this your idea or Henri's?"

"Both. My point is, it's meant to put the past to rest."

I knew she was under Henri's spell—otherwise she'd never be so naïve. "Yet all it will do is keep their memory alive."

"Alive, yes, but not part of us anymore. It will be out there, not in here."

She pointed at the room, at herself, and for a moment I was tempted to believe it—that we could externalize our fears, plant them and trim them and pull them up by the roots if they grew too wild. But that's not how it worked. "No," I said. "You'll become a parasite on Father's memory. One of those children who . . ."

"Stop it," she said. "I told you I want this antagonism to end."

"That's not really up to you."

"Don't do this, Milo."

"Or what? You'll investigate Mother and Father's death? Show that I was responsible? Is this what you'll have over me for the rest of our lives?"

She put her hands over her ears. "Stop!"

"Maybe you believe it. Maybe you believe the lies of someone you've just met over your very own brother. Maybe this is your idea of family loyalty."

"I don't even know you anymore. All you do is hole up in the study."

"I'm working."

"On what? Stupid models nobody cares about?"

I rose to my feet and rushed across the room and ejected the DVD. Before Klara could reach me I'd bent it in half. "And who cares about this?" I shouted. "It's nothing but a disc of plastic!" She tried to take it away. I wouldn't let her. "Nobody cares what you do either!" I yelled as she loomed over me. "Nobody has ever cared except me! Don't you understand?" I never saw her hand. All I heard was her athletic grunt; all I felt was the dry-ice sting across my cheek. I dropped the disc. She snatched it up. She glared at me stone-faced, then turned and marched away, her pale ankles churning up her skirts. So this is what we've come to, I thought. Full-circle back to the physical memory of pain—to the days of the baton.

The Master was an ancient man, voice cracked and grinding,
And when our man, our Keith, did find him
Holed up inside his attic heaped with art, he smelled the paint,
And glue and clay and wax, and that decayed and languid taint
Of something else. Burnt flesh? Singed hair?
'What are you doing there, and there?'
The Master asked, while tossing down two photos,
Keith's latest work, the Faulkner twins, extinct as dodos.
They're propped beneath a pair of trees, and facing one another,
FACING OFF, the work was called, because—how clever!—
They had no faces anymore, he'd cut them both right off
  their heads
And hung them limp from branches over their death beds.
'Too neat! You're showing off!' the Master snarled
And bade him try again, but Keith just gnarled
His fists and said: 'You're old, you can't see genius anymore.'
The Master paused, and nodded, his eyes keeping score.
'You know that everything is language, grammar,' the old
  man said,
'Take murder, stories, art—they're all the same. And
  when you've seen and read
As much as I, you realize that genius is quite rare.
Most people just manipulate the forms they're given. No one dares
Do anything that's new. The forms are comforting, a
  blanket to a child.'

'A child?' Keith said, unable to believe his ears. 'A child?'

'A faceless figure?" shot The Master back. 'You're copying
  Magritte.'
And that's when Keith first knew he'd need a wholly new
  conceit.

ALL NIGHT LONG THE SHADOWS CREPT ACROSS MY BEDROOM WALLS. Elaborate shifting shapes that reached to me with rotten-leaf arms, yearning hollow eyes. I told myself: *they're only shadows, only figments of my imagination.* I even glanced out the window and saw how the shapes were formed—by the trees and moon. Yet when I turned back it was like they mocked me: *So you see what made us. So what? We're still real.*

This was what haunted me, the notion that they could be both shadows and real. That the shadows were like their camouflage—that they hid there waiting for the unsuspecting, the confident sunny daytime people who couldn't see the magic until it was too late. In the same way I imagined Keith had been waiting, hiding in plain sight, that he was both a fiction and real somehow. I tried to look at the situation logically, telling myself that perhaps I was just afraid of Henri—of this former investigator now investigating me. But there was too much else. Too many signs. I'd unlocked their mystery. I'd seen behind their façade. Logic was almost a debasement now, a violation of the sacred vision. I knew well what horrors Keith was capable of—using his knife, his teeth, even on one occasion an overgrown fingernail, to disembowel his hapless victims:

> *A stroking curl of finger down her skin,*
> *And then surprise! A thrust, a gouge, until he'd limned*
> *Her belly with her own dark seeping juice*
> *Of life, of death, an open sluice*
> *To bathe his hands in . . .*

I pictured Henri's hands—hand smeared with dirt that very first day. I thought: *he was showing me already.* Yes, every part of him seemed ominous now—his teeth, his lips, his nose. For Keith, killing was an intimate art. He literally burrowed himself into it, hoping to excite all the senses. What had he said once? That a warm body was like pudding to a child? Half the fun was getting it all over yourself.

Yes, I knew there was more—things I couldn't yet see. I was still an initiate, finding my way—the light remained dim. Father loved to embed his novels with puzzles and red herrings, unexplained phenomena and unreliable narrators and even private jokes, like the time he'd named a heinous villain after an editor who'd dismissed his work. About Keith's origins he'd written only that he'd been raised

By good and caring folk with only one small minor flaw.
You see, they liked their infants raw.

I'd always wondered what this meant, whether to take it literally, as in *Keith's parents ate babies*, or more symbolically, as in *they didn't school their children.* I vaguely recalled some academic dust-up over this point, and in the grey early morning hours I crept downstairs, where I found a volume of scholarship by the first professors to take Father seriously. Of course I gleaned nothing from them. They were critics, not prophets. Their greatest enlightenment was that "*a large share of Keith's horror lies in the fact that he appears* sui generis, *a self-created monster*" and that "*like all agents of divine wrath, Keith is more force of nature than man.*"

I thought of this last line as he came to us in the crisp early-morning sun—his car gleaming, his smile a crooked gash—like a force that would always return: a battering wave, a Northern wind. He parked in front of the garage. He was alone. I watched as he opened the garage door, careful not to make a sound. I could see him in the Volvo's bay, kneeling on the concrete floor, running his palms over the grease spots like a painter or a priest. He spent several long minutes in there. Then suddenly he glanced up. He was studying the wall: the exact spot where the wire-cutters and Chilton's Guide had hung. I thought: *how did he know where they'd been?*

He quickly exited the garage and closed the door. He came into the house with his key. He must have surprised Klara in the kitchen. I heard a clattering pan. She sometimes made oatmeal for herself on the stove. They talked. I couldn't hear what about. They were whispering, and I discerned only the occasional word: "*expert,*" "*study,*" "*proper.*" I tried to form sentences out of them: "*experts study properly*" or "*we could hire an expert to study the garage and send the results to the proper authorities.*" Anyway it didn't matter. The image of Henri kneeling, almost genuflecting, in the Volvo's bay had given me an idea, a way to divine more.

I hurried down the long hallway to Mother and Father's room.

Nothing had changed from the night of their deaths, nothing removed, not the yellowed newspaper that lay folded on their bed, or the dusty curtains or Mother's night-time glass of lithia water or the worn leather slippers, the jars of perfume and skin cream and tubes of crumbling lipstick. It was like a mausoleum to *before.* I threw open the closets. There were Mother's sequined dresses. Father's old black fedoras. Shoes I was sure Mother had never worn and a white tuxedo that I recalled vaguely from old wedding photos. But it was Father's more pedestrian attire that I pulled off their wooden hangers. A tweed jacket, rumpled Oxford shirt, corduroy trousers.

While Klara and Henri were engaged in more kitchen-*klatsch* I brought these items to my room and carefully arranged them on the bed. I wasn't sure whether I ought to say something or make some sign. In the end I just closed my eyes and breathed, then pulled the needle and thread from my nightstand drawer.

One of the benefits of making models is that I've never been intimidated by fine manual work. I was always the one to fix Klara's buttons or sew a ragged sleeve. To her the work was demeaning—*women's work*—while to me it focused the mind. It soothed.

I quickly sewed together the trouser bottoms and sleeve ends. Then I tucked the shirt into the tweed jacket and sewed the trousers to the shirt, leaving the shirt a little unbuttoned. Only after-wards did I realize that I'd forgotten one of the fedoras. I went back into the hallway. Still empty. Again I heard their voices. They were no longer in the kitchen. They seemed to be in the entrance hall directly below the stairs. I heard Klara say in a low voice: "I have to know. I'm sorry. I can't do anything until I find out."

"You are not responsible for what Milo did or who he is."

"Not directly, no, but it's possible that everything stems from my own negligence."

"You are looking for reasons, explanations."

"Please don't try to talk me out of this." I heard a jangle of keys. "I shouldn't be long. Will you be alright?"

"I am not afraid of him," he said, "not for myself."

"That's another thing I need to find out, whether we should be, whether he's capable of . . ."

"And you think this doctor . . . ?"

"Zeiss. I talked to him years ago. He wanted to do a scan. You see? I was negligent even then. I didn't want to face the truth. But now I have no choice. After yesterday . . ."

The rest was lost as they made their way out the front door. For a time I just stood there, wondering what my sister could be talking about. It wasn't the first time she'd referred to her own responsibility for me. But I'd never heard her talk about a doctor before.

I hurried back to my bedroom just in time to see her bouncing away in the old MG. Henri remained at the edge of the driveway. He was hunched, coiled like a question mark, his thumbs looped into the pockets of his faded jeans. He watched her go just as I watched him stay, and suddenly I was conscious of how alone we were—no Marta, no workmen, not a soul within miles. Just me and this infamous psychopath sprung to life from the pages of Father's book.

He turned and made his way slowly back to the house. And to me. He'd expect me to be in my bedroom, where I'd be trapped, at his mercy. I picked up Father's clothes and raced into the hallway. I'd just managed to duck into my parents' room when I heard footsteps on the stairs—the loud, shuffling boot steps of a man with no need for stealth.

In a few steps I crossed the room and grabbed the fedora, then I was back at the door, watching through the slit. In the dim, shadowy light of the hallway I saw his white shirt pause at the top of the stairs and those eyes glance up and down. He was drawn to the portraits. He reached out and touched the first one. Then he called out: "*Milo? Do you want to come out and play? It is just the two of us. No use pretending anymore.*"

It was the mocking tone of the bullies that had once tormented me. And like the worst of them, Henri knew just where to strike:

"*I know you believe in me. Come, let me show you.*"

Where could I go? He was blocking the stairs. I began to perspire. That's when I remembered the narrow winding steps at this end of the hall. The ones we never used because they remained unfinished—a vestige of Father's aborted attempt to build a tower like in the castles of his native England. They were only accessible from a low passage that ran alongside Mother and Father's room. With the clothes and fedora in my arms I slipped down this passage, immured in stone, lost in shadows. I felt the walls. There. The wooden door. I turned the rusted lock and pulled.

"*I also know you are not really afraid. This is all exciting to you.*"

It creaked open. I slipped through and hastily closed it behind me. Now I was in total darkness. I felt for the brickwork, then cautiously advanced, but caution meant little under the circumstances. The first stone step crumbled immediately underfoot and nearly sent me tumbling—only the narrowness of the staircase saved me. The next few steps were solid, and I was just getting into the rhythm of the descent when suddenly…nothing. No step, just empty space. What could I do? I teetered, then gave myself to the pull of gravity and jumped.

I didn't fall far before I landed on what must have been a slope. I landed on my bottom and began to slide, finally stopping in a pile of leaves. No, not leaves. Paper. Mounds and mounds of paper, redolent of ink and dust. I picked myself up, shedding them, wanting them off me, I didn't care if they were old bills, though I knew they weren't. This was where Father had once tossed his unfinished, unwanted drafts, here in this unfinished tower. I stumbled forward and saw a crack of light, a metal door.

I turned the handle and pulled. It screamed against its hinges. I blinked, I was free, at the side of the house near the woods. I'd lost the fedora, but I didn't care—I still had Father's clothes, and they were enough. I ran.

The sun shone through the forest canopy in strobes and beams. I soon found myself back at the old Indian wall. I tossed Father's clothes over it. Then I climbed after them and crouched behind the mossy stones. I could no longer see the house, just a screen of twisted trees and underbrush. Still I remained alert to him, to that terrible voice, as I began gathering leaves, stuffing them through the shirt buttons I'd left open. A faint scent of Father lingered in those clothes, but it was soon masked by the smell of so much mulch.

When I'd finished I quickly buttoned the shirt and tweed jacket and hauled Father deeper into the woods. There was no path anymore, just damp hilly earth, and I dragged him by the shirt collar, leaking leaves like a decapitated body might leak blood. I was nearly out of breath when I paused, sensing something ahead of me, something *unnatural*. There, behind a screen of trees. Encased almost entirely in vines and weeds. The rusted hulk of an old farm truck.

I dragged Father to it. These relics were more common in the Vermont woods than one imagined—the legacy of so much farmland turned to forest. I managed to pry open the driver's door and peer inside. The leather bench seat had been eaten away to reveal rusted springs. The steering wheel was gone, the dashboard slick with moss. The entire interior had the crayon odor of old diesel fuel.

"Isn't this fun?" Father asked.

"Vroom, vroom!" I said.

I grabbed Father and wedged him into the driver's seat. *"Is this what it was like? Were you sitting just like this?"* He slumped forward. Leaves tumbled out of his open neck. Then came a breeze, pulling more leaves out of him. I picked up a handful of them from the ground and threw them in the air, and they scattered over him, a bloody mess of leaves.

"I always helped you, you know," I said. *"Now I need a favor in return."*

Silence. Was he really dead? Just a pile of leaves stuffed into clothes? But by that token Jesus was just a carpenter nailed to some planks of wood (and why has no one ever seen the irony in that?). Then all of a sudden . . . A cloud moved in front of the sun. Everything became dark and the breeze died away. I felt oddly cold. That's when I heard his voice:

Son.

I opened my mouth. Not a sound emerged. This was what I'd wanted, I told myself, why I was here, yet I still couldn't form the words. Finally I managed: *I'm in the middle of a plot. It's out of my control. I don't know what to do.*

You need my advice?

Ironic, yes, but I didn't know where else to turn. I closed my eyes.

Did you manage to create Keith for real? Bring him to life like you'd never been able to do on the page? And then did he turn on you?

In a manner of speaking.

How do I defeat him?

How do you defeat a fiction?

That's just it. I don't know.

Where do fictions live?

In books. So I thought. But now . . .

No, not in books.

Then where?

In the mind. Of the reader.

What are you saying?

Do you believe?

That's when I remembered the reviews of Father's early work, how critics said he *strained credulity* and *invited disbelief.* Yes, I saw it now, the way out of this novel I was trapped in—out of the entire mental architecture I'd built up and only now realized was a cage . . .

All at once I snapped out of it. I opened my eyes. There it was again.

Snap.

A branch, a twig. I turned around. The trees shook, jeering at me: *over here, over here.* "I know who you are," I called out to the

mute woods. Another snap. I whirled the other way. He was circling, toying with me. "And Klara does, too," I went on. "I told her."

It doesn't matter. She doesn't believe you. She thinks you're *the fictional character.*

I picked up a stone and backed into a tree. All at once I turned
and yelled and hurled it. It bounced harmlessly through the underbrush. I ran back to the house, leaving Father behind, bursting through the door and up the stairs. I locked myself in my
room and stumbled to the window. I was never so glad to see
Marta's station wagon or the old MG in the driveway, to realize
there were people nearby, even ones who doubted me—anything
to escape my relentless imagination.

In the mind. Of the reader.

I opened my door and heard Klara and Henri in the living
room and Marta humming in the kitchen. Their voices girded me even though I could hear the conspiracy, the overbearing *concern*, in Klara's low tones. I went to the bathroom and
splashed my hands and face and scrubbed my muddy shoes.
Then I removed my clothes. I changed into pajamas and spent
the rest of the day in bed.

I told Marta I wasn't feeling well and instructed her to leave
soup and crackers before my door. In the evening I drifted early
to sleep. My dreams were of Henri again. He stood in my room,
looking down at me, hanging his head. "*How can you possibly
expect to defeat me? You'd have to defeat yourself first.*" I stirred
awake. I was laughing, giggling. Yes, I thought, I could defeat
myself, my own belief, because really it was absurd to imagine
that Henri was Keith somehow brought to life. I laughed at the
shadows, at the window, at the moon-glow and rustling trees,
laughed at my slender bed, thick walls, my antique dresser and
night table, laughed at everything but the smell, which I suddenly noticed rising from beneath me, the smell of earthworms,
maggots, decay. The smell that quelled my laughter, though not
my nerves, the smell that forced me, slowly, to look down and
see on the floor a badly sewn-up arm protruding from beneath
my bed, the arm of Father's shirt stuffed with its damp and rotting leaves.

THE MORNING WAS COOL AND BRACING AND BLUE, AND I WAS SUR-prisingly calm given that Father remained beneath my bed, leaking and smelling of decay. I suppose there's a comfort in having the worst actually happen and realizing that you can sleep right through it. I felt refreshed, rested, ready to tackle the question of exactly how Father had gotten there, or rather why Henri had done it (as it could only have been him) other than to frighten me into realizing that he'd followed me into the woods and could enter the house and my room at will. Yes, I sensed already that there was another motive at work, another element in his designs. Yet it wasn't until the police arrived shortly before breakfast that I realized their full and threatening intricacy.

I'd just thrown open the window for some fresh air. A few streaky clouds marred the sky. I could just see the distant road to Rutland. I was wondering what easy morning rituals its residents might be enjoying—wolfing down greasy plates of bacon or combing *The Rutland Herald* for shopping mall coupons—when I spotted a metallic glint through the trees. It was coming up our driveway. Henri? Marta? No, it was a vast American sedan, and when it finally emerged I knew right away what it was. Why are unmarked cars so obvious? The police ought to use beaten-up little Fiats. It rumbled to a stop in front of the garage. For a minute or so no one emerged. Then the door opened. Out he climbed. Heavy-set, with a tight-fitting sports jacket that bulged where a shoulder-holster hung. Another cliché. He hitched up his pants by the waist and lunged straight for the house.

And, I knew, for me.

I opened my door and heard a knocking downstairs. I pictured the huge clown-head knocker that Father had installed years ago.

I told myself I should run and stash Father in one of the guest rooms. Still I couldn't move. I was succumbing already to the lure of giving up, how easy it would be. I remained rooted there, imagining the officer's surprise on seeing Father beneath my bed and my half-hearted attempt to make light of the situation: *Oh that? It's nothing, a scarecrow, I've been sewing it in my spare time. Boo!* I even opened my door a little wider to make it easier for him, to show him I had nothing to hide.

I waited. More knocking. *This is a lot of knocking!* I could almost hear the officer's gruff voice as he asked for me, and Klara's innocent-seeming reply: *"Is there a problem?"*

"I need to ask him some questions, ma'am. We've gotten new information about the accident. Is he home?"

He'd trudge into my room and see Father right away. Then would come the questions. The almost wolfish disbelief when I told the truth. Followed by a pat on the shoulder, a not-so-gentle request to *come to the station for a little talk about your parents*. It would be the opposite of all those parent-teacher meetings where the teachers wanted to ask *them* about *me*. And I'd go. What choice would I have? I'd take one last glance over my shoulder at Father lying there and hear the officer's reassurance that *it'll be there when you return*, even though I knew I'd never return and that a forensics team was already on its way. Would Klara finally get what she wanted, then? To have the estate all to herself? To be alone with Henri?

Where was she? I gazed at her room. Her door was open wide. "Klara?" I called out, still not daring to leave my room.

The knocking stopped.

I braced myself. I hadn't heard the front door open. Yet I couldn't be sure. Any moment now I might hear footsteps. Up the stairs, some heavy, some light, and Klara's shaken whisper before they turned the corner: *"He's right up here, in his room. Be careful, he's not well."* But no. The house remained quiet as a grave.

I drifted back to the window. Was I surprised to see them at the garage? *They*—Klara and the officer both? The officer was inspecting the garage door's lock, running his thick fingers across the plate. He talked out of the side of his mouth. Klara nodded.

She must have been behind the house, must have heard the knocking and come around. Now she stood beside him, arms folded against the morning chill. Finally he lifted the door. He did it with a quick motion, as if it were nothing for him, then pulled a flashlight from his belt. Into the darkness he plunged, the flashlight's beam dancing while Klara remained outside, a stone-faced statue in the breeze. She didn't even flinch when a rabbit darted across the driveway not three feet from her. They always look so guilty, rabbits, as if they've just devoured your vegetable garden. This one seemed worried for its life.

After a short while the officer came back out holding a clear plastic bag. A shriveled lump of blue lay at the bottom. A pair of latex gloves.

My gloves.

I've already mentioned this, I know: how I often wore surgical gloves when working on my models, how I'd been wearing them on the day Henri first arrived. He must have noticed this—as he noticed everything—must have catalogued it in his evil brain. I pressed my hands against the window as the officer held up the bag for Klara's inspection. She recoiled a little. Eventually she nodded: *Yes, those are Milo's.* I scrabbled against the glass. I was being buried alive, my *character* assassinated before my very eyes.

She came to me several minutes later, knocking gently on my door. By then I was back in bed, curled beneath the covers, staring at Father's protruding sleeve and the sewn-up stump where his hand ought to have been.

"Milo? Can I talk to you?"

At first I didn't respond. But she persisted. What could I do? I didn't dare let her in. It would have been the final nail in my coffin—the one she herself was fitting for me.

"I have a headache, Klara."

"You're not feeling well."

It was a statement, not a question, and I let it go unanswered, because that was what she obviously needed to believe. Yes, everything we knew was just a matter of belief, I saw that now, not just about fictional characters but real people too. And for a moment I was tempted to believe her: that I was *sick* and *not right* in the mind. *So how did Father get beneath my bed?* I wanted to scream. *Am I dreaming him there?* No—I couldn't ask this. I could only listen as she whispered *"I'm sorry"* as if it were all her fault. Which in a way it was, though I didn't know yet how—didn't know the full extent of her own terrible guilt.

I had no idea how long I remained in bed. It felt like days. Every time I heard a car I imagined it was the police. I almost longed for them to come, just to relieve the suspense. But they were only gardening trucks. They arrived in the morning and remained like slumbering dinosaurs until the sky was evening-purple. What happened in between was vague. I couldn't sleep. I leafed through military manuals and historical texts. I read about the invention of the phalanx by the little-known Epiminodas of Thebes. At one point I thought I saw the Mormon boy hiking up our driveway, but when I looked there was no one—just Henri's workers pulling assault-like implements from the trucks and carrying them on slings around the house. I felt their din from my room—a slight but unmistakable tremor whenever I pressed my head against the wall.

Still I began, despite everything, to plan. Not consciously—more in the way a small animal might plan when trapped in a hole, eyes shifting frantically to calculate the angle of its one last chance to escape. Again I thought about smuggling Father into one of the guest rooms. Only I knew Marta would find him during her very next deep cleaning. Even at her age she was remarkably thorough, sticking that feather duster everywhere. There *was* one place I could stash Father where she wouldn't find him—yet this was the one place in the house I was reluctant to go.

In the end I might never have made an attempt at that black lacquered door—might have succumbed to the gallows or wherever accused murderers go these days—if I hadn't seen them the following afternoon. I was still in bed. Still expecting the police. I kept picturing overweight officers with their feet on their desks reading pornography and fingering their guns, just waiting for the signal to pounce. I decided that the rotten-leaf odor must be getting to me, so I opened my window, and that's when I noticed them, Henri and Klara, against the iron fence below. Henri had his sleeves rolled up and a blade of grass between his teeth. His self-confidence was palpable. He must have known the police would return soon enough. Klara was huddled next to him, fingers at her temples. Another headache was coming on. I wasn't surprised. He was steadying her, a hand on her shoulder, yet I could already see the impatience in the gesture. He didn't really care about her. He was doing it because it was expected. "Everything will be alright," he said—the emptiest words I could imagine. He didn't even bother to remove the blade of grass. "The important thing right now is to learn all the facts."

She nodded and touched his tattoo.

"You are interested in my tattoo?" he asked, silky smooth.

"It's just . . . Milo had this crazy idea . . ."

Henri smiled. "Just before I moved to southern Vermont, I received a letter from an old friend, an ex-Legionnaire. Saying that a mutual friend, one I was with in Chad, had died. I did this to honor him."

Relief washed over Klara's face. "I'm sorry to have doubted you," she said. "I'm such a fool."

He narrowed his eyes like a watch-maker studying an intricate Rolex. "You are under a great deal of strain."

She shook her head. "I just don't know what to think anymore. Or what to do."

"Listen. What we have created together is beautiful. Even more beautiful than before the sodium nitrate. You see? Out of death comes a new and better life."

She rubbed her eyes and nodded, and for a moment I was taken by the notion that he meant *me*, that out of *my* death would come her own blossoming.

"Your vision, the color and harmony in your daffodils, the perennial border on the south side, by the Helen Traubels—these are touches of sheer brilliance," he said.

"Flattery will get you everywhere," she murmured (and this from a woman who hated clichés!). Henri began curling her hair behind her ear. She gave a shiver and hardly moved, but didn't pull away either. "Should we do more?" he said. "Expand the garden here, to the front of the house?"

She nodded.

"We make a fantastic team," he went on. "I do not want it to end."

"Me neither. It's just . . ."

"Shh." He leaned over and kissed her, a furtive, pecking affair, engaged in shyly on her part and with a good deal of flushed awkwardness. "Not here," Klara gasped. A smile cut across her face. She clutched his hand and led him across the grounds, toward the woods where I'd seen Father with that grisly raccoon, and where (the memory came back to me now) I'd once, years earlier, seen him with her.

I tried to bury this memory by staring at my posters of antique cars. But all their bumpers were lips, all their lights Henri's piercing green eyes. I opened my night table's drawer. *Is this a dagger which I see before me, / The handle toward my hand?* Yes. I snatched it out of its case, an old bayonet I'd found in the basement years before. I knew I wasn't thinking straight, yet I couldn't help myself. I didn't even change clothes. I ran out of the house in my elephant pajamas and slippers. I ran toward the woods, waving the bayonet over my head, yelling nonsense about driving a stake through evil's heart.

They were easy to spot, huddled against a thin white birch, Klara's blouse falling off one shoulder—gently teased down by Henri's fingers.

"Milo? My God, what are you . . . ?"

There was genuine terror in her eyes. But I refused to look at her. I was watching Henri—watching as he whirled around, eyes hooded with excitement, hair falling in his face. "It's you," he said.

"Be careful, Klara," I blurted out through the trees. "He's dangerous."

But he just laughed at me—laughed in his smug smooth way, a bubbling brook of laughter. "I'm not the one with the bayonet."

I looked down. For the first time I saw myself through their eyes: jealous, unhinged, obviously capable of heinous crimes. I knew I'd just made things immeasurably worse. "Sorry," I said.

"Go home," Klara said. "Right now. Before I call the police."

Home. Where was that exactly? I paused at the front door like I'd always done when returning from school, bracing myself for Mother's neglect. Then it came to me. I knew what I had to do. I hurried up to Klara's room, bayonet still in hand. I searched her night stand and dresser and behind her dolls and porcelain figurines. Beneath the bed I rummaged through her old photo boxes and pulled out her white leather jewelry case. I opened it like an accordion and fingered aside the pearls and earrings and her old wedding band and engagement ring. I was about to close it again when I noticed a gap between the inside and outside bottoms. My heartbeat quickened. I picked up the bayonet. I slipped it into the gap and pried. A false bottom. Beneath it was a silver necklace and a dangling brass key. She still had it. I knew she would.

I carefully put everything back together before fetching Father and dragging him to his room. I closed the door behind me. I didn't turn on the light. The room was dim and shadowy. I walked to the base of the ladder. The attic door hovered darkly overhead. I remembered, after the funeral, Klara admonishing me to stay away from it, implying that a museum might be interested in what it contained. Even at the time I could hardly believe that any self-respecting historical institution would be interested in Father. For all his acclaim he was nothing but a glorified hack. Perhaps it was a museum devoted to hacks? I wouldn't have been surprised. After all, America was the land of strange museums— The Tupperware Museum of Historic Food Containers, The Barbie Hall of Fame, The American Sanitary Plumbing Museum. Why not the Museum of Hack Writers too?

I clutched Father in one arm, bayonet still in hand, and began my ascent. One step and I was airborne. Two and I was floating giddily above the objects below. Three and I was like a space-walker on the loosest of tethers.

By the time I reached the top I could hardly breathe. It felt like I was on the moon. Still I hesitated, wondering if the attic would smell like Father—a peaty odor to turn my stomach—or contain ground-up corpses in the walls (as in *Bricklayer, Brickslayer*) or rusted man-traps and spring-guns (as in the aptly titled *The Man Upstairs*). I reached forward and found the lock, felt its rough unused edge. I fit the key inside. It turned easily. The door popped back with a whoosh, as if pulled by an escaping ghost. But no one was there. No smells, no arrows, no man-trap shots. Just an inky blackness pierced by the gleam from a slatted window. I saw myriad shapes—patches of shadow that might be a desk or a bookcase and others like lines of fluttering flags. It wasn't until I reached along the inside wall, found a light switch, and (holding my breath) flipped it up, that I saw what they really were.

There is, I'm sure, a stereotype in all our minds of what the sanctum of a famous horror writer ought to look like. Red velvet chairs, high bookshelves, carved wooden desk with odd "horror writer" ornaments like a skull or a set of old pistols in glass cases—all familiar from many films on the subject. Equally familiar, from the same source, is the lair of the stereotypical serial killer with its walls covered by newspaper cut-outs and photographs of past and future victims.

Once my eyes adjusted to the light from the track of bulbs (only about half of which still worked) that ran along the pointed ceiling's spine, it was some mixture of these two visions that I beheld. What had appeared to be flags turned out to be sheet after sheet of typewritten paper pinned to a clothesline. Beyond it, on the far wall, beneath the slatted window, was Father's desk, on which stood an old manual typewriter with a half-written sheet of paper still lodged inside. The walls on either side were cut like triangles to follow the sloping roofline and were covered with bookshelves of various heights arranged pyramid-like to match the space. There was also a day bed in one corner and a bronze statuette of a blindfolded woman holding a set of scales—the traditional embodiment of Justice he'd once been given as a prize at a mystery writer's convention.

I pulled Father toward the day bed and managed to wedge him underneath. Then I closed the door. It was the desk that drew me. The desk where Keith had been set down, sung into verse. For a moment I wondered if there were notes, drafts, where Father had planned his return, his *metamorphosis* into something real. Or perhaps journal entries describing how Keith was somehow haunting him? But no, it wasn't so simple. What I saw was an array of photos in dusty frames. There was an infant Klara; Klara in pigtails; Klara bending into a Christmas tree; Klara in a plaid skirt hugging a notebook, earnestly delivering the high school valedictory, wearing her Harvard graduation cap with that Brazilian hovering beside her.

There was not a single one of me.

I turned away and gazed at the clothesline. On wooden pins hung several sheets of paper with the beginnings of an unfinished novel entitled *Halfway to Paradise*. I tore them down, reading frantically. The first thing I noticed was that it wasn't in verse. He'd finally decided to write a novel without his trademark gimmick:

Where was he? His hand floated up to his shirt pocket. One thing he loved about Egypt was that everybody smoked. Not like the States, where people were health-crazed and afraid to die. He didn't trust anyone who was afraid to die.

I crumpled this page and tossed it to the ground, certain that Father had been afraid to die when his Volvo plunged over the edge of the ravine, that the terror had finally inflicted its most enthusiastic maker.

The sun was hot. Like a heat lamp. The old woman's black cloak and head covering stuck to her skin. She was pulling sheets and pants from the clothesline and watching the mud hut's door. She'd been doing this too long. She glanced at her Rolex watch.

Finally she saw the girl. Dark, skinny, one of her best. She squeezed out the door, then shut it again. She was wrapped in a grey cloth, much too big. She had to hold it against her body with one hand as she walked. She walked jerkily, knock-kneed. When she was close the old woman gave her the usual look-over and held out a hand. The girl produced a wallet. The woman smiled, tucked the wallet into the folds of her cloak. Then she held out her hand again. The girl gave her a bloody knife. The woman smiled and put the knife away too. Then she held out her hand a third time. This time the girl opened her mouth. At first it was like she was smiling. But then she kept opening it. Blood dripped down her chin and she gagged as a lump of red flesh pressed out, as if she was giving birth. Then the man's kidney dropped into the old woman's hand. It was smooth with bits of darker flesh still stuck to it.

"Very good," said the old woman.

My head began to throb. It had been months since I'd been subjected to Father's imagination, but it seemed like only yesterday. I tossed these pages aside and returned to the desk. I ignored the photos, turning them around as I opened the drawers. There were many more drafts of Father's work—some in verse and some not, some typed and some handwritten in marbled composition books. I threw them all aside. There were other odds and ends—pens, pencils, crumpled packs of Craven cigarettes, a flashlight, a pair of slim binoculars—that I didn't bother with, and several more framed photographs of Klara that I hurled against the wall.

There must be more, I told myself. Private notebooks, diaries. What had Klara been searching for shortly after the accident? I recalled how she'd sneak up here in the middle of the night—the creaking door, footsteps overhead. I peered behind the bookshelves and beneath the day bed. I began opening books and feeling the bottoms of drawers and pressing the cushions on his chair. I walked every square inch of that place, knocking on walls and ceiling beams. But there was nothing—just an empty attic in which a man had dreamed terrible tales. I sat on the day bed, defeated, ready to give up, when I noticed a corner where the wall-to-wall shag carpeting was coming up. It was a little thing, a curl of fabric. Still it made me curious. I approached it and pulled. It came back easily. There was a square of carpeting that was not nailed down. Beneath the carpeting lay a floorboard that didn't match. I tried to pry it loose with the bayonet, only the blade was too big. I had to use his old letter opener with the sea horse handle.

There, in a little well, lay a stack of letters.

I recognized Klara's handwriting at once—her neat slanted print. Many of the envelopes had postmarks spanning the years she was teaching those delinquents in Ohio. But unlike her postcards from that place, these letters were addressed to a post office box in Battenkill near where Marta lived. And many of the letters were not addressed at all—they just said "Father" on the front, evidently to be hand-delivered.

I opened the uppermost one. It was dated May 14, 1999, just a few weeks before her return from teaching.

Father,

It is settled, then. I shall return at the beginning of July. In some ways it gives me such great relief to write that! The weather here is becoming unbearable already. They say that summer is coming earlier and earlier these days because of Global Warming. I do believe it.

I cannot escape feeling like a failure. I will go, but it will be with my tail lodged firmly between my legs. Chancellor Smith has asked me (again!) to reconsider, but I've told him I simply cannot stay. I feel I've done nothing for these poor children. I just don't seem able to form a pedagogical connection to them. They come from such alien worlds. I don't blame them. I shudder to think what has been done to them throughout their lives. It's a wonder they're even alive, the way society treats them. Society! Their own families. It's shameful.

This is why they deserve so much more. They would be better off with someone who understood them and can help them or at least someone with the energy to maintain their interest throughout an hour-long class. I don't seem to have that energy. I'm exhausted all the time. Perhaps I'm too old for this—the younger teachers, the ones right out of college, seem to fare much better.

I'm sorry to be repetitive. I know I've said all this a thousand times. But you seem to be the only one I can talk to. Mother doesn't really say anything in her letters except "Keep a stiff upper lip!" and Milo just wouldn't understand. He's been sending me the strangest letters, you know. Have you spoken to him lately? I suppose not. He's impossible to talk to. He exists in his own little world. His letters aren't really to me, they're to himself—like a one-sided conversation in his head. He keeps telling me all the technical details of his model warships—how many rounds per minute their guns can fire and so forth—and about these battles he's still so obsessed with. Do you know he's learning the name of every American soldier and sailor who died in Pearl Harbor? He says there were only 2,280 of them so it shouldn't be that hard. 2,280! And this is what he does in his spare time? I worry about him. When he was younger this all seemed more natural. All boys are fascinated by war. But now? It keeps getting worse. He needs a friend. Someone, anyone. Do you know he's never had a girlfriend? Never had a real relationship with anyone? I asked him about girls once and he just looked at me as if I'd said something horrible. I wonder if he needs medi-

cal help. There are drugs that do miracles these days. Perhaps we should have done this years ago, after what happened when he was small—that terrible incident that haunts me to this day. You see, you aren't the only one to blame for how he is.

I'd be happy to call some doctors myself, only Mother would have to take him to the hospital. Perhaps she can say she wants to buy him a book, then at the last minute make a detour? Or is this too scheming? Would it be better to be honest with him? I only fear that honesty would be lost on someone like him.

Love,
Klara

I spent an entire era staring at those words:
Someone like him.

No one enjoys being referred to in the third person. Especially in letters. It's like being present at your own funeral. But this was another kind of death altogether—that of the deepest, blackest betrayal. And by whom? The person closest to me in all the world. The one I was trying desperately to protect. I felt like a formaldehyde frog splayed open for dissection, utterly helpless, with steel pins through my limbs and a cold light shining in my eyes, only half-obscuring the clinical smile of the scientist I'd thought to be an ally.

Drugs. She wanted me on drugs. She wanted me to be *different* than I was, to be *altered chemically*, because she thought I needed a *miracle*, otherwise I'd remain monstrously strange and *impossible to talk to*. Yet isn't that all I've ever wanted? To talk to her? To live in peace and quiet where we can hear each other speak and where we understand what lies unspoken between us? How could she claim I'd never had a real relationship? She and I had lived together nearly all our lives.

My hands shook as I put down the letter. I was tempted to burn it, to burn all the letters, to burn everything—the attic, the house, the woods. Burn it all to cinders and let nature start anew. But would anything be different next time? Or was this just how people were—selfish, untrustworthy, *scheming*?

And there was more: the awful *incident* she'd obliquely referred to, the source of some haunting guilt. I didn't want to know what it was, but I had to. There was no longer any turning back. Still I sat there for a time, not reaching for the next letter, letting the future, the past, everything coalesce into a hazy, disconcerting *now*.

May 21:
Father,
I wasn't blaming you for Milo. Not entirely, anyway. If anyone was responsible, it was me. I am speaking of course about the "incident." Although it occurs to me now that perhaps you never knew. It happened when he was just learning to walk. You and Mother were away at a reading. I was taking care of him. I always had a difficult time with him—he used to scream and scream for no reason, and I'd have to bounce him and rock him and swing him around until he stopped. Was something wrong with him even then? Or did things go wrong only after that night? I was too young to tell. And I couldn't ask. Mother was useless. She seemed afraid of him, like she wasn't sure where he'd come from. And you—you were preoccupied with the children of your mind.
It started just after you left. We were in the kitchen, eating at Marta's table because Mother hated the dining room getting messy. He was eating mashed-up pears from a jar. I remember that because I wondered if he was allergic to them. He'd had pears countless times before, but never before had he started gagging like he did that night. He was making funny faces too, and I wondered if he was teasing me. Have you ever heard of a 1-year old teasing? I turned away, stopped paying attention, hoping he might calm down. It didn't work. I don't know which came first, the screams or the throwing up. They seemed to fly out of him at the same instant—a throw-up-scream that sent pear everywhere, all over my new dress, my hair, the table, the wallpaper. I was angry. I can admit that now. I was angry and I picked him up. I rocked him and I shook him and my hands became slippery from all that pear. I was crying when I dropped him, when I heard that awful smack of bone on tile. Then everything became quiet. He just lay there, arms out at his sides as if soaking up the sun. He looked peaceful, more peaceful than I'd ever seen him, even with that pear smeared across his face and sticking in his hair.

I don't know how long he was out. Minutes felt like hours. I was convinced I'd killed him. I was a terrible big sister. I hadn't taken care of him. It was all my fault. I shouldn't have fed him those pears, shouldn't have turned away or gotten angry at his screams. I held him in my arms and I knew he was dead, because hadn't I held him more than anyone else? Wouldn't I know if he was still alive? Then all of a sudden he was looking at me. I nearly dropped him all over again. He hardly blinked, just stared with those haunted eyes, and in that moment I loved him and hated him more than ever, because I knew I was now responsible for him—that I'd blame myself for anything he did from then on because I'd dropped him and damaged his brain. Would it have been easier if he'd died? It's terrible, but I wonder that sometimes. He would have been a memory, and it's easier to love a memory.

I have no memory of this. None at all. Her letter was the first I'd heard of it, and I just held it in my hand, my numb hand, as I took it all in. Would I have been better off dead? Would I have been easier to love? Or just easier to forget? It made me think of something I'd once overheard Mother say, that she loved her children most when they were asleep. Because in sleep—as in death—she could imagine any child she wanted without having to face the actual, messy, incorrigible human being.

I nearly cried. I might have, too, had I not forged ahead—had I not decided to mask this pain by inflicting more. I want to think that nothing had prepared me for what I was about to read, but I'm not sure if that is accurate. Once I knew the sort of betrayal she was capable of, nothing surprised me anymore.

There was a gap of some months before the next letter.

August 3:
Father,
Chancellor Smith asked whether you might be interested in giving a reading even if I am no longer here. He thought it might inspire the children to see an actual writer, especially one whose work they might have heard about or read. I told him I didn't know whether you were still doing that sort of thing. I hope so. You are such a wonderful reader. I'll never forget the time when I was six

years old and Mother was in the hospital with Milo and you spent all night reading me Grimm's Fairy Tales. I couldn't understand all the words but the way you read it made everything clear. I have this vivid memory of you jumping onto my bed, grabbing the bed-post, and pretending you were Rumplestilskin. I don't think I've ever laughed so hard.

What has happened to us since? Why are we no longer as close? I guess the easy answer is that you became famous and self-ab-sorbed. But it wasn't just that. It was how you became famous. You must know what I mean.

Your idea for the new novel Queen Dad sounds wonderful, and the first few pages read beautifully. I can tell already I'm going to relish the rest of it whenever you'll let me read more. I've told you over and over that you should publish these more serious works. Why keep them hidden away? Don't let the reception that Museum Collections received discourage you. You've written others that are different and far, far better. Let the world see what you can do! You can even write them under a pseudonym if you're nervous.

I should tell you that I've begun writing, too. Just notes so far. It's to be a novel, a family drama. Based on us? I suppose that's inevi-table. Everyone will read it that way, anyway.

I didn't really understand the end of your letter. You do want me to come home, don't you? Forgive me if this is a silly question and the result of a misunderstanding. When you wrote that your work was all-consuming and that you didn't think you could see me un-til you'd gotten it out of your system, I wasn't sure. I know how im-portant your work is to you. But does it really have to come at the expense of those who love you? I'm sorry to press this. I'm happy to have Marta pick me up from the train station, but can't you at least let me come up and say hello? Things are a bit overwhelming right now as I try to finish classes and pack and say good-bye. I'm tired. I can't sleep. I have these splitting headaches. These are not as bad as Mother's, but I do worry given the family history. Anyway, I apologize for how scattered this letter is. I just opened yours and wanted to reply right away.

The next one didn't have a postmark on it, nor a stamp, and was dated September 11, after Klara had already returned home.

Father,

I found my old music boxes again. I took two of the handpup-pets from the wall—the Cheshire Cat and the beetle—and had a little performance on the bedside. Too bad the music boxes were out of tune. For the finale I opened them all at once and it sound-ed like something dying. Oh well. I wish you could have seen it, though. It seems silly to keep writing like this when I'm home. If it's your work that's keeping you, you could at least send a short note through Marta telling me that. And if you've got any more pages from Queen Dad, *I'd love to see them.*

What did you think of the pages I sent you?

September 15:

Father,

I'm starting to wonder what to think. This can't possibly still be about your work, can it? Even if Queen Dad *is difficult, I can't be-lieve you haven't had a moment free for the past week and a half. Is it about what I've said regarding Milo? You need to face this, just like I have. Your own complicity. Or is it about what happened before I left for Ohio? I don't feel bad about it, Father. I really don't. And I don't think you should, either.*

Let's talk, shall we? Have you read about how SUVs are causing so many deadly accidents on the roads? I'm enclosing a newspaper article from yesterday's Boston Globe *that made me think of it. Is Marta still bringing up your newspapers every day?*

I'm also reading an article about the so-called "Prison Industrial Complex." So many of the boys at school still end up in prisons that I had to read about them. Apparently states like New York and Cal-ifornia are using prison-building to bolster the economies of their rural regions. Draconian sentencing laws are meant to supply "raw materials" for these prisons in the form of young African-American and Hispanic men. It's all very insidious. I'm so glad Vermont doesn't have these problems. Or does it? Do you have any thoughts on this?

I also just re-read The Taming of the Shrew *as you recom-mended, and I think you're right that Kate's final speech in Act V is much too long and involved to be anything but ironic. Methinks she doth acquiesce too much!*

Enough of this. I guess I'm just a little starved for conversation with only Milo and Mother around. I'm also at loose ends with this so-called novel of mine.

September 18:

Father,

I've come to the end of the article about prisons. The irony seems to be that they don't end up helping the rural communities that much. Except for prison guards and prison builders. They seem to be the real roadblocks to reform. So it's nothing but petty self-interest after all.

Milo has been acting especially strange these days. I came across him in the study, hunched over a model aircraft carrier and making little airplane and explosion sounds. He didn't even hear me when I spoke to him. Afterwards I looked up the word "peculiar" in the dictionary. Did you know that it has the same root as "pecuniary"? It turns out that they both come from the Latin "pecu," meaning cattle. What does "cattle" have to do with these derivations? Cattle was what wealth consisted of in ancient times, and then the word was used to denote property of one's own, or one's "peculiar" property. Isn't that fascinating? I knew you'd appreciate it.

September 19:

Father,

Mother is hardly ever home these days. Not that she ever was before, but on my first day back, do you know what she said? She said she'd taken down one of the pictures in my room—that drawing I did in third grade of a Cardinal—and was going to try and sell it. She thought I'd be happy about that. Apparently one of her artist friends told her that Cardinals were "hot" right now. I think it has something to do with a baseball team. Anyway, I let her take the drawing. I don't know what happened to it. I helped her pack up the car this morning but I didn't see it. Those other paintings, though—they're the same ones she's been trying to sell for years. I mean literally they are the same exact ones. It's eerie. She loads them in the car each morning and then takes them out each night. I don't know what to say. Can't you call someone and have them buy those things from her? She won't have to know it's you.

September 20:
Father,
Maybe you're right to hide in the attic. Milo has become even more insufferable lately. Sometimes I hardly want to come out of my room for fear of running into him. It doesn't help that he looks like such a little fascist in those jackets and ties. I find myself blowing up at him for the smallest things and then feeling bad about it afterwards. This morning, for example, after Mother left, he deliberately smashed one of the handmade vases in the entrance hall. I watched him do it. He looked down at the thing for the longest time and then laid it on its side and just stepped on it. I was in the kitchen at the time, helping Marta, and I saw the whole thing. I ran out and asked him what he thought he was doing. "Modeling," he said, in that annoying way he plays dumb sometimes. "No," I said. "I mean what are you doing with that vase? How could you smash it like that? I'm going to tell Mother." And you know what he said? "You don't have to tell her," he said. "I told her I was going to do it before she left."
Help!

September 22:
Father,
Sometimes I feel I'm in this house purely by accident. As if I've wandered into some stranger's place and taken up residence. I wander between rooms, feeling like an empty husk of clothing nearly indistinguishable from the wallpaper. I sit on the stairs and wait to see if anybody notices me. I try to write, but nothing happens.

September 23:
Father,
Maybe you're ashamed of how you used Milo. But let me make something clear: you didn't use me. I shouldn't have to tell you it was alright, but it was. You always said you didn't have to worry about me, that I was the one person you didn't need to protect yourself from, and you're right. I am alright, except that I'd like to talk to you.
And why should what happened between us be so taboo, really? I mean nothing else in society is taboo anymore, so why should this

be? It's in the Bible, after all, right there in Genesis—Lot and his daughters. And they are the ones who survived the destruction of Sodom and Gomorrah! Anyway we were already so close mentally and spiritually. Everything else just seemed natural.

But please let's talk. Please?

September 24:
Father,
What happened between us happened. I wasn't a little girl. I knew what I was doing. We were adults, two adults together. You said once that societies have always tried to dictate how people express themselves but that we, in our private world, in Vermont, can see things our own way. One time, during, I looked at the wall next to me and saw our shadows there and thought: We could be anybody. That's how I saw it.

September 25:
Father,
I've been re-reading Milton. Sin says to Satan that she's "a Goddess arm'd / Out of thy head I sprung." Was I just some notion that sprang out of your head too? Some notion of sin? Sin goes on to say that "I pleas'd, and with attractive graces won / The most averse, thee chiefly, who full oft / Thyself in me thy perfect image viewing / Becam'st enamor'd." Is that true, too? That you were enamored of me only because you saw yourself? Your own "perfect image"? Your student? And now? "Hast thou forgot me then, and do I seem / Now in thine eye so foul, once deem'd so fair / In Heav'n"?

Forgive me, it's late, I've had trouble sleeping and I'm probably not making sense. I don't know whether I'm even going to send this.

October 2:
Father,
I haven't written to you in a few days. I wonder whether I should wean myself off the habit. I've noticed you pull up the attic ladder these days so I can't even get close if I wanted to. Is that what you're afraid of? Closeness? It's a shame. You know I'm not going to force myself on you. You should know that more than anyone.

Or is it the sequel to A Portrait *that's consuming you? The one your fans have long demanded? Sometimes I wonder. You're not working with Milo again, are you? You couldn't possibly . . .*

October 6:
Father,
I've started inviting old acquaintances to the house again. Frankly I could use the company. Do you hear them from the attic? I suppose not. We sit downstairs and have tea and chat. They're not the sort of stimulating discussions you and I used to have, but they're something. My old English teacher, Mrs. Fitzpatrick, came yesterday and we talked about Macbeth and silk scarves. She's always had a somewhat Calvinist view of the play—Lady Macbeth as an example of the "temptation of evil" and Macbeth as the "fallen hero," that sort of thing. But I've always liked her and we had a nice time. She's taken to wearing the most beautiful scarves. She was wearing a rich blue one with silver ends. She says that everyone in Vermont wears only wool but that silk is so much prettier and you can wear it all year round. I don't know if it's quite my style, but I had fun trying it on. I didn't have the heart to tell her I wasn't going back to Ohio to teach, at least for now. She's always wanted me to be a teacher.

It's refreshing to see other people. Especially when the only ones in the house are Milo and Marta, and occasionally Mother. I suppose you're technically in the house all the time. I don't count that. I don't know how you can isolate yourself like you do. Is it me? Is it because I'm here? Do you want me to leave again? Would that help?

October 11:
Father,
I've decided I'm going to keep writing you these letters until you tell me to stop. Are you afraid Mother will find them? I'm not. She's lost in her own world, driving around to all her friends. I'm not even sure she'd care.

I just re-discovered the china shop in town. Do you remember that place? Myrtle's? I can't believe it still exists. And Myrtle herself is still there behind the register, as imposing as ever. It's like going back in time forty years to see her in that pillbox hat.

You don't have any friends anymore, do you? Do you think that says something?

I love you, you know, no matter what.

October 17:
Father,
I didn't mean to make you miss supper last night. I'm sorry. I was only sitting there, after Marta left your tray, hoping to talk to you when you came out. But you must have seen me. Would you really rather starve than talk to me?

October 31:
Father,
Happy Halloween. Let me guess: You're going as a ghost. Ha, ha.

November 8:
Father,
It's funny how we can get used to our lives. No matter what they are. Especially out here in the woods. Is that what's happened to you? Staying in the attic is just your routine? And I'm not part of that routine, am I? I threaten it somehow.

My days feel so terribly slowed down. At least I'm getting more sleep. I only wish I could be more productive. I've been sending small donations to Catholic Relief Services and Doctors Without Borders, but I fear that just sending money to these far-off places is too easy, too abstract, that there is something missing, something more immediate that I'm not doing. Maybe I should go back to teaching. I did enjoy it for the most part. Maybe I'd be better off in a private school. Or even in Memorial School in town. I don't know. Whenever I think about it I start getting a headache.

That's how I feel about Marco, too. I can see now what a terrible mistake he was. It shocks me, how blind I can be. Did you ever suspect that he was only using me to get a visa? Milo said something to me once, but I dismissed him out-of-hand. I wonder if everyone does that too easily. He says things in such an odd way. But I'm surprised how perceptive he can sometimes be. The other day, when I was staring out the window, he asked if I was looking for you.

November 16:

Father,

I'm helping Marta more around the house. She looks at me strangely these days. I can't describe it. It's in her eyes—a sort of all-knowing dullness. Why did you suggest her as a go-between? Were you afraid Mother or Milo would intercept my letters? I never really understood.

Yesterday I polished all of the silver. Today I dusted the book-shelves and cleaned the entrance hall tiles. You should have seen me, down on my knees, scrubbing away. It takes my mind off things. Off you, I suppose. Maybe that's the problem, that I've never worked with my hands. All my life I've done nothing but work with my brain. Didn't Karl Marx say we should each do a few hours of intellectual work and a few hours of menial work each day? Or was it Tolstoy?

Maybe I should suggest some menial work to Milo. Who is going to take care of that boy in the future unless he starts taking care of himself? Yesterday he showed me his plans for a bomb shelter. There was a long tunnel going into the side of a mountain and then down several hundred feet. The tunnel had maybe fifty or so doors, all electrically wired and elaborately encrusted with spikes and daggers and trip-wire-activated machine-gun barrels. It must have taken him days to draw it all. Then at the end of the doors was a little room with a light bulb and a table and chair and some stacked provisions and, of course, more guns. There were also two long tubes that ran from the room to the top of the mountain—for air, he said, one to let the air in and the other to let the air out. He seemed so proud of this design. He even drew himself, in his jacket and tie, sitting at the table in that room, smiling. He was smiling, Father. In the picture he was sitting there all alone behind those fifty doors, just smiling. He said he was finally safe.

I wonder if there's a reason why he feels this way, if something's been happening . . .

November 18:

Father,

I'm not angry. No, that's not the right emotion at all. I'm worried. Don't you see that? Milo has been getting worse again. He won't even respond when I talk to him. But the other day he let slip that when he was a boy you asked him to write things down in that diary of his. Horrible things that he saw or felt. "For the material," you kept saying.

November 20:
Father,
Mother told me that you've agreed to do a reading at the Barnes and Noble in Manchester next month—that you'll be previewing the long-awaited sequel! Have you finished it? I'm excited for you, really, but I also can't help wondering: Does this have anything to do with how Milo is acting?

My old friend Missy Saberhagen was going to come over for tea tomorrow, but I've told her to postpone it because of the expected snowstorm. She's married now and has a brood of little ones. I think about children, sometimes.

November 22:
Father,
I asked Milo to have tea with me and he looked at me like I was speaking Chinese. "Are you inviting another of those stupid guests?" he said. I said no, that no one was coming because of the snow but that he and I could have tea if he wanted. I want to get him used to social situations and to interacting with people in more normal ways. It's good practice. I didn't tell him this, of course, I just said that Marta had made some biscuits and that it would be a shame to let them go to waste. To my surprise, he shrugged and said OK. I sat on the sofa and he sat in a chair and we had tea and biscuits. He was generally well-behaved. You know he can be well-behaved when he wants to be. We talked about normal things like the weather and politics. He said he hoped the Republicans would do well in the next election because of all the scandals involving Clinton. I made sure to tell him that while it was certainly unseemly, what happened, I hoped people would focus on the candidates' specific policies. He needs to hear that sort of thing, I think, just simple reasonable conversation. We didn't exactly see eye-to-eye, but he managed to carry himself in a polite, civilized way. Maybe he's learning.

But then at the end he said something strange. He said you couldn't write anymore, that your sequel was garbage, but that he could. What does this mean?

I want to meet you after the reading. I'll wait for you in the attic. We could finally talk. You can't ignore me forever, you know.

November 25:

Father,

It was so good to finally see you today. It really was a Happy Thanksgiving. You're looking well, surprisingly well for being cooped up so long. You have a few more grey hairs since the last time I saw you, but not too many more. You just need to brush your hair down a bit so it's not all over the place. For the reading, I mean.

I'm sorry supper was so awkward with Milo. I suppose he still has a way to go in his social development. It was unintentional, I think, his spilling gravy all over my dress. At least he seemed to feel bad about it. He was actually quite contrite in his way. He came up to my room afterwards and looked at the floor and said he was "very sorry about the dress." He even offered to clean it. I just laughed and said no. Then he asked if he could stay in my room while I read. I said alright, and he asked if he could take a look at my photo boxes. I gave him the boxes and he just sat there flipping through them one-by-one. When he was finished he put the lids back on and stared out the balcony door. It was nearly midnight when I said it was getting late, and he jumped up and left, murmuring about having work to do.

December 1:

Father,

Is it just on holidays, now, that you come down? Am I going to have to wait until Christmas to see you again?

December 4:

Father,

Suddenly Milo is worse again. For the past few days he's been constantly scribbling in his diary. He's got that excited horse-laugh of his.

It makes me ill just to hear it. It's his "work," he says, and I know he's not talking about his models. He's talking about you. And yes, I understand, you're scared now—you don't want anyone to know what you've been doing with him. To him. You don't want to destroy your reputation. But I can do that as easily myself. If you won't stop this, I will have to. You will leave me no choice.

December 6:
Father,
Mother tells me the reading is next week. I'm not even going to ask anymore. I'm just going to say that before you return, I'm going to go up into the attic to wait for you. You owe this to me. You can't expect that we could share what we did and then simply cut everything off. It doesn't work that way. It's not that simple. There's something I never told you that I have to tell you now.

December 12:
Father,
Milo says you're afraid of something. But he doesn't know what. Is it me? Are you thinking of backing out of the reading tomorrow just to avoid seeing me afterwards? You can't hole yourself up there forever. Anyway Mother would never let you off the hook. Not this time. She's gotten it into her head that she might be able to sell her own paintings there, to feed off of your celebrity. That's what I suggested to her, anyway. A little insurance, I suppose.

Don't think me manipulative. I just want to talk to you one more time, alone, like we used to do. That's not so much to ask. I'm thinking of returning to teaching again. Chancellor Smith says I can have my old position back. Maybe I should give it another try. So one more conversation, Father. I think you already know what I have to tell you anyway. I practically gave it away a couple of months ago with the Milton. "Thyself in me they perfect image viewing / Becam'st enamor'd . . ." You know how the rest of it goes. I know you know it: "and such joy thou took'st / With me in secret, that my womb conceiv'd / A growing burden."

It never grew very much. I never let it get that far. There was a clinic near school. It's where they send the girls. It was easy to say I was visiting one of them. There are always a few there at any given time. The doctor was named Sylvia Jones, a tall African American woman with short curly hair. She smiled a lot in a wide, easy way, which took me by surprise a little bit given the sort of work she does. But then I saw why. She took me to her office, a small white-washed room with harsh lighting. But behind her desk was a child's drawing. "Yours?" I asked. She nodded and showed me a photograph of her with her husband and children—two daughters, aged thirteen and ten, and two sons, aged seven and three. Then she asked which of the school's girls I was there to talk about. She had all seven files on her desk. I looked down and saw their pictures clipped to the front. They were smiling. I realized it was because they were so young, they had the habit of smiling for the camera no matter what it was for. That's when I started to cry. Something came over me at that moment. It was so terrible, I thought, all that smiling. It must have been what had gotten those girls into trouble in the first place.

I also remembered how, when I was a little girl, you said I smiled coolly, like a queen. You didn't like it.

I'll be there waiting.

Waiting. She'd been waiting. In the attic. To confront him. He'd been afraid, distraught—I could see his pale hands clutching the steering wheel, his eyes flickering in the reflected light of snow. One turn of the wheel would be all he needed. One turn to escape, to write his own ending. Because now I saw the truth. He hadn't needed to bring anything to read because he'd had no intention of ever getting there. Had I suspected? I must have. For all Klara's haranguing of me and accusing me of unnaturalness—for all her claims to be protecting me against Father—*she* was the most unnatural one. *She* was the one whose relationship with Father was horrible. Yes, I finally saw her for who she was— someone who could never accept that Father needed *me* more than her, who'd manipulated him into loving her no matter what twisted form that took.

I pulled up the wastebasket and vomited. For the longest time I hung my head, breathing through the acid chunks of food. Then I took the letters, all of them, and flung them into the bilious muck. I swept in the photos before continuing to the bookshelves, hugging the putrid receptacle to my chest. I was determined that nothing should remain—certainly nothing Klara might care about. The marbled notebooks I stuffed down in a giant handful. Then came those precious unknown literary works. I tipped them in one at a time. When the basket was full I kept going, spilling them onto the floor, glancing at their titles typed neatly across the spines—*Stopping By Woods, National Geographics, Doors, The Stranger, Sleeping on Trains, The Gemini*—all those early books that would never grace a bookstore's shelves, all those stories that would never, ever be available to redeem Father's miserable critical reputation. Not that I thought they could. For years I'd seen first-hand what an awful writer he was, how like a blind babe he was without me. I found *Queen Dad* in a box stuffed into the top of the shelf and quickly read enough to see its prose—yes, prose!—was dead, desiccated, unworthy of repeating. I won't even excerpt it here. I'll just leave a blank to show its nothing quality—a soothing, merciful void like this:

I scattered its pages across the floor, then kicked them and fell to my hands and knees and began ripping them to shreds, stuffing the smaller bits into my mouth, chewing them to a pulp, swallowing them down, down, down, until I vomited them up all over again. What had Father once said, quoting Whitman? *Here the frailest leaves of me and yet my strongest lasting?* Frail, yes, but lasting, no. No one would ever read them now, just like no one would read the awful early drafts of the novels he did publish, the onionskin pages he'd hoarded for years on the off-chance that history should look kindly on his work. I hurled these against the walls, then took the letter opener and mangled the keys of his Remington typewriter. I thought to myself: *I'm protecting him.* And: *I should have done this ages ago.*

I don't know how long I stayed up there. Time meant nothing anymore. Hours swam by like elusive fish. By the time I clambered down it was early evening. The shadows were long, the daylight a dying red—the red of police lights, cooling embers, solitary traffic signals in the rain. I went to my room and peered out the window. The gardening trucks were gone. Only Henri's Peugeot remained.

159

That's when I heard his voice.

Not Father's but Henri's.

He and Klara were coming up the stairs. I couldn't make out their words. They were whispering. Then they saw me. They stopped. I laughed. She must have thought I was having a nervous breakdown. But I was merely trying to stop myself from weeping.

"Are you alright, Milo?" he asked. "We are worried about you." I laughed again. It was the we that got to me—the we that spoke of plans, hushed conversations, fake teary-eyed concern.

I looked down at my vomit-stained pajamas. "It's funny you should say that," I managed. "Because I feel the same way about myself."

Henri tilted his head to one side. He was doing a magnificent job, really—his hand clutched tenderly atop Klara's, eyes benevolent with care. Even his sleeves were no longer rolled up. Still I sensed that tattoo.

"It is a good sign," he said. "That you are worried."

"You think it shows I'm redeemable?"

"That you will accept help. As a former soldier, I know how important this is. Those who are alone . . ." His voice drifted off.

"Help from you?" I said, making it sound like a joke.

Now it was Klara's turn to chime in. "From professionals," she said. "Doctors or psychologists."

"You can go to them," Henri added. "And tell them everything."

Everything?

Suddenly I saw it, the most terrifying element of their plan. That I'd become so frightened that I'd leap at the opportunity to tell someone, especially a supposedly benevolent professional. And where would that lead? What further confessions might I make? Even a simple revelation of Henri's supposed "evidence" against me might be enough to brand me as *dangerous* and a *threat*, might vitiate any doctor-patient privilege and lead me straight into the arms of the police.

I realized I was holding my breath. The audacity, the subtlety of these designs nearly overwhelmed me. It almost made me wonder whether Henri really had been a police investigator—it was a trick worthy of a professional.

That's when I noticed Klara staring at me. She looked worried. Paradoxically this gave me hope. I blurted out: "He's not who you think he is." There was more desperation in my voice than I'd intended. But she just muttered: "I'm sorry, Milo. You're the one with the over-active imagination."

The beautiful imagination that created me.

He was smiling.

I had no choice. I closed the door on them. Then swallowed down the bile rising ineluctably in my throat.

Eventually I heard him leave. He strode out to his car with a slow, jangling stride, limbs loose, hair loose and hanging messily across his face. It was obvious what he and Klara had been doing in her room. Still he glanced up at me as if to say: *You're creating me even now, don't you see?* He shook his head and dragged a boot heel across the gravel. At first I thought he was making a symbolic line I couldn't cross. But he didn't stop there. More lines came furiously, and when he was done he laughed and hopped in the Peugeot and drove away, leaving those etched symbols behind, which eventually coalesced into a single dreadful word:

LIFE.

Water, that necessary ingredient to life, was coursing through our old pipes. Klara was taking a shower. The pipes were humming. No, she was humming. Beethoven? It didn't matter. Afterwards she knocked on my door and asked matter-of-factly if I was hungry. I said nothing. I was still staring out the window. Her footsteps faded down the stairs. At one point I opened my door and heard the television's high whine. I'd always suspected she watched it while eating alone. I did the same whenever she left me.

I waited until she'd gone to bed. Then I went outside. The word was still there. I thought about photographing it as proof, but I knew Klara would only think I'd done it myself. So I kicked gravel over it and went back inside, up the stairs, down the hallway and into Mother and Father's room, straight up the ladder to fetch the wastebasket. I lowered it onto the bed. Papers spewed everywhere. I stuffed them back in. I thought about dumping them into the turret, but I needed to be sure of their fate. So I carried them outside, across the patio, and emptied them into the ditch where I'd once burned my baseball uniform. Then I strode up for the next word-filled load. I did this nearly twenty times, thankful for our old stone walls—and for Klara's oblivious exhaustion. I hauled down everything, including Father himself, who'd grown mercifully silent, until the bookshelves were bare, the desk devoid of everything but the old Peruvian shrunken head and that famously negative review of *Museum Collections* by *The Boston Globe's* A.W. Peer: "*What John Crane has given us seems, like many an item in museum collections these days, to be nothing more than a dead object from a dead age. His attempt to reincarnate the Victorian social novel has only resulted in the creation of an ugly, inarticulate Frankenstein. We should all do ourselves a favor and put it out of its misery.*"

I thought about that last line as I poured modeling turpentine over everything. Its dizzying stench nearly overwhelmed me. I stepped back and lit a match. The flame pulled to one side. I was afraid it might go out, but it didn't—it burned right down to my thumb. Only then did I drop it, a little falling star, exploding the darkness with a conflagrant roar. I jumped back, shielding my face, watching the ivy on the wall shrivel and brown. Glowing bits of Father and his opus mingled with Klara's hopeless missives, curling together into the half-moon night, their embers like vanishing fireflies.

Afterwards I stared at the moon and the darkly swaying trees, the wisps of high cirrus clouds. Would they come with lights flashing and sirens blaring? Guns drawn, charging into the house? Soon—I knew it would be soon. Everything was coming to a head.

There was no time for sleep. I pilfered several of Marta's rags and scrubbed every bare surface of the attic. Scrubbed it with bleach to destroy every last molecule of dust: of Father's hair, his skin, the threads of his threadbare clothes. Back downstairs I drifted through the living room and into the study, past the ticking clock, the crumbling *Encyclopedia Britannica* in the bookshelves, the moonlit reflections of the long-dead day painted in the china cabinet's glass. I began with the trireme. I swaddled it in rags. I hoisted it up the ladder in a wicker basket and installed it atop the desk, where its hull matched the exposed overhead beams. Then I returned to the study for more parts, loading these into the basket with my scalpels and brushes and paints.

I spent two tireless nights hauling everything up—the galleys, dromans, cogs, schooners, destroyers, battleships, submarines—my entire gun-bristling armada. The basket fit everything but the larger vessels: the battleship *Missouri* and the aircraft carriers *Enterprise* and *Kitty Hawk*. For these I had to use cardboard boxes from the basement—a damp low-ceilinged place at the bottom of the stairs whose door I had to force open with my shoulder because no one had been down there for years. Certainly I never had. Not since I was a child, when Klara had locked me inside after I'd cut out the eyes of her frog doll—and I'd scrabbled at that door until my fingernails bled.

I found a box of old Christmas lights near the door. I emptied it and ran back up. Like a resourceful Robinson Crusoe I poked holes in it to string a clothesline through. It was large enough for everything but the *Kitty Hawk*. For that I had to descend once more. I waded through mounds of dilapidated children's furniture and saw an old bassinet, a low table, metal desks and stools. There were also rusted farm implements that looked like medieval torture devices—the rack, the brank, the neck violin, the strapedo. Finally, beneath a pair of oversized shears, I found a cardboard box. The word "school" was printed on the flap. I hesitated, then pulled open the flaps. I saw a marbled notebook, PHYSICS printed in my own blocky hand. A rush of nostalgia came over me—for the ruddy Mr. Mora and his lab benches and formulas containing all the secrets of the universe. $F=ma$: Newton's second law of motion relating force, mass, and acceleration. $t=2\pi\sqrt{m/k}$: describing simple harmonic motion. $E=mc^2$: unlocking the key to nuclear bombs.

I pushed the notebook aside. There was our high school yearbook, *The Green Mountaineer*, from 1988, Klara's senior year. I flipped through it, cracking the spine, until I reached the class photos in back. She looked younger than I remembered. But her gaze had that familiar half-mad intensity hidden behind a prim smile and horn-rimmed glasses. Below her photo someone had written, in a hasty boy's hand, *Don't forget about us all at Harvard!* —*Mike B.* Other students had written similar notes below their own photos:

You've been so great on The Falcon [this was the student newspaper]. *I know in a few years I'm gonna read about all the great things you're doing. PLEASE keep in touch, OK?* —*Wanda Cuxhaven.*

I flipped to the middle-school photos. These were much smaller. There was me in skinny miniature, frowning beneath a shaggy curtain of hair, my shirt collar hanging loose despite being buttoned and clasped with a tie. A few pages later came little Lizzy Meecham. I could hardly believe my eyes. Her perky smile and pigtails revealed no trace of the mammoth Elizabeth Silfer.

I was about to close the book when I spotted, on the inside cover, a drawing of a novel—I could tell it was a novel because it said "A Novel" across the middle—with "by Klara Crane" printed beneath and "In bookstores soon!" written in a loopy, exuberant hand (not my sister's) across the bottom. I didn't want to be reminded of Klara's so-called ambitions—the "family drama" she hoped to write, the one she was in a sense trying to write now. So I dropped the book in the cobwebbed crevice between two milk buckets. Then I paused. I thought about a different plot. Or maybe it was the same one? I emptied the remainder of the box and shunted it upstairs. My mind was furiously churning. I realized that Henri wasn't the only one who knew a thing or two about investigating.

The next day I managed to take the MG without anyone noticing. I returned to the library. A perky young librarian directed me to the annual reports of the Vermont Gardening Society: large green volumes full of pictures, tips from local gardeners, obscure horticultural awards. "Of course you can get all this information on-line," she informed me, pointing to a bank of shiny new computers. But I just smiled and said: "It's the historical material I want."

It went back several decades. I saw the name Henri Blanc beginning in the mid-1970s and continuing until just after publication of *A Portrait of the Artist as a Young Psychopath.* Then there was nothing, a blank (Blanc?), until he reappeared only a few years ago, winning awards such as "Best Floribunda Spray" and "Best Miniature Rose-in-a-Bowl." And the garden owners? Marybeth Bliss, Peggy Sporleder, Phyllis Green, Yvonne Dutton. All female. I wrote them down. One of the names was vaguely familiar. I asked the librarian for help. She typed the names into the computer, and there it was: Peggy Sporleder died from an overdose of sleeping pills shortly after finishing one of the largest private rose gardens in the state.

I closed my eyes and imagined it: the pill bottle on the floor, a pale limp hand, glassy eyes, flowers swaying in the window. A scene right out of Father's early novel, *Bloodless Sacrifice.* "Can I find out more about this?" I asked.

Further searches turned up little else. Ms. Sporleder had been discovered by a house cleaner. There was a vague allusion to debt, to living beyond her means—just like the victim in Father's book.

Another kind of answer arrived that afternoon, in a thin *Confidential* envelope that I immediately took to my room and propped upon the windowsill. I sat on my bed and stared at it, almost *through* it with the outside light. Finally I tore it open. CarInfo was pleased to serve my needs. The Peugeot was registered to Henri Blanc.

I dropped the letter. For the longest time I didn't move. What if he really was just a gardener? Then another possibility occurred to me. One that managed to be both strangely reassuring and more disconcerting than anything. That he was *both* Henri and Keith. That he (Henri) was deliberately copying Father's psychopath. And that *that's* how I'd been creating him as Keith—by believing him to be.

That night I lay in bed, turning this idea over in my mind, thinking of all the possibilities it offered. I thought of similar artifices in *The Wizard of Oz* and *The Hound of the Baskervilles*—stories of *seemingly* supernatural beings that turned out to be fake, to serve very worldly (and in the case of the hound, nefarious) purposes. But what was Henri's purpose in this case? I imagined him trying to seduce Klara for her newfound wealth. It must have been irresistible to him, a story Father himself might have written—how a con man pretended to be one of Father's most nefarious villains in order to exploit his only daughter. But would Henri really take such a risk? He must know we'd eventually recognize him—we'd see every little sign. Unless this was part of the game . . . Yes, I could see him even now, raising his arms to show-off that tattoo—how he *meant* to frighten me so I wouldn't interfere with his plans. And Klara? Klara too. This was his genius: to attract her despite her fears. To tell her to her face that he'd fleece her dry or get me hanged for murder, and still have her swoon over his accent and his ponytail.

Keith by another name exactly.

Suddenly I heard a footfall on the stairs. I paused. I wondered if he was still in the house. I crept to the door and opened it just an inch. I peered into the hallway. The portraits hovered in the gloom. The rows of low dark doors were all quiet and shut up. All except Klara's. Once my eyes adjusted I could see that it was ajar. I imagined he'd just departed, making it the perfect time to confront her. She'd be tired and wouldn't expect it—her defenses would be weak. Perhaps I wouldn't even have to say anything—just look at her and *know* whether she was a villain or a fellow victim here.

I watched the stairwell until it seemed to change colors, acquiring hints of green and blue. Then came another footfall. Next the translucent outlines of her nightgown. Floating back up the stairs. She wasn't wearing a robe. How odd. I saw how loosely the nightgown was held together, barely covering her pale naked belly. There was also something else, but I didn't realize it at first—didn't see her hand thrust through the folds, those cagelike fingers clutching a trembling rose atop her pubis. This was a picture that crystallized in my mind only after she was gone, when I was left with nothing but her scent on the still night air, and a sense that while one sort of climax had just occurred, another was drawing fatefully near.

MORNING BROUGHT SOME CLARITY. FOR ONCE, IT WASN'T WELCOME.

Click.

I opened my eyes. Sunlight flared orange across the wall. I ran a hand through my disheveled hair. I heard it again: a click, followed by a muffled metallic rush. For a moment I was confused, then I shot up, recognizing the sound.

I stumbled to the window. The sedan. The heavy-set policeman. He stood in front of the garage with Klara. Henri lurked nearby, poking the soil with a spade. He seemed to be disinterested, minding his own business, only I knew better—I knew who was turning the screw. *Are you sure I'm just acting the part of Keith?* I put my hands over my ears, then grabbed the bayonet. I could force the issue. One mad rush, and I'd know for sure. Then I noticed Henri looking up at me, his eyes shimmering like on the very first day we'd met—full of curiosity, eagerness, even sympathy. *"There was a Turkish word, Keith knew, for right before a climax, / That moment of surrender, triumph, life so sweetly axed."*

No. I wouldn't give him the satisfaction. It would only vindicate his and Klara's manufactured truth—about how *crazy Milo was unhinged*, how *he'd knocked his head as an infant* and was *never right after that*, how *everyone* knew he was *off* and should have used *drugs* to escape the *dark place* his mind was in. I'd become a cautionary tale, the subject of raised eyebrows and feelings of moral superiority, the dull rural folk hitching up their pants and thinking: *at least I'm not suicidally violent like that Milo Crane. He attacked a cop with a bayonet!* It might even cause renewed interest in Father's work, speculation that I was the model for his psychopaths. I pictured magazine articles with color photos of the house, book club guides, Cliffs Notes, an essay or even a long-awaited book by Klara herself, all slotting me neatly into Father's work.

No.

I backed away from the window. I'd had a close call, yet there was no time to relax. Klara and the man were already approaching the house. Henri was a few steps behind. After a moment's hesitation I reached beneath my bed. The lock-box. Where was it? I scrabbled around. I must have pushed it to the back when I'd hidden Father. Finally I found it. I fumbled with the combination, all 9s. My lucky number. Inside was my secret diary. And beneath it lay *A Portrait of the Artist as a Young Psychopath*—the first copy to come off the printing press, the one I'd kept all these years for myself.

I turned to the interrogation scene and began to read.

"Milo?"

I tucked the book beneath my pillow. "It's not locked."

My room was narrow, too narrow for them all to stand in. Klara entered first. The man remained in the doorway. I took this as a hopeful sign. "A detective is here," she said in a low, deliberate voice. "He's been asking questions. It seems there are a few loose ends from the accident. Can he talk to you, as well?"

She was a terrible liar. I could see the worry on her face, but also a flicker of hope. A hope to be rid of me? Was this what she really wanted? If it was, I knew I'd succumb after all, hurl myself against that detective and force him to destroy me, because I wouldn't be able to go on like that. "Does he have to?" I asked.

She paused, then saved me—saved us—by what she did next. She stepped forward and touched my shoulder. A gentle, reassuring touch that spoke volumes. She said: "I don't know, but I think it would be very helpful."

"Of course," I said. "I have nothing to hide."

The man had a craggy Italian face and a habit of wiping his forehead with his sleeve. It was obvious he was no match for me. Still I had to keep my guard up. He flipped through his notebook as if searching for something that puzzled him. I wanted to laugh—it was the oldest trick in the book. In all the books.

"You work on models, right? You ever work on model cars?"

He had all the subtlety of a blunderbuss. I kept my answers strictly to "yes," "no," or "I don't know." This was harder than I'd imagined. *Confess*, Henri's voice kept whispering, *and you'll be free.* Instead I asked about the gloves.

"We ran some tests," the officer said.

"Ah." They must not have found any brake fluid.

Then the detective said: "I've read all your father's books. Interesting stuff."

"Some people like them."

"You don't?"

I shrugged. "He wasn't the best writer."

He glanced around my room, his eye caught by my stacks of military histories. "I couldn't help noticing how often he thanks you in the acknowledgements."

"He needed my help."

"Yet he hardly thanks your sister."

"He needed her less, I suppose."

He chewed his lip. Something bothered him, yet he couldn't articulate it, and I wondered if I'd said too much—inadvertently started a chain of reasoning that would circle back to snare me.

"Thanks," he said, standing up. "We'll be in touch."

Then he was gone, in a huff and jangle of keys. I heard him downstairs talking with Klara—their whispered overbearing concern—and that's when I realized whom I didn't hear: Henri. He'd lurked in the hallway while the detective was with me, but by the end of the interview he was gone. I crept out into the hallway. I sensed him—I always could. A little farther. There. In Klara's room. He was staring out the window, hands behind his back, surveying the garden, and I began to study him: the curve of his back, his thin tanned neck. Searching for weaknesses, human vulnerabilities, some sign of what he really might be. What if I fetched my bayonet and rushed him? Would I find out then? I wonder now how everything would have turned out if I had. Yet part of me was convinced the bayonet would go straight through him or that he'd turn upon me a horrible decomposing face with gaping blanks for eyes—like the mask Keith once wore to literally frighten a woman to death.

So I did something I never should have done. I left him and retreated to the attic. I wanted time to plot. To plot my plot, I suppose. I sat at my desk and stared at the trireme. That's when I realized something profound. Ancient Greek rowers weren't chained to their benches. That was a Late Medieval practice. The model was anachronistic and false.

I swept it off the desk and brought my foot down upon the hull, over and over, smashing it to bits. I knew then that history itself was becoming corrupted, revealed to be nothing more than the lies we all share. How could I have been so blind?

Late afternoon. I finally ventured back down. I heard Klara's voice from the stairwell, bright and tinny and false. She was describing what a "miracle" the garden was, how "excited" she was to "share that vision" with others. Or some such claptrap, for it was difficult to distinguish precise words amid her general effluvium of nonsense. But underneath it all I could sense her sadness, worry, even panic.

About what was happening to me?

I wondered.

I peered into the living room. She was standing on the other side, against the patio doors, her face gripped in such obsequiously forced cheer that it looked paradoxically like an expression of tremendous grief. She wore a flowing blouse and looped earrings that dangled from plastic clips. In front of her were two men dressed in black. At first I thought they were more detectives. Then something gave me pause. They had their backs to me. I couldn't see them clearly. The nearest one had blotchy, pinkish skin and a close-cropped red beard, while the other had a right earlobe that gleamed with a diamond stud.

She touched the bearded man lightly on the shoulder. "Let's see it now, shall we?" She turned and swung open the doors. She marched out, hands raised like a waiter holding up two trays, the loose sleeves of her blouse falling nearly to her pale elbows.

I realized then what I hadn't seen for the past few days. I'd been too preoccupied, or willfully blind. But there it was, in all its splendor—a vastly improved garden filled with roses and sunflowers and lilies unfurling in great swaths of color, everything from red to yellow to white to green. There were new bushes and trees and a flower-lined path winding up to a small artificial rise, where a trellis remained under construction. I could barely make out a figurehead on a pedestal up there, a strange sight until I glanced at the banister and realized with horror that it was the head of the old Roman, removed from his post, banished to this distant decorative pavilion.

After a few moments Klara and the two men came into view again on the path. They were small, frail-looking figures—the men like mosquitoes in their black clothing and wide black eyes that must have been sunglasses, Klara like a little sparkling Christmas ornament, a miniature magus, with the way her blouse shimmered in the sun and her sleeves hung with wizardly slackness.

"Oh Milo, you feeling better?"

I turned. Marta was making her way toward Father's old set of Dickens with a feather duster. Her hobble was almost totally gone.

"Tell me," I said, ignoring her query. "Why have they been working so quickly? Why all the rush?"

"It's for the television show."

The television show. I thought of Keith filming his victims—documenting the horror and sending it to nature museums: "*It's nature pure and simple, atoms rearranged, / And bodies feeding bodies. Not so strange!*" Marta moved the feather duster like a pom-pom or Fourth of July sparkler. Then she noticed me watching her. She froze, her face a nervous rictus, a snapshot of unease.

Had she also looked like that years ago? When she'd passed along Klara's letters?

I drifted into the empty study and ran a finger across the dusty shelves, waiting for Klara to come. One last model battleship graced the uppermost shelf—the USS Arizona, a ship bombed in

Pearl Harbor. 1,177 men perished inside its hull. It still lies at the bottom of the sea as a memorial to that infamous stealth attack. I stood on a rickety chair, snatched it down, and set it on the desk.

By the time I looked up she was in the doorway. She was glancing around, her eyes wide and dull. Something wasn't right, she could tell, but she didn't know exactly what. "Cleaning?" she said with a vanishing smile.

"Something like that."

"Where are your models?"

"I've moved them."

"Are you feeling any better?"

It was the same question Marta had asked, as if my wariness were like a stomachache or the flu. Only Klara's hands, held gnarled at her waist, betrayed her. "You know you can always talk to me, Milo," she went on, when I didn't answer.

I nodded. "I didn't kill Father," I said. "You've got it all wrong."

I don't know why I bothered. Her eyes didn't see me; her ears didn't hear. In her mind she'd made a marionette of me, and she beheld only that. Whenever my mouth moved, she started pulling the strings, and if I said something she didn't want to hear, she simply pulled a different way. "There's evidence," she said. "But I know how difficult things were for you. There were . . . mitigating circumstances, as they say."

"You don't understand." I tried to smile. "Henri is putting these notions in your head."

"But that's not why I'm here," she said, gazing out the window. "I wanted to talk to you about the television show we have planned."

"I have evidence, too," I said. "He's preyed on rich single women before. I can show you their names. And their obituaries. Even if he's not Keith, he's Keith by another name, and just as deadly."

"Don't worry." She laughed nervously. "You'll only go in front of the camera if you want to. And you wouldn't have to talk about the garden at all. They just want to know about us for background purposes. I thought you might show your models. Thousands of people on television could see them."

"Did you hear me? He doesn't care about you. Not really."

"You might even start a modeling club. Be with others who have a similar interest."

"He'll frame me for murder and then what?"

"You might have them over to the house. We could throw combined gardening and modeling parties."

"Then you'll have exactly what you want. But it won't be what you think. He'll drain you of every penny. He'll toy with you. Promise you things. And when you're too much trouble? He'll kill you. At best he'll leave you scarred and disfigured and too embarrassed to go to the police. And what will you have left? More bitterness and disappointment? The hard truth of your greatest failure yet?"

She turned and looked at me curiously, like I was talking gibberish.

"Ask him about Peggy Sporleder. She was so in debt after he'd finished her garden that she killed herself. Or so they say. Is that what you want?"

She opened her mouth, but before she could respond the two men came in from the patio. "Here are some people I'd like you to meet," she said. "Milo, Angus, Leo."

"Delighted," said the one with the diamond earring, who I think was Leo, smiling beneath a cloud of well-shaped hair. "Your sister has told us so much about you."

"I suppose it's my turn to tell you things about her then."

Everyone laughed in a polite, bubbly drone. Even Klara, whose smile had hardened into a rocky formation amid the folds of her cheeks and chin.

The second man, Angus, began to speak from the moist pink spot in the center of his beard. He told us the opening segment of each gardening show contained a brief portrait of the owner, and while this portrait didn't normally include siblings, Klara had convinced them it would be nice to have an interview with me. He said this in a way that made it clear he didn't agree—that I wasn't *interesting* enough for his precious show.

"Now we won't be talking to you about the garden, at least not at first," he said. "We'll be trying to get a sense of you, of what you like to do, what your hobbies are, sort of thing. Klara says you like models, you have a collection of them?"

I nodded.

"We can talk about that, you see? You can give us like a guided tour of them for the camera. Leo, make a note, we contrast his

173

building models with Klara's building a garden. Brother on the inside, sister on the outside, sort of thing."

He had a tendency to stir up his hands when saying "sort of thing," the phrase a generic stand-in for whatever he was too impatient to express.

"Anyway, my point is you tell us a little about yourself, show us what you do, a few models, sort of thing. We don't need to get into the garden. We'll ask you about it at the end, but it'll just be a general question or two. So don't worry if you haven't been involved."

"And the editing?" whispered Leo.

"Oh yeah. We'll shoot a bunch of film, then edit it down, so you also don't have to worry about saying things just the way you want them the first time around. Now we're not going to have all day, so don't think we can keep shooting until we get it perfect—this ain't a movie. But if there's something you think about as we go, something you really wanted to mention earlier on, just say it, and we can work out the sequencing later on. Understand?"

"Just behave yourself and everything will be alright," added Klara, which was gratuitous, even for her.

I turned to her. "Will they be able to get those cameras into the attic?"

She froze, as if hearing my words for the very first time. "What are you talking about?"

"Because that's where I've moved everything," I went on.

"You've *what?*" she said.

"I work up there now."

"How did you . . . ?"

"I found your key."

"Are you . . . ?"

Crazy was what she wanted to say, but the word lingered stubbornly on those painted lips.

She returned shortly after Angus and Leo had departed. I knew she would. I was still in the study, boxing up the *USS Arizona*. I sensed her hovering in the doorway, the rasp of her breathless rage.

"What have you done with Father's things?"

She'd visited the attic. I hadn't locked it for just that reason. I laid the *Arizona* diagonally across the box. It barely fit.

"I burned them in the ditch alongside the house. I'm surprised you didn't notice. I suppose you had other things on your mind."

I glanced at her. I could see she was tempted to rush outside. But her legs wouldn't comply, rooted to the same floor where she'd first told me of the accident. "I don't believe you."

"You don't *want* to believe me. That's becoming a habit. So look for yourself. I covered the ashes with soil but it's not terribly deep. And Father's typewriter only melted a little bit. Those old things are quite impervious to heat."

"There were manuscripts. Unpublished work."

How she clung to him, his precious *work*. Did she have any idea what it took for him to write it? Or was she just unable to face the truth, that Father was now one step closer to being gone for good, that there was nothing left to preserve or curate or even visit in the night? "The world is better off without it."

"That's not for you to judge."

"Actually it is."

"He should never have asked you to help him."

"*Help* him?" I said.

"You were the one who needed the help. Especially when you were little. But it's not too late. Have you considered what I've said? About seeing a professional? I wonder if this is all one big cry for help."

"*This?*" I said, forcing it out of her finally.

"The accident. Isn't that what you did to get back at him?"

I shook my head. "You don't understand. I've tried to tell you."

"Tell me what?"

"That's not what I'd do if I wanted to kill Father."

"So how would you do it?"

"You'd have to . . ." I began fiddling with my battleship.

"To burn his things?" she pressed. "Destroy his work?"

"That would be a start."

"And then? How would you finish the job?"

You don't, I wanted to say. *You can't ever kill a writer. Unless . . .* "You'd have to find a way for people to forget him. To erase his memory."

"That's why you moved your models into the attic and cleaned out all his things."

She edged closer, holding out a hand, not threateningly—no, not like those times with the baton. I was tempted to believe she understood—that she saw me for who I was, that I wasn't alone. But then I remembered.

"No," I said. "Exactly the opposite. I was trying to *preserve* his memory."

"How?"

"Did you ever read what Father wrote? I mean what he wrote on his own?"

"Those early novels," she said, still speaking slowly, patiently, as if to a child.

"Awful, right?"

"Go on."

"Did you ever wonder what happened?" I asked. "What changed?"

She was almost touching me. Her fingers reached, exploring the air. "Say it, Milo. How he used you."

I sighed. "*He* was the one who needed protection, not me. *He* was the one who needed saving."

"From whom?"

"From himself. His belief that he could write. And then, at the end, from you."

She must have heard something in my voice—something that *knew*. Her eyes shifted. An almost imperceptible movement to the window and its promise of escape—a mad dash through the woods to the distant gorge, then a step, a flutter of clothing, a thud against the stones.

"Me?"

"I found them," I said.

Her hand wavered.

"Under the floorboards," I went on. "He had a secret hiding spot."

She bent slightly forward. Gravity was exerting itself. She was losing the will to resist. She had no idea about any floorboards. He'd never hidden anything from her before. Had she admonished him to destroy them? Was his keeping them itself a betrayal? I thought not. It was only my discovering them that made her afraid.

"He was always tucking little things into corners," she managed.

"Not like this. There was a whole stack of them."

"Books?" she said, not even believing her own words anymore, just expressing hope out of an old undying habit.

"I don't know," I said. "Could they become a book? I think not. But people publish all sorts of things these days. Private letters, anything. The more bizarre the better, I suppose, in order to sell, sell, sell."

"Letters."

"Your letters to Father, Klara."

I let that statement do its work, draining her face, emptying her eyes, robbing her body of equilibrium and balance. Her sudden listlessness made her reach out a hand for support, only to find nothing there. She stumbled before righting herself. One of her earrings clattered to the floor. She didn't bother to pick it up, just said after smoothing down her blouse: "Where are they now?"

"Burned along with everything else. You might at least thank me for that."

"It was a difficult time for me, Milo."

"A lot of people have difficult times, but they don't . . ."

"I needed someone to talk to."

She remained absolutely still as she said this except for the tears running down her face. They descended like streaks on a wet window, falling with that same haphazard quality, here and there through all the dark lines and grooves—grooves cut by years of unhappiness. Yes, I saw it now, how unhappy she'd been—and Father, too—and for a moment I thought of his last desperate pleas to me, how he'd kept saying how *awfully sorry* he was for what he'd *had to do.*

"No." I shook my head. "You couldn't stand it. How he needed me more than you."

"I was looking out for you."

"Then why didn't you ever talk to me? Ask me how I felt? Oh, that's right. Because I was impossible. I was damaged."

"Milo, I never meant to suggest . . ."

"Do you know what I kept wondering?" I said. "At the end?"

She shook her head.

"Why. Why he was so afraid to write. Why he could hardly look at me anymore."

"I didn't tell him . . ."

"That I was a *freak*? That he was *abusing* me? When all along *you* were the horrible one? What you and Father did . . ."

She began to nod.

"Do you want me to tell a story, Klara? About the so-called accident?"

"Don't do this." She was nearly whispering now. "Please."

"You must know it already. How he drove the car into that ravine on purpose. To avoid facing you that night."

"What should I have said? Father couldn't live with the shame? That maybe I was the one who'd killed him? I've carried this with me for so long and still I can't decide . . ."

"It's not something you decide. It's something you just know."

She nodded again, a stubborn gesture—a last little act of both defiance and resignation, a surrender on her own terms.

"Now I know, too," I went on.

I moved forward until she was only inches away. She looked like she wanted to say something. Yet she couldn't find the words. I put a finger to her lips, and then, against every instinct of revulsion, took her in my arms and pulled her close. For the first time she gave herself to me, let me hold her like that. I don't know how long we stood there *embraced, engirdled*, before I realized my own tears were gushing down. Was this shared grief? Or a glimmer of impossible hope? In the end it didn't matter.

"I know, too," I said again, whispering it now into her ear. "And don't worry. Your secret's safe with me."

'It's hardly something new in all of Art,' Keith said,
'Although I've tried.' He looked resigned, and took her by
  the hand, led
Her down into his basement studio.
She wasn't too reluctant, no,
She thought Keith was a real artiste,
A budding oils-on-canvas man, the new Matisse,
Until she saw the horror: Cubism of the Flesh,
The dripping, fused remains of Allison and Beth.

And then she panicked, shot Keith with her pepper spray
And somehow managed it, a frantic get-away.
The stairs she climbed, the hall she crossed,
Expecting every moment to be tossed
Back into Keith's most hellish dungeon,
Where she'd be cut and stretched and bludgeoned,
Become a terrifying form for human beings to take
Unless you loved what nature couldn't ever make.

Already opening his thick front door,
She heard it, from the basement, this otherworldly roar:
A sound to wake the dead, to scatter all the ghosts
That crowded in her mind and make her focus on the most
Important choice of her entire boring life.
Because she knew she'd never get away, this town was rife
With evil, always had been underneath its veil.
So there, she turned, and saw the phone, and made the call,
Long-distance, said his name and set it off the hook
And waited for the monster down below to write his own
  doomed book.

Father was the public figure. The writer everyone knew. I was in the background, part of the scenery, and happily so, for what did I want with all those fans and interviews and awards and acclaim? They would only sap my strength, dull my ferocious edge. I was the purest of writers, penning lines in my secret diary for the value of the work itself, to hear the music of my language come alive, those polysyllabic words that became *oh-so-real* worlds in my mind.

Just how real became clear the following day. I slid the lockbox out from beneath my bed, hoping to describe my conversation with Klara—to capture every satisfying detail. Yet something gave me pause. I had the odd feeling that another voice was creeping in, threatening to take over, using my own words against me. Whose voice? Not Klara's, I was sure. Not after yesterday. That left only one possibility. But how?

The box was heavy, with a combination lock. The click of its wheel fly had always sounded reassuring before. Now it was like an invitation to thievery—listen for the click that's different, that tells you the notches are aligning. The lid creaked when I opened it. There was *A Portrait of the Artist*, crisp as the day it was printed. I picked it up. I already knew. There was nothing underneath. My secret diary was gone.

The trucks arrived mid-morning: camera trucks, sound trucks, catering trucks, trailers, the whole film-making circus that traveled like the US Army, distrusting the local terrain, hauling everything from home. Klara was trying to direct them but was mostly ignored, a gesticulating ghost, as waves of men and women in black tee-shirts that read "America's Best Gardeners Speak Out" and "Crew" streamed into and around the house. By the time I saw her again, in the living room, she was sitting in a chair beneath a spotlight as a woman smeared make-up on her forehead. I hardly recognized her. Her hair was a Jackie Onassis helmet, her clothes a bright blue blouse that plunged like a waterfall in front. But underneath I could see the truth. She was stiff, listless, dead, imbued with all the sadness of a clown.

"Is Henri coming today?" I asked her.

All she could do was nod.

Of course he was in a buoyant mood. I could see it from how he parked his car, carelessly, in the middle of the driveway, from how he'd dressed in a loose linen shirt and a leather necklace with something dangling at the bottom. A shark's tooth. How apt. I had to give Henri credit, he never tried to hide who he was—he gave us all the signs. He sauntered into the house with a smile, the rugged Frenchman at ease with his surroundings, greeting people in the entrance hall as if he already owned the place.

"Ah, Leo! How is everything?"

"Crazy. Like usual, crazy! Listen, we need to find a place to do your makeup."

"Klara will not mind if we use her room."

Footsteps clomped up the stairs. Henri was talking, saying there wasn't another garden as elaborate anywhere else in Vermont. "It is incredible!" He even began suggesting camera angles. "You should shoot the Helen Traubels against their primrose background and the hybrid teas straight down. Because they have already opened up and will fill the frame with color that way."

"I think you may have missed your calling in the television business," remarked Leo.

Laughter.

"Actually, you know, when I was still in France I did a short film about several small gardens in the Montorgueil Quarter of Paris."

"Really? You know I spent two weeks in Paris recently? Stayed right on the Rue Montorgueil. A fabulous area. But I didn't see any gardens."

"Most of them are private. I'll have to show you my film. I think I still have a copy at home."

Their voices echoed in the hallway, then died as they entered Klara's room. "Very good," I heard as if from far away. "I'll tell Alicia, from makeup. She'll be right with you." One set of footsteps back down. I knew I didn't have much time. I remained close to the wall, letting the interior of Klara's room gradually unfurl: the glass balcony door, the figurine-topped dresser, the foot of her bed, the hand-puppets hanging on the wall. Henri was behind the half-open lavatory door, rummaging through Klara's medicine cabinet with the cold professional regard of a pharmacist.

He shut the cabinet. I froze. One glance up and he'd see me. But he was staring intently at a pill bottle as if he didn't understand its language. Was there a single one of Klara's seducers not foreign born? I wondered. How curious. I stepped forward, pausing at Klara's bedside. There were more letters on the table. These looked different than the ones she'd written to Father, in heavier cream-colored envelopes. She seemed only to tell the truth in correspondence, so I quickly snatched them up and placed them in my blazer pocket. Just then I heard a rustling and saw, in the mirror, a flash of ocular green.

"Hello, Milo."

Had those eyes seen me take them? No. There was a different expression in them, one that told me he knew that *I* knew about the diary. But I couldn't confront him about that yet. There were some nagging details to clear up first. "Do you need something from Klara's medicine cabinet?" I asked.

"Only her vitamin tablets." He put the pill bottle into his pocket and drifted out of the yellow bathroom light, into the pale sunlit room. He paused before the dresser and gazed out the balcony door. "You know I have many more stories I could tell you about the Foreign Legion. We should sit down one evening with a bottle of wine, fine cheese. I can tell you anything you want to know."

"You're a storyteller, too," I said.

He smiled, a thin tight gash in his rugged face. "I am sorry, Milo. It seems we have had many misunderstandings, you and I."

"But you're ready to put those behind us."

"If you wish."

"Did you know my father?"

He hesitated, fingering the shark's tooth, pressing his thumb onto the point. I wondered what my mention of Father would do. I didn't have to wait very long. He pushed on the tooth. Carefully, until it just broke skin. "I knew his work," he said.

"Not the man?"

He waited until a drop of blood formed. Then, to my surprise, he pushed harder, grunting until I heard the crunch of bone. It went clear through, bulged out the other side beneath the nail, which turned almost instantly black.

"Was there much difference?" he said calmly as the blood welled up and began dripping in Rorschach patterns across the floor. "I suppose you, of all people, ought to know." He smiled. I blinked furiously. Was he showing me this to prove he was a fiction—a *character* capable of anything? He twisted and pulled the tooth back out. Blood leaked across his hand. He gave a grim thumbs-up. *You see?* he was telling me. *You wanted a story, but I have given you something better: a demonstration.*

"I just wondered if you'd ever met him," I said, determined not to be afraid, telling myself: *He's only hurting himself. He's only hurting himself.* I tried to find it funny. Only I couldn't bring myself to laugh. Still he must have noticed something, because he put the thumb into his mouth like a perturbed infant, and when he pulled it out again it was perfectly normal. Even the nail was back in place, with no sign of any harm. He seemed disappointed.

"Ah." He wiped his thumb on his pants. There was not a trace of blood. Even the stains on the floor were gone. "No, I never had the pleasure of meeting him."

"Before *A Portrait of the Artist* he drove around looking at gardens. Ones he could use for the settings of his book. I wonder if he ever saw yours."

"He inspired me, it is true, but no, I did not inspire him."

"Inspired you to become Keith Sentelle?"

A deadness suddenly clouded his eyes, like a curtain falling. "Excuse me?"

I must have felt reassured after making those visions go away, after *disbelieving* them. I said: "There was a gruesome dismemberment in a state park near Burlington. This was shortly after Father's book came out. A copycat murder. The killer was never found."

A curl of hair had fallen across his cheek. He didn't bother to push it back. He was looking straight at me, giving nothing away. "Klara tells me you have your father's imagination. So tell me more, *create* me in the image you see."

I hesitated, which was of course what he wanted—to fill me with self-doubt. But I quickly found an added reservoir of strength. "Maybe you did it as a sort of *homage*. A way to show how much the book meant to you. And you knew just how to do it. Your time in Africa must have taught you that."

"You make me both grateful and interesting."

"Then you disappeared for a time," I went on. "And when you returned you'd stolen the identity of this older gardener, Henri Blanc. Did you know him? Or was he just the perfect person to replace—one who could help you become Keith for real?" I paused. "No matter. This new Henri Blanc got exactly what he wanted. To work for lonely disposable women who wouldn't ask too many questions." I thrust out my fingers one at a time. "Marybeth Bliss, Peggy Sporleder, Phyllis Green, Yvonne Dutton."

"You have found the names of my former clients," he said carefully. "Congratulations."

"They're all rich like Klara."

"Most clients of serious gardeners are."

"Did you seduce them too?"

He picked up one of the figurines on the dresser. I could see the anger in his hands, and for the first time a touch of fear.

"Yes, you're seducing Klara and trying to scare me off," I went on. "*All by the book*, as they say. Were you attracted by Klara's wealth? And by how *fitting* it would be to turn Father's most famous character against his own grieving children?"

"Grieving?" he said, suddenly perking up again. "An interesting choice of words."

He gave a slight smile as my mind raced in many directions at once. "You met Klara when you were both up in Burlington," I said. "Was she the one who introduced you to Mrs. Silfer?"

Another shot in the dark. He looked at me curiously.

"What I can't figure out," I went on, "is whether Klara helped you plan all this. Or is she a victim too?"

He turned the figurine over in his hands. It was a unicorn, I noticed. "I suppose your story remains incomplete," he said, "if you cannot answer that question."

He set the figurine back on the dresser, facing away from me—all I could see was its white porcelain tail. This too helped me disbelieve. "It doesn't matter," I said. "Even if she did help you, you were the one pulling the strings. You're a con man and a killer."

"If you say so."

Yes, I said it over and over to myself: he was just a con man and a killer—one who'd become enchanted by the notion of becoming this famous fictional character and acting out his peculiar brand of manipulative horror. Still it was difficult, especially when he turned the unicorn around. Now its horn was facing me, shining in the light. *What if he were Keith for real?* I wondered. "Anyway, what is a *con man*?" he went on. "One who *pulls the strings*? Where do you get such notions?" He shook his head. "Don't you see? You can't ever escape playing the roles that others have written."

"Unless I'm the author."

He sighed. "You think of an author as a god. A creative genius. But what is that? Another story. Nobody creates anything new. All writers do is rearrange old plots. In a way it's like nature. Our own bodies. Every atom inside us is borrowed from somewhere else."

"There you go again. Sounding just like Keith." I couldn't take my eyes off that unicorn.

"You keep returning to this character," he said. "Trying to change me into someone I am not."

"He was a good liar. Just like you."

"And a good storyteller? Just like *you*?"

I looked at him—his weathered face, depthless eyes, bunched-back hair. I thought of his creativity as a gardener. Also what Leo had said about him *missing his calling*. "You're the one trying to tell a story here. About me."

"Ah." I watched a slight smile creep across his face. "You do not need my help for that. You tell the story quite well yourself. In your own words."

The diary. I could see it clearly now. How he was determined to twist this tale, to cast *me* in the role of villain. Again I thought of Keith. His murders had also told stories, imposed narratives on the unwilling.

"I don't know what you're talking about," I said.

He glanced around. "There is no one here to fool. Only me. And I know what really happened."

"Because you read my diary? It's just words. Just stories, as you say."

"It is an admission, as *they* will say."

"No one will believe it."

He sighed. "It is in your own handwriting. Klara herself can authenticate it."

"She wouldn't do that. I'm her brother."

"Don't be naïve," he said, flashing a sad sympathetic smile, as if he really did feel sorry for me. "She too finds your tale irresistible."

I don't know what I would've done if Alicia, the makeup artist, hadn't arrived at that moment—if I hadn't seen Henri's face change into a placid mask, his demeanor into the charming Frenchman. I might have lost control, attacked him or broken down. Perhaps that's what he wanted, to bring matters to a head, to force me into rash, unconsidered action that would only validate his story. *And whose side would Klara be on? Which tale would she believe?* These were the question he'd planted in my mind. I'd been so sure, after yesterday's embrace, of her allegiance. But now I began having doubts. Had he shown her the diary already? Pointed out the relevant passages and had her confirm that *yes, it's him, it's what he must have done?* I didn't *know*, and not knowing made me anxious, made me beat a strategic retreat to the attic where I might think and plan for every contingency. And it was there, under those exposed beams, that something occurred to me, something that gave me pause. He was bluffing. He hadn't had any time alone with her today. And yesterday, when she'd confronted me—when *I'd* confronted *her*—she'd hardly acted like someone who'd just read my secret diary.

Even so, I knew it was only a matter of time. No matter what I did or said, he'd show her—and the police—my diary eventually.

And it was this prospect more than anything else—the prospect of losing control of the narrative, of losing everything—that made me remember the letters in my pocket.

The first thing I noticed was that they were not *from* Klara, they were *to* her. I saw her name printed in old-fashioned script across the envelopes: the swooping *K*, Crane's dying *e*. They were recently postmarked and bore no return addresses and had all been slit open across the top. The paper was thick cotton bond and didn't slide out easily. I had to pinch the envelope and pull hard to get it free. I opened the topmost one that way, surprised to see only two sheets inside. The paper was cream-colored, like the envelopes, and had a visible weave. Clearly designed to impress. I unfolded it.

My dear Klara, the first one began. It was dated some weeks before.

I wanted to tell you again how excited I am at the prospect of our working together. I have spoken to Elizabeth Silfer and she can do without my full attention for the summer. What I wish you to do now is to visualize and to feel. I have sketched a little idea of mine on the next page, but I do not want you to look at it yet. First think back to childhood. We were all a bit more liberal with our imaginations then. What has always been your ideal garden? We all have an ideal garden in us, le jardin idéal, I am convinced of that. That picture, once you have it in mind, will not be the end of the process. It will be a beginning, the seed from which our garden will grow. A flower is not just a picture. It is the translation of a picture into a real object in space. Always remember that.

Yours,

H

On the following page was an ink sketch of a trellis full of hanging flowers in front of a mass of jagged pines.

Now walk over the places where these flowers will go—touch the soil, feel the sun on your face, breathe l'air frais. Do not be afraid to sense the environment! Use all your senses! Smell the flowers, feel them, hear them in the breeze. Taste them. Have you ever tasted a rose petal? I will show you how.

This would be just the thing to appeal to Klara. Tasting the flowers. I could imagine exactly how she'd do it, closing her eyes and placing a rose petal on her tongue, letting it bathe in her mucus without chewing as her mind sought the appropriate metaphor. It was also a nice touch to add a little autobiographical sketch in the letter that followed.

I am reminded of the very first garden I ever helped design. I had just gotten out of the military. Did you know I was in the military? I was a Legionnaire, in my wilder days. I was an ordinary soldier at first, with my special carte d'identité and my uniforme and all the rest. What a silly boy I was. I look back and I think: was that really me? Was I really so brash? I was, until it came time to actually fight and kill and die (yes, we did some of that). You will be happy to learn that as soon as this time came, I knew right away that la vie du soldat was not for me. Perhaps I was not brave enough, or strong enough, but one day, watching my friend John get shot in the leg and nearly die on a dusty African street corner in the middle of nowhere—it was enough to show me how precious little of "la vie" was really in this life. It is a cliché, I know, but you never get over the sight of a man so helpless. His leg was soaked in blood. It was like somebody had poured the blood on top of it. And he was so scared, twisting in such indescribable pain, and the leg kept shaking and twitching and he kept grabbing it to make sure it was still there. He was afraid someone was going to cut it off. All he wanted was to save his leg. We carried him back to our base. The other men with me said he'd be fine and that we'd get the one who did this to him. But they were saying this only because they'd heard it said in movies. In truth we were all shocked. John never really recovered. He became bitter. Years later I visited him in London, and he was selling pornographic magazines from a little sidewalk stand and limped away when the police came. He never opened a bakery, which was his dream.

And I? I transferred to another unit and became a military policeman. I don't know why I thought this would be better, that I would be able to do some good. We worked under impossible conditions. Fly-eaten bodies in the streets, people on either side shouting and pointing fingers. Ancient tribal hatreds, not to mention the cruelty of my fellow Legionnaires. Still I did it for several years. I investigated murders and so-called war crimes and all the darkest, most malevolent things that men can do. I wrote reports. Sometimes things happened to those responsible. Sometimes not.

Afterwards I returned to Paris with the vague notion of doing something else entirely, of helping to nurture life instead of destroying it or watching it destroy itself. But I did not know how. I considered becoming a nurse or even a doctor. Then an old friend went on holiday and left me in charge of his garden. It was full of bright lilies and sunflowers and was so peaceful and delightful. I spent entire afternoons there. I also went to the library and read everything I could, not only about taking care of flowers but about what flowers meant to people, what they stood for. When he returned I told him I had an idea for how he could better take advantage of the afternoon light in order to make the flowers glow. He allowed me to suggest some small improvements. In the end he was so happy. He recommended me to someone else, and violá! A gardener was born! But what I wanted to say was that this first garden of mine also suffered from the problems of allumer et l'ombre that we discussed last time. What I have tried to show you on the sketch on the next page is how we can better . . .

And so on. How extraordinary. I'd never quite believed in Henri as a real person with a past, etc. But here he was, nearly leaping off the page. It made me realize what an effective writer he was—a dangerously seductive storyteller. But was this true? It occurred to me that Henri may have made it all up to prey on Klara's sympathies for *victims of violence.* After all, it was the first rule of writing: *know your audience.* It was also the first thing that Keith always did before selecting his victims: research.

Then I saw his most recent letter. *Dearest Klara*, it began.

I cannot tell you how happy I am with the progress of the garden. It is everything we dreamed about. And the vision you have contributed has been breathtaking. It is like you were meant to do this, like you are finally becoming the person you were destined to be. This is obvious by how you are blossoming as much as any of the roses. Blossoming in every way as a woman. As a creative spirit. I simply cannot get the feel of you, the scent of you, off my mind. When I leave you I am in a stupor. I long for your passion. There

*is so much life in you, Klara, that has been waiting so long to come
out. And it is that way for me, too. I feel I have been waiting for you
my entire life. Everything I have achieved as a gardener was only
a preliminary to you. I imagined you before I saw you, and when
I saw you I knew.*

I quickly stuffed the letter back in its envelope, burying these
words, these manipulations, which I saw now were such obvious
contrivances. And the proof was right there, in the invoices that
accompanied them. The first one was for $1000 for a "creative
consultation" and the next nearly twice that for "imaginative design." Each letter extracted just a little bit more, until by the end
she'd been billed nearly a hundred thousand dollars. It took my
breath away.

I was just replacing the other letters in their envelopes when I
turned one of the envelopes around to get a better angle. On the
back of it, European-style, was the return address: *H. Blanc, 54
Walcott Way, Battenkill, VT 05284.*

I smiled.

THE AFTERNOON WAS FILLED WITH FILM CREWS AND MOCK INTERVIEWS, false faces and cardboard façades and even falser words: "*That's so interesting! A wooden horse?*"

"*A Trojan Horse. I was working on it when the accident happened.*"

"*And what's this?*"

"*Pieces of a Greek trireme. It wasn't exactly right. I had to start over.*"

"*Wow. Now that's dedication. Still, it's all Greek to me.*" [Cue laughter].

Otherwise it was a day of planning, thinking, imagining the surprise ending I had in store for him. I read. I thought. I observed. In the late afternoon I saw them arguing on the patio, under a fly-eaten sun. Klara had her hair set in cascades of curls with that ridiculous white streak prominently displayed. Her eyes were glassy and distant like those of her porcelain figurines. "Are you alright?" Henri asked, his shirt open at the collar. But he was all business. The shark's tooth necklace was gone. A sheet of paper dangled from his fingers.

"Fine," she said.

"Do we have a moment? For a little communion with nature, so to speak?"

He didn't seem terribly enthusiastic about the prospect. He raised his eyebrows, but it was a forced expression—his eyes didn't go along. He looked almost relieved when Klara turned away. "I'm sorry, Henri. I'm not in the mood."

"Is something wrong?"

"Just stop haranguing me. Please."

Her vehemence took him by surprise. Even from my vantage point on the balcony, I could tell he was annoyed. He cocked his

191

head to one side as if to behold her from another angle—as if that might clear things up. "I have never seen you like this."

"I suppose we haven't known each other very long."

"I had no idea you felt that way."

She sighed. "I'm sorry. I'm not feeling well. It's Milo again. He's . . . I'm worried. It's worse than usual."

"Listen. I am certain he will be better soon. In fact I'm sure of it."

"If only I believed that."

"Trust me. He will not bother us much longer. I will ask Marta to make you hot tea. Biscuits. Yes?"

She shook her head. "Maybe later. What do you have for me?"

He glanced at the paper as if noticing it for the first time. "Unfortunately it cannot wait," he said in a low voice.

"What is it?"

"The underwriting agreement. For the new television program we will do together. Leo wanted to have it finished before he drives tomorrow to New York."

"Just leave it. I'll read it over and give it to him myself."

"Yes, of course. Only…if you sign it now, I can save you the trouble. Especially in your current state, you should rest."

"Have you read it?"

"Everything is as we discussed. Here, use my pen. A quick signature on this line, and *violá*, it is done."

I watched her look at him for a moment—his earnest smile, his ponytail, his impossibly green eyes. The paper and pen were on the table. She bent over them like an old woman. Her hand shook as she scrawled her signature. Henri immediately snatched it up and folded it in half, beaming, while she slowly raised herself. "You seem happy," she said.

"I am happy for us both." He folded the paper into his shirt pocket. "And you? Are you happy?"

"Yes, of course."

Then he was gone, with a quick peck on the cheek, and I could see how she watched him—the hope and fear and loneliness in her eyes.

By the time I went downstairs she was shuffling among the roses, brushing her fingers against them, not enough to feel anything but like she didn't expect to—like she was trying to convince herself to care.

I strode into the garden myself. The first thing I noticed was the smell, a heady mixture of sweetness that reminded me of those times when, as a boy, I'd stuff a handful of assorted candies into my mouth. Still I put my head down and ventured deeper. The paths twisted and turned like a labyrinth between the flowers and perfectly manicured shrubbery. I saw Klara in the distance. I wasn't sure how to get to her. I soon found myself on the small hill. Several paths led into the woods, connecting the cultivated world with the wild. And there, in the pavilion, stood the old Roman with a ridiculous garland around his head.

"We can always move it back, you know."

I whirled around. Klara had appeared so far away just moments before, but I realized now it was just an illusion caused by all those winding paths. She was mounting the hill by a different way. She wore jeans and a red checkered blouse and was shading her eyes with one hand.

"Excuse me?" I said.

"The bust of Marcus Aurelius," she said between breaths.

"It's not Marcus Aurelius."

She chuckled—a sad kind of laugh. "Henri called him that and I thought it was funny. Don't you think it's funny? He does look so stoical."

"He looks nothing like Marcus Aurelius," I said, knowing I sounded pedantic but unable to stop myself. "Maybe you want him to be Marcus Aurelius because of all the things Marcus Aurelius did for the poor, but he looks nothing like him. And Marcus Aurelius persecuted Christians. He threw them to the lions. If you thought about it even a little bit I'm sure you wouldn't want him to be Marcus Aurelius."

She'd reached the pavilion by then. Her face gleamed in the sun. It was another moment before she spoke, this time in a lower tone. She must've heard something in my voice.

"You'll be happy to know that the filming's almost finished," she said.

"So what comes next?"

"You get your peace and quiet back."

"For how long?"

"As long as you need."

"You mean until the police return?"

She glanced away. I waited for her to reveal her knowledge of the diary, but she just bit her lip and said: "Why would they do that, Milo?"

"Did Henri find anything else here?" I asked, glancing toward the woods. "Any other so-called evidence of my guilt?"

She shook her head. "This was never about you. Or me. No one was responsible for their deaths. I've had time to think about it, and I realize that now. It was an accident. Accidents happen."

Was it that easy? I wondered.

"That's why I think it's time to put everything behind us," she went on. "I mean the garden shouldn't be a memorial to Mother and Father." She gazed out over it. From this vantage point I could see the intricacy of its maze-like paths—a perfect Henri creation. "We'll still talk about Mother and Father for the sake of context," she said, "but the garden is no longer about them. I thought, well, that it really should be about the living, not the dead. That we should care more about the living."

"How poignant," I replied.

"Henri and I are also discussing a business venture. I thought you ought to know. It would be our own television show about gardening. To demonstrate what's possible even in soils like this."

Could she really be so blind? "I suppose he's asked you to finance it."

"I don't see what that has to do with anything." She looked at me. "He wants us all to live in peace."

"And you still believe him? After everything?" I shook my head. "He's writing fiction, Klara. Sweet-sounding lies. About your future together. Just like he has about the past."

She narrowed her eyes. But didn't ask me to explain. And what would I have said? How could I have convinced her?

After all, I was a fiction writer myself.

Had she really seen my diary? That's what I wondered as I left her. Whether it was my own words coursing through her mind. Words that would have come as a welcome relief to her, that would have alleviated her own sense of responsibility. Words that were so easy to misconstrue, to see as an admission of *my* guilt, when *guilt* wasn't what they were about at all. They were about stories, about Father's new book, the one he'd been working on at the end: the long-awaited sequel to his most famous work. About the struggles to make it the greatest sequel ever written, one that readers everywhere would never forget. Could she ever understand that? No. She wasn't a real writer. She couldn't comprehend the sacrifices that had to be made in the name of craft, art, a higher calling—the loss of yourself that comes when the narrative takes over.

11/30: THERE IS NO ESCAPING THE PAST. STILL WE ALL WONDER ABOUT alternative histories. Had I been more physically fit I might have been a naval officer in some distant port-of-call and none of this would have happened. Had I been anyone but Father's son I might have escaped this house, been a stockbroker or a lawyer or a pharmacist who didn't live in constant fear of shadows and midnight voices. Whose only involvement in a plot was buying a modest plot of land to call my own.

In the early days, when Father struggled with a particularly difficult scene, he'd pluck me from my childish activities, lifting me by the top of my shirt and making it impossible for me to do anything but gape at what I was leaving behind: the tin soldiers arrayed carefully across the crumbled patio stones, the Encyclopedia Britannica opened to an article on catapults in a spot of warm sunlight on the living room floor, or the vast army of wind-rippled trees I'd been admiring from the window of my little room. He'd carry me like that into the study, close the door, and there visit his terrible creations upon me.

I became his habit, a tool he couldn't do without.

12/3: The one time I tried to resist he grabbed his scissors, held my head back, and thrust them up my nose, tearing through hair and mucous membranes and residual snot until the cold metallic tips were lodged at the base of my brain itself. "Now are you scared?" he asked, his voice coming through the hollowness in my ears. My entire face felt clogged with his violence, and the thin metallic taste of blood dribbled into the back of my mouth. He glared at me. I tried to glare back, but his face was a distant blur, a hazy collection of features somewhere beyond the looming mountaintops of pale bony knuckle.

"Are you?" he insisted.

His face moved closer, gaining a terrible visual coherence. His breath billowed hot and acrid against my forehead as his eyes searched mine. I didn't meet them. Instead I concentrated on the looping metal handle pressed into and rather stretching my nostrils. His hand began to tremble, causing the scissors to scratch across my deepest sinus cavities and my eyes to squint. Then he put both fists together in preparation, I felt certain, for the final deadly thrust, but still I said nothing, and we remained there, inches apart yet intimately connected through this instrument, until his breathing began to slow and he fell into something of a reflective mood.

"Please don't let me down, Milo," he said in a softer, gravelly, and more plaintive voice. "I count on you, you know."

Silence.

"I'm sorry this is a little hard on you sometimes."

He slowly extracted the scissors along with bits of hair and membrane and dropped them clattering to the floor. I closed my eyes. I saw nothing but little swirling stars. Then came a sniffling sound and I opened them again and witnessed the one and only instance I ever remember of Father crying. He held his fist up to his stubbled chin. His eyes were clenched shut and his head nodded rapidly as if in vehement agreement with something. I just sat there for a time not knowing what to do. I recall thinking that from a man who terrorized not only me but also millions of readers, this was a curious sign of weakness. Of course it didn't last. After a week he came to me again, this time at night. He wore a plastic Halloween mask of a vampire. Soon he dropped the mask. He didn't need it any longer. His face itself had become a mask— impassive and dead to what he was doing. He still apologized sometimes, but he never meant it anymore. He seemed to look right through me, seeing only his own words, hearing mine only when they painted the proper pictures.

12/5: Or should I say when they painted A Portrait? Because it was then, during the writing of that novel, that he killed me for *good. Nothing as dramatic as the incident with the scissors, more like a gradual drowning. But I didn't really die. I was reborn, into a different kind of life. A writer's life.*

12/6: Today I told him my idea for a sequel to A Portrait. *I described it for him in excruciating detail, letting him know exactly how it had to be. Yet to my surprise he said nothing at first. He just gave me an odd look, then dismissed me out of hand, saying I wasn't to think of such things anymore. He actually let slip that he was working on a sequel of his own, that he had his own ideas. His own ideas? I was shocked. "What on earth do you mean?" I asked. He refused to elaborate. But I saw something in his eyes. Something that told me he was afraid of me, or worse: disgusted. By what I'd become. By what he'd done to make me this way. Eyes that were like a pair of mirrors saying: "I don't recognize you anymore." That was when I knew our collaboration was over—that we couldn't go on this way and there was no turning back. Only I still don't know exactly why, what might have prompted such an utter change of heart.*

12/7: Perhaps I ought to be happy. But I'm not. I haven't suffered all these years to let him throw away what he once called my gift. I keep thinking of the sequel I have in mind. A book to elevate horror to new heights, to make the novel NOVEL again. I have the perfect beginning. Will he see the beauty of it? How another kind of death will lead to another kind of rebirth? I imagine he will. Because in a way it was inevitable all along; it was always how the narrative had to go. He'll know what I have in mind soon enough.

12/9: Master cylinder, brake pedal, brake lines, drums. Brake lines made from 87% copper, 10% nickel, 3% iron/manganese. A strong alloy with good resistance to corrosion. Wrapped in a blue rubber jacket. Accessible near the shock absorbers behind each wheel. Ordinary pliers or wire cutters would do the necessary work. Just press until you feel it start to give, until the metal braids begin to fray. Nobody realizes on what thin threads our lives depend. Lines set down by others, which we can't appreciate until they go awry. I wonder whether anyone will ever see the irony in that.

I PEERED OUT MY BEDROOM WINDOW. THE MOON MOVED INTO and out of the clouds. I thought of the "fissure of the arched and ponderous roof, through which heaven darkened and blazed alternately with a gloom that wrapt every thing" from Maturin's late-Gothic classic, *Melmoth the Wanderer*. It was one of earliest books Father read to me, curled trembling on his lap. Father himself would describe this night more simply, in his trademark style: "*The moon behind the clouds did dart, / And night came blacker than a witch's heart.*" A witch's heart? Despite everything, Father was susceptible to cliché. Suffice it to say that I didn't know what was in a witch's heart, but I knew what was in mine: excitement, a sense of purpose finally. Here was the moment around which so many other moments would turn. *Climax,* as the ancient Greeks would say.

I waited until an hour after the light beneath Klara's door had disappeared. Then I made my way down to the kitchen. In a drawer I found Mother's art scissors. They were solid metal and weighed almost two pounds, with tips that could lance a boil. She'd always said they'd make a formidable weapon, even thrusting them into air once or twice for emphasis. I slid them carefully behind my belt.

The front door creaked. Cool air enveloped me. My footsteps growled over gravel. The iron gate squealed. Crickets shrieked. The garage door didn't wake anyone, not even the dead.

I hunched over the steering wheel and went through all the motions: ignition, clutch, shift. The M14 was a moon-river of concrete. My headlights blazed into the mist. I drove at exactly the allowable speed. It was hypnotic, freeing in a way. I was a soldier, an unthinking instrument. Of what? Fate? Again I thought of the ancient Greeks, of the inevitability that marked their tragedy, and of poor Frankenstein's monster, doomed to brutishness by own creator's abhorrence of him: *"when I looked upon him, when I saw the filthy mass that moved and talked, my heart sickened . . ."* I moved, how I moved, and talked constantly to myself, and my heart sickened too as I was drawn to Walcott Way like a magnet. Was I the monster? Or Dr. Frankenstein himself? I didn't know, didn't care anymore. I saw a barn-shaped mailbox and the number "54" reflected in my headlights. There was a screen of trees behind it and the windows, some illuminated, of a small, gabled cottage.

I snapped off the headlights and rolled to a stop. Silence. More crickets. My hissing breaths. The clacking engine. I unclasped the seat belt: *zip*—into the bolster. My mind's word-hoard went blank—I thought of nothing but the physical world around me, of the scissors pressed into my kidney and my fingers on the cool metal door handle. The rush of air as I stepped out—like a gasp, a recoil, an awe-stricken sigh when the hero shows his face to his mortal enemy.

The driveway was smooth, gleaming, recently repaved. Halfway up I saw the ghostly outline of the Peugeot. I ran a hand across the question mark I'd gouged in that hospital parking lot. But my eye was soon diverted by a second car, somewhere in the gloom—a Saab.

I crept around the house, remaining near the trees, a spirit in their penumbral shadows. I couldn't see anything except indistinct shapes through the nearest window. I hurried across a small patch of open grass, suffused a dark blue by the interior lights. That's when I spied several wooden masks along the wall and a cabinet full of statuettes. I moved closer. The masks were African in origin, with huge lips and slit-bulb eyes and protruding tusk-like teeth. And the statuettes were Hindu dancers, their multiple contorted arms shooting out like sunbeams. I remembered them from Mitchell's *Gods, Goddesses, And Other Deities*: the elephantine Ganesh, and Shiva, god of destruction and cosmic dissolution, in his incarnation as Nataraja, Lord of the Cosmic Dance. All the famous shape-shifters.

A path led from the driveway to the front door, a path lined with roses. Even by the light of the windows it was too dark to see their thorns. I quickly became entangled, thinking of those medieval paintings of Saint Sebastian, tied to a post, full of arrows. Only I was no martyr. I took out the heavy scissors and hacked my way through.

Stone steps do not creak. With a whisper I was atop them. The windows on either side revealed a living room with a camelback sofa and frilly lamps. On the wall behind the sofa hung a black-sheathed sword. I could tell it was of Sikh manufacture. As a boy I'd gone through a brief Sikh phase, falling in love with those distinctive curved weapons.

Then I was arrested by the sound of voices. They seemed distant at first, but grew in leaps. It took a moment to realize they were coming down stairs. I moved back and lowered myself into a well between the steps and a bush. That's when I heard, through a cracked-open window above me, Leo's voice as if it were not five feet away.

"She's really gonna finance the whole thing?"

"I have the signed contract."

"You amaze me, man. How do you do it?"

"Charm, *mon ami*. Simple old-fashioned charm."

"Well you play the game better than anybody I know."

Laughter. "Tell me Henri, are you really fucking that thing?"

"When you close your eyes, they are all the same."

More laughter, the kind I remembered from college: "'*What's wrong with blazer-boy's head?' 'Dude, it's square.*'" Then came the gruff intonations of Angus, which made me even more grateful that I hadn't gone inside.

"You'll still need to partner with a local gardener in each location, someone who knows the conditions, sort of thing. Leo has already been researching that."

"I've found some wonderful people already," Leo said.

"But the show is still mine, yes?" said Henri.

"Chill out! Of course. You're the host. They're just guest stars."

"So where will we begin?"

"Someplace warm," Leo said. "Florida or California, for the winter."

"Perfect."

"Especially if your company pays the way, right? So tell me, is Klara really willing to be on the road that long?"

"She has already told me so."

"And the brother won't get in the way? I assume some of the money is in his name."

"Trust me. He will not be a problem."

"You sure? This isn't Africa, man. You can't just do whatever you want."

"You'd be surprised."

By the time the door swung open I could hardly move. I heard: "Let me get the light." In an instant I was flooded with a harsh glare; my white shoes glowed like beacons. What an idiot I was—not to have changed out of them. Leo and Angus descended inches above my head.

"Watch your step," said Henri.

His piston-like breathing continued as their footsteps died. I imagined him staring down at me, snickering at my curled, fetal form. I started counting primes, trying not to scream like in Dracula: "*a scream so wild, so ear-piercing, so despairing that it seems to me now that it will ring in my ears till my dying day.*"

The Saab hummed to life. The cottage door closed. Still I didn't move. Suddenly I gasped and coughed. I realized I'd been holding my breath. I tried to muffle my mouth with my sleeve, but it was no use. Did Henri hear? The interior stairs creaked. I braced myself.

Nothing.

I opened my eyes. The lights were off. I raised myself up, saw shades of furniture in the darkness of the windows. The sword was lost amid the inky muddle. There was a far-off sound. *A dog barked in the distance.* Life imitating cliché. Not a peep came from the house.

I waited. And waited. No lights, no more creaks or dogs or anything else. Just the crickets, as ubiquitous and full of song as a Greek chorus. I knew I'd just *dodged a bullet*, as they say. Henri must have gone upstairs to sleep. Yet a part of me still distrusted the silence, even as I approached the front door. It had a round brass handle. I thought about fingerprints and turned it with my sleeve.

It wasn't locked.

My head started pounding. I admonished myself to act, go inside and do it. But I couldn't. Everything was suddenly too real, too imbued with consequence. What was I doing here anyway? I felt like an actor who'd forgotten his lines. I had to concentrate, making the whole universe small, nothing except the action that lay immediately ahead. I imagined it in words: *In one swift motion I threw open the door and strode in.* It worked. Before I knew it I was in the living room. *My heart beat like a war drum.* There was the sword—a black smiling gash on the wall. I laid the scissors on the sofa's arm and reached up, allowing my fingers to find the hooks, to study them, before lifting and releasing it. I backed away from the wall—the moment of truth—while keeping it cradled above my head. Only when I was certain that it was free did I lower it. It was heavier than I'd anticipated. Much heavier.

I curled my fingers around the handle and pulled. It slid out reluctantly. It was no longer a much-used weapon. But once free of its covering it seemed to dance through the air. I imagined the sense of power that must have girded the man who'd once wielded it in earnest. For a moment I was tempted to run off with it, declare victory and go home. But what would I do in the dead of winter if Klara were gone? I imagined lying in bed clutching the steel blade, the wind howling all around me. "*A howl swept through the wintry night, / A forlorn cry, so full of fright.*" I thought of a long ago winter's night when Mother and Father had gone out on a social engagement. It had snowed so much that they couldn't return until the following morning. Great drifts blocked the roads and piled up nearly to my window. I stood gazing at it, keeping watch, not for them but for Klara, who'd sneaked off with her drama-friend Jane shortly after they'd left. Every groan of the roof and creak of a floorboard told me I wasn't alone. But who else was there? That's what I never knew. I peered behind doors, opened closets, scanned beneath beds. Still I was suffused with doubt. The attic? The basement?

No.

I couldn't go through that again. I'd come too far to back down now. I retraced my steps to the hallway below the stairs. I paused, wondering whether something less than total violence might suffice. Perhaps I might just steal the contract? Or merely frighten him away, the way he tried to frighten me?

In the end I had no choice.

"Looking for me?"

The next few moments flew by in a blur. These words—"*Looking for me?*"—sounded like something out of a Humphrey Bogart film. In the first shock of hearing them I remember wondering which film it was. And why were the words coming from behind me? Did Henri have a second staircase?

My head exploded. I heard the sound of shattered porcelain as if from far away. Pieces rained down, glittering in the diffuse and bluish light. I remember thinking it was almost beautiful in the moments before the spasms hit. Then I bent over, convulsing wildly. I began to panic. I knew the next blow would end me.

But there in my hand lay the answer.

I whirled around like a dervish. The sword must have taken him by surprise. I could hear him stumble and a crash of glass and furniture. Had I done it? Gotten rid of him for good? I staggered forward until I'd found the front door. I burst outside, running wildly over the spongy grass.

I was nearly at the tree line when the outside lights popped on. In a quick backward glance I saw Henri's shadowy figure limping down the stairs. Limping? "*Utterson thought for a moment that Hyde was limping. But it was only his eyes playing tricks on him. Hyde had a strong, forceful walk.*"

He was coming straight for me.

I knew I couldn't possibly find, unlock, start, and drive off in the MG before he reached me. I scrambled past the trees and down the sloping lawn. If I couldn't lose him I might at least discourage him by running as far as I could. Of course he might not give up if I had his sword, so I stuck it into the ground—upright, so he'd see it—in an open patch of lawn.

Of all my mistakes that night, that might have been the worst.

After another hundred yards or so I glanced back and saw him in hazy silhouette against the house lights, yanking the thing out and continuing on. I ran harder. My legs were a discombobulated mess. My breath was a wheezy dying train. I tasted blood. My tongue was swollen where I'd bitten down on it. Flutters of panic began to overcome me, weakening my knees and nearly causing me to hyperventilate. Where could I go? Marta's house? I had a childhood recollection of a tiny, tidy cottage—yellow-painted wood with a crucifix on the door and plastic-covered furniture, Marta hovering over me with a tray of almond cookies. But I saw nothing like that, just more trees and the outlines of roofs with an occasional haloed light. So I kept running, taking the streets more or less at random, until I was lost, hoping that if I couldn't find myself, he couldn't find me either.

How wrong I was.

The footsteps only grew louder. He was gaining on me. I had to hide. I veered toward the vague outline of a sign. Its familiarity drew me. *Girardi & Sons.* I crunched up Phil's driveway and nearly tripped over the flowerpots. Where was the office door? There. But it was locked. I hurled myself against it, over and over, with an abandon I didn't know I possessed. Something splintered. I pushed and it gave way. The footsteps were close. I saw him out of the corner of my eye. Stumbling up the driveway like a drunk. I plunged inside, toward where I remembered the secret door. How did it work? I clawed the lines in the paneling. Come on, come on. Finally I heard a pop. I pulled back and slipped inside and quickly shut the door behind me.

It was pitch black until I found the light. It nearly blinded me. After the first blinking moments of visual adjustment I hurried to the wall. The .45 caliber revolver. I fumbled with its chamber, trying to recall from my military textbooks how to open it. I pulled the pin and dropped it to the right. There were no bullets inside. My hands shook. The vintage bullets on the wall were much too large. I glanced around, my eye finally resting on the dresser where the bullet-riddled helmet lay. I tore open its drawers. In the bottom one, beneath a folded pair of military underwear, was a small patriotically colored box. I took this out and opened it. One bullet fell to the floor. Another remained inside.

I hastily chambered this bullet.

A strange sense of calm came over me then. I spun the cylinder to line up the bullet. I cocked the gun and leaned my head against the wall. Henri's feet padded across the office floor. I hardly flinched. Not even when I heard him scrabbling against the wood-paneled door. I was at the center of a great stillness now. There was nowhere to run, no more decisions to make. I raised the gun to my temple. What would it feel like? In the end I didn't want to know, didn't want to indulge the cliché. "*It is a tale / Told by an idiot, full of sound and fury, / Signifying . . .*"

"Milo?"

I opened my eyes. Henri was standing in the doorway, his hair disheveled and the sword lowered in front of him. A large cut ran across his upper leg that gave him the air of a stagy buccaneer.

"Don't hurt yourself."

"I won't," I said, lowering the gun.

He seemed relieved, running a hand through his hair and taking deep billowing breaths. "My God, I thought you were a thief."

"I took your sword."

He waved away our antagonism like it was yesterday's joke. "It doesn't matter now."

We remained silent for a few moments, *the silence of the grave*, as both of us glanced around this strange room we'd found ourselves in. "We have been at each other's throats, you and I," he went on. "Perhaps it is time to end this game, yes?"

"You have my diary."

He shrugged. "I could have turned it over the police, but I did not. I am giving you a chance, you see?"

"To do what?"

"To leave us. Klara and I. We only want a little freedom. We have great plans."

"I've heard."

Henri's smile wavered for just an instant. His eyes darted to the walls. "*It was a trap, Keith saw it now: police with shields and pistols drawn, all strewn / Around the room, its walls now witness to his fate, so small, so drab, a little ruin.*" "Klara must have told you," he said, attempting to regain his charm.

"She tells me everything."

"Ah, we have no secrets then."

I wanted to laugh, but something held me back—the pressure in my head again. "*Keith sprang at them, but seemed to freeze, defiance in tableau, / It was his final work, himself, before his deathly throe.*" I blinked. Henri edged closer to me. "*Keith sprang at them . . .*" "Have you ever written fiction?" I asked.

"When the characters and plot just take over?"

Another step forward, hands outstretched. I clutched my head. "*Keith sprang at them . . .*"

No! It was getting worse. Other novels crowded in, not just Father's but all the books that influenced him. *Dracula:* "*There was something so panther-like in the movement—something so unhuman, that it seemed to sober us all from the shock of his coming.*"

"I am not a character," he said. "And this is not a plot."

"*Now* you want me to believe that?"

"It is the truth."

"The truth is you've been acting like Keith. Trying to make me *believe.*"

"Everything is going to be alright now." He reached for me in the same way he reached for this cheap optimism. "Trust me, yes? Here, let me give you a hand."

Matthew Lewis's *The Monk:* "*He overtook her; he twisted his hand in the ringlets of her streaming hair, and attempted to drag her back with him to the dungeon.*"

I raised the gun. He stopped.

"Milo?"

"Everything is not alright," I said. Because I realized what he was doing, trying to suck me under his spell by pretending sympathy, pretending he understood. "You had it all plotted out. How you'd get rid of me. Then bilk Klara dry. Maybe kill her when you didn't need her any longer." "*Then throw her to the wolves, the birds, the trees, / And let cruel nature claim her fee.*"

"That was only in your mind, Milo."

I waved the gun. "What difference does that make?"

"I am truly sorry if I . . ." Suddenly there was a hint of fear in his voice, as if he realized he was no longer in control—that neither of us was. Then who? Father? I wondered that, too. Maybe he wasn't dead. Maybe he wasn't even done writing. Maybe he'd set this all up as *his* sequel—his last and most horrifying game.

But no. I shook my head. "You were acting a role," I said. "With the tattoo. The scar. It was a game to you. You knew Klara wouldn't see through you—she'd be too blinded by your charm. And me? You'd scare me, make me wonder if you really were Keith so I'd be too afraid to oppose you."

"This is your imagination talking."

"Do you know what my father taught me?" I went on. "His greatest lesson? That all life is what you imagine it to be."

"You are getting excited. Perhaps you would like to lie down? Have a rest?"

"You said Father inspired you. He inspired me too. Literally, as in breathed life into me. But you know what? I inspired him even more."

"I am leaving Vermont. You see? There is nothing to worry about."

"But you're taking Klara with you."

He shrugged.

"Florida? California?" I said. "I overheard it all."

"She is a business partner. She will only be gone a few days at a time."

Liar! On all sides, Phil's Father stared at me heroically. A real-life war hero. "You're a con man. You knew Klara would be an easy mark. Were you even in the Foreign Legion? It doesn't matter. I'll leave it ambiguous. Readers like that sort of thing."

"Readers?"

"What do you think I'm describing here? This is an outline. For a book. *My* book."

I could see it in his eyes—the sudden realization that he was just a character after all.

"Do you know what Father's literary agent will find when he goes through the attic?" I went on.

He paused. "Klara said you had burned everything."

"No, not everything. There was one thing I missed. In the floorboards. The long-awaited sequel."

He opened his mouth and closed it.

"It will be the greatest literary discovery since the lost manuscript of Shakespeare. I've already told you the plot."

"Do not do this, Milo."

"Should I change the names? That's what I'm still unsure about."

"Nobody will believe it."

I laughed. "I'm calling it *The Garden of Blue Roses*. Do you like it? The title, I mean? It comes from you, you know."

He shook his head. But I could see him inching closer. On all sides, Phil's Father stared at me heroically. A real-life war hero.

Or was that, too, just a *story*?

"This is crazy, Milo."

"Well in that case . . ." I aimed for Henri's heart.

"Milo?"

"Tell me your name. Before you changed it to Henri."

"You know my name."

"You stole someone else's identity. An older Henri Blanc."

"That was just a coincidence."

"There are no coincidences in novels."

"But this is not . . ."

"Say it! Say: 'My name is Keith Sentelle.'"

"But that is not true."

"Keith sprang at them . . ."

I squeezed the trigger.

> *Blood spurted from his gaping chest*
> *As Keith did finally come to rest,*
> *All that natural, killing, cold philosophy*
> *Stopped dead and leaking, gurgling red. Catastrophes*
> *Averted, that's what everybody gathered had to contemplate*
> *Now that this evil monster had met his fate.*
> *Or had he? Could a bullet really stop him?*
> *That was the question as they watched, so grim.*
> *And then, from somewhere in Keith's throat*
> *They heard strange noises--not a snicker or a gloat,*
> *Just childish crying, fear of being all alone*
> *When this sad story ceased and he was gone.*
>
> *And somewhere far away, the Master stilled*
> *His hand, his canvas half-undone. He willed*
> *Himself to listen to the silent, eerie absence,*
> *The ineluctable transcendence*
> *Of rotting flesh, so slowly growing cold.*
> *The Master, too, then closed his eyes. Keith's tale was told.*
>
> *Or so he thought.*

I covered my ears. I couldn't hear a thing. My eardrums felt like they'd burst, oozing liquid silence. I was underwater, floating in another realm: graceful, easy, buoyant. I lowered my hands. I was free. I was just standing there being me, as people say, in this room full of someone else's memorabilia.

Even my memories grew distant. "*Keith sprang at them.*" I remembered it as something that had happened ages ago: how I'd seen Henri's action before he moved—seen the idea of it as it made its way from that brain down through his legs. I'd reacted. My hand had jerked back. Now all that was left was his blood dripping down the walls like moisture on a wintry window.

And a pair of boot-shod feet sticking through the doorway.

And my breathing.

And the dull throb of my ever-insistent heart.

But nothing else. No stories. No authorial voices. At last.

Until . . .

Until a different plot intruded—a not-so-distant cry: "*Did you hear that?*"

Phil.

Suddenly a more primal fear took over. I pictured the Italian detective picking over the scene, teams of forensic scientists in white jumpsuits and masks piecing together their own kind of story. I wiped the gun clean with the end of my blazer. What else had I touched? The drawers? The sword? I took the olive drab underwear and wiped down everything. Everything? No. I knew I was bound to miss things. I tried to find some turpentine and a match to burn away the evidence, but I saw only a fire extinguisher in the main office. Good enough, I thought. I stepped over the feet. Henri. Keith. The name didn't matter anymore. It looked like a skinny fish, the head twisted to one side, the face mercifully hidden by the office's shadows. I grabbed the fire extinguisher and sprayed down the entire room, letting chemicals destroy anyone else's attempt to write this past. I alone would be its jealous guardian.

Then I wiped down the handle. I hurried away. At the bottom of the driveway I turned. I watched Phil burst out the main front door. The lights were on. They looked like shining stars. I wrapped my arms around my chest and lunged away, suddenly so very cold, an astronaut light-years from home.

ANGUS AND A SMALL CREW ARRIVED EARLY TO TAKE ADVANTAGE of the morning light. The filming was almost done. All that remained was to take morning shots of the garden. And to film an introductory sequence with the program's host, Wilhelmina Cottrell. She looked even more imposing in person than on Klara's DVD—an old battle-axe with sausage legs and sharp drooping eyes.

It was the longest day of my life. I hadn't slept at all. It took ages to find the MG. Then it wouldn't start. I nearly screamed, coaxing the thing to life. I drove to Henri's house and stumbled through those dark and unfamiliar rooms. Where would he keep it? There were flowers everywhere and expensive furniture and a startling lack of books. There were no stories here.

Except one.

I found it in the refrigerator, in the shadow of flavored tea bottles and hunks of local cheese. I was tempted to destroy it—burn it page-by-page—but I didn't, for I needed it: I needed the *material*. I slipped it inside my blazer pocket and closed the refrigerator door. I wiped down the refrigerator handle and the front door's knob as I left.

I stopped at the Baylor's Massacre site. I tossed my shoes and blazer into the trash. By the time I got home I was delirious for lack of sleep. Somehow I inched the car back into the garage and stumbled upstairs and hid the diary inside my model Trojan Horse. Then I went to the bathroom and took several anti-inflammatories and a sleeping pill. They didn't work. I lay atop my bed and blinked at the ceiling. I watched the hours flash by on my clock. I had to ruffle the sheets at dawn to convince myself I'd slept.

The television crew. For once I was thankful for its distraction. It was a relief from the penitentiary of my own thoughts. Everyone scurried around like black-clad ants. At one point Angus noticed me. "Would you mind holding this?" he asked. He held out a book. Ms. Cottrell's Bible. How ironic. It was the one thing I'd never believed in. Ms. Cottrell smiled as I took it. I was strangely touched. So was Klara.

"I'm glad to see you're finally getting involved, Milo. It will do you a lot of good."

I wished I could say the same about her. She wore a flower-print dress that hugged her hips. Already she was worrying about Henri. "He was supposed to be here hours ago," she whispered to Angus.

"He probably forgot. Or maybe he got distracted by some wonderful perennials. You know him, always looking for something new."

The afternoon became increasingly hectic with preparations for the supper party. I'd forgotten all about it: the dinner Klara had promised for Henri's gardening clients. Marta was like a workhorse in the kitchen—beating eggs, washing lettuce, trimming steaks. I don't think I'd ever seen her so busy. I shocked her by offering to chop onions, taking a great armload of them to the small table and cleaving them to bits. My arms and shoulders ached and my eyes dripped like a fountain, but I didn't stop until every last one was done. I stood there, crying like a babe, as Marta thanked me for being so helpful.

I haven't cried since.

The first guests arrived at seven o'clock. By then I was back in my room. I was staring out the window. Every criminal makes at least one mistake, I knew, and I'd just realized mine. The scissors. I'd left them on Henri's sofa. Would anybody take fingerprints? Could they connect those prints to me? I had no idea. What if someone had seen my car parked at his house? What if I'd dropped some traceable item—a library card or bookstore receipt—during my frantic scramble around Phil's office?

There were endless ways I could be damned. But now the facts existed *out there*, beyond my reach, and no amount of editing could alter them. I bathed and changed clothes several times just to give my limbs something to do. For luck I pinned a submarine officer's insignia on my blazer's lapel: a gold-plated submarine flanked by dolphins, those mythical attendants to Poseidon. They were symbolic of calm smooth waters, and I closed my eyes and imagined myself floating deep beneath the ocean, the raging storms above just a murmur.

Then they grew louder. Engines rumbled up the drive. I opened my eyes and saw them: the great Buicks and Dodges of the doddering garden set. They staggered out and pushed their trembling feathery forefingers against the doorbell. They laughed and chatted as if they'd been enjoying this one long conversation all their lives. In the meanwhile I kept waiting for more ominous noises: the scrape of a detective's shoes on the stairs or Klara's hushed voice: "He's in there."

Mrs. Silfer was among the last to arrive. Her massive Ford rumbled to a stop in front of the garage. I watched her great bulk heave itself out of the vehicle and wobble to the door.

The bell rang three times. *Ask not for whom the bell tolls.* Moments later Klara opened the door. "Elizabeth!"

"Sorry I'm late," she huffed. "My son Todd was playing hide-and-seek in the clothes dryer. Kids these days!"

Klara called out: "Milo! Elizabeth Silfer is here and wants to say hello!"

I was halfway down when I overheard Klara ask Mrs. Silfer whether she'd spoken to Henri. "Not in ages," came the reply. "I thought he'd be here."

"Me too," said Klara. "I've been waiting since morning."

Guffaw. "Artists."

"I tried calling his mobile phone."

"Are you kidding me? He *never* answers his phone."

I did my best to smile as Mrs. Silfer noticed me. Her eyes widened, her arms surrounded me in a pillowy embrace. I held my breath.

"How are you?" Mrs. Silfer shrieked. "Isn't the garden awesome? Didn't I tell your sister how awesome Henri was?"

I shrugged, still not trusting my tongue. Thankfully Mrs. Silfer didn't seem to notice. She grabbed my arm and led me into the living room, smiling and waving to the crowd. "This is Milo Crane, Klara's younger brother, he and I went to school together," she'd emphasize before turning to me and uttering the name—which I promptly forgot—of whatever dull, unremarkable-looking person was standing there. It was no wonder Henri had been a rock-star among this set. Klara was off in the corner making small-talk. To anyone else she would have seemed the picture of the perfect hostess. But to me, who knew the signs, every glance at her slender watch or the window spoke volumes.

The dining room table had been expanded to its full length (which I'd only remembered happening once before, when Mother had displayed several of her oversized paintings for an effete New York dealer who promised to get back to her and never did). At the far end of it a group of plump, aging bachelors were heatedly discussing the aesthetic qualities of *Digitariasanguinalis*, or crabgrass.

"A weed by any other name," declared one of them.

"To hell with taxonomy," cried another.

"Well I for one agree it's ugly," said a third.

"Absolutely hideous, yes," agreed a fourth.

"Underrated, underrated in its usefulness!" said a fifth.

With this and several other conversations going on I nearly didn't hear the telephone. I was sitting at my usual place, wondering how I'd make it through an entire supper with these people. Klara leapt out of her seat. My heart nearly leapt up with her. I glanced to my left, where an old woman in a flower-print dress was sliding awkwardly toward me along the bench, and to my right, where another was doing the same, virtually indistinguishable from the first except that her dress was one solid color and had ruffles in disconcerting places. Mrs. Silfer stood in the doorway beaming at us, a pocket camera dangling from her puffy wrist. Marta was just coming through the kitchen door with a giant soup tureen.

Klara returned after a few minutes. She looked catatonic. "Is everything alright?" asked Mrs. Silfer. Klara's mouth began to move. But no sound emerged. I hung onto that soundlessness as if for dear life. Was it true? For a moment I had a strange sensation. That Henri really *was* a fictional character. That as soon as I'd left that blood-spattered room he'd dusted himself off and laughed and loped away. Mrs. Silfer guided Klara off into the living room. Everyone else fell silent. I watched Marta put down the soup and a few people cough and finger their napkins. Then Mrs. Silfer returned. She was quivering like an earthquake. She managed the following words: "I'm sorry. It's Henri. He was . . . shot. Last night. He's—oh God." She put a hand over her mouth and groaned and finally spoke the words that made it real: "He's dead."

The room exploded with questions and shocked ejaculations, only dying in time to hear, in a faltering tone, Mrs. Silfer's next six words—the six words which were, in truth, the most bittersweet I'd heard in all my life.

"They think it was Phil Girardi."

They think it was Phil Girardi.

They *think* it was Phil Girardi.

They think it was *Phil Girardi.*

Were they not sure? Would they come for me yet? Had they done so already, and was all this a dream? *Yes, we discovered the car, we know it was you, you're here in prison, for the murder of your parents as well as Mr. Blanc.* Memories or imaginations surfaced in my mind: of that Italian detective and some other man, bald and thin, questioning me in a windowless room, playing Good Cop and Bad Cop, smoking incessantly and drinking sour coffee and hunching their shoulders as if readying themselves to fly into a rage. And my incompetent lawyer (Father's rube) picking at his fingernails, lodging an occasional dreary objection but otherwise more concerned with not missing lunch. *Take the deal*, he said. *And save your life.* My life, the one I no longer recognized, the one that Klara would memorialize in a hopelessly false and sensational book that would win her fame at last, newspaper articles, TV specials, devoted fans of her own.

But no.

It never happened.

Not that way.

Phil's trial came late in a wet and miserable autumn and lasted nearly two full weeks. The entire town turned out to witness it, and everyone had a theory as to its merits. Some opined that the evidence of motive was weak and that Phil was not a violent man. Others said it was just as obvious that Phil was guilty because it had happened in his own office, with his own gun, and he'd known and done business with the victim.

But only one opinion mattered—that of the jury. Oddly enough, I was nearly selected for it myself. I don't know how they got my name. I've never even registered to vote. I was only spared that awkward ordeal when I described how the victim had worked for my sister in some vague capacity (so I said). Of course the police already knew this—they'd interviewed Klara shortly after the shooting—but the investigation turned up nothing. Still they had their suspicions. The Italian detective in particular seemed to wonder if I was being honest when I'd said I'd hardly known Henri. But without any solid evidence they soon focused their attentions on Phil and on a series of late payments Henri had made. Suddenly there was the foundation for another story: one of anger, revenge, a business deal gone awry. A more familiar story, perhaps, to these country police.

The jury took four hours to acquit. It wasn't nearly as divided as the general public. When polled, they said they couldn't fathom why Phil would shoot Henri in his own office. The fire extinguisher also troubled them. Why would Phil have set it off? To remove evidence? But why not do so in a quieter way, since it was his own house anyway? It was heartening to hear such faultless logic. It actually restored a modicum of my faith in human nature. Still I couldn't help feeling a twinge of doubt. Would the police now re-open the case?

Two weeks later they finally came to me, but it wasn't at all like I'd imagined. The Italian was no longer there. There was a shiny young detective I'd never seen and an older female partner. They sat in the living room, where Klara served them tea. "Just gathering up loose ends," they said, and began asking me about something they must have known all along—my little interview with Phil.

Klara said nothing. If she was surprised that I'd asked Phil about Henri, she didn't show it—just sat there with her hands in her lap, occasionally offering cream or sugar or buttery Danish biscuits.

"I just wanted to make sure Henri was legitimate," I told them. "That was my right under the will."

"Did you harbor any ill-feelings toward the deceased?"

This was the young detective. He must have come straight from Detective School on the first public bus. He had an earnestness that made you almost want to break down and confess, realizing he needed the help. "I hardly knew him," I said slowly, as if to a child. "That was why I was asking questions."

"Mr. Girardi says you thought he was overcharging your sister."

Beware the older woman, the harridan, I told myself as she leaned back into the sofa and eyed me, her chin multiplying alarmingly and her brow furrowing beneath that limp policewoman's hair. She lived for this, I could tell, but it was sad because she was no match for me either. "I've never been interested in money," I said truthfully. "Anyway Klara and I are very comfortable, and our needs are few."

"Did you know that Mr. Blanc was accused of overcharging other clients in the past?" she croaked.

I shook my head.

"One of them even ended up dead," she went on.

"Then I suppose he must have had lots of enemies," I pointed out.

"Sort of like in your father's books?"

I shrugged. "I'm sure it was nothing like that."

The charade finally ended when the young detective confessed what a fan he was of Father—and how sad Father's death had made him. I nodded and said that I was sad too, but that Father would, like any author, live on in the hearts of readers like him. I smiled. In the end I wished them well. Klara and I stood in the doorway, watching them go. "You never mentioned seeing Phil," she said in a monotone.

"I must have forgotten. We had so much else going on then."

"Yes, we did."

I didn't think much of this last statement until a few weeks later. Winter had arrived with a vengeance. Snow piled up everywhere. The one-year anniversary of the accident came and went, and then, just before Christmas, Henri's house and its belongings were put up for sale. Mrs. Silfer convinced Klara to go to the auction and procure some remembrances. She reluctantly agreed. I remember there was icy rain. She nearly didn't go because of it, afraid she'd be stranded somewhere. When she returned I thought she'd seen a ghost. I asked her over supper what was wrong. She became absolutely still for several seconds before excusing herself and hurrying to her room. She hadn't touched her food.

On the following morning I saw them, in their old drawer, in their old leather case. The scissors.

What could I say? I pulled them out of their sheath. They were smooth and worn and cut like a whisper. Everyone had their secrets. Now Klara and I did, as well. We were like a secret society, bound by what we could never discuss. *The Order of the Blue Rose*? Father had once written a book about a band of murderers fashioning themselves after the Knights Templars, whose symbol was also a rose. These men killed innocent people as an initiation rite, a way to seal their bond. I was tempted to bring her a copy, explain how Henri's death might be our own initiation, might bring us closer even though he wasn't exactly innocent.

But who really was? Innocent, I mean?

For days she locked herself in her room. I began to worry. What if she never came to her senses? There was much she could do to implicate me. I saw myself as one of those grizzled murderers shuffled into a courtroom in a bright orange jumpsuit and leg irons. I'd seen such men on television, mostly from inner-city Boston. They didn't look at all like me. Still, I began having doubts.

Finally she came down for supper again. She wouldn't even glance at me. Her face was gaunt and waxy, like she'd been suffering from the flu. She picked at her food. Then she turned her heavy eyes to me and asked: "Do you know why Henri had our scissors?"

I looked her directly in the eye and forced myself to believe, in that moment, that I'd had absolutely nothing to do with it. It was a moment of great realization for me. One might call it an epiphany. Honesty, I saw, is just a matter of faith like anything else. That's what Father had meant by saying that life is what you imagine it to be. How do you ever really know you're telling the truth? You don't. It's merely a conviction.

"No," I replied.

What should I have said? That the scissors found their own way to his house? That they'd exerted a vague pull, a demand for stabbing, ever since the days when Father visited me at night? No, it was impossible. She'd never understand. I'd tried telling her when we were children, but she hadn't wanted to hear, and now she never would. Let her think she herself was responsible—she who knew Father as an author, a parent, a horribly forbidden lover, when really he was much less than anyone knew. Anyone but me, that is.

I tried to keep the memories at bay. I closed my eyes. It didn't work. It was like a dam had finally burst—everything came flooding back. I heard my bedroom door creak open and the soft padding of his slippers in the darkness. I felt the weight of him on the mattress. "Milo?" he'd whisper, and I'd pretend to be asleep, but it never worked because he'd say "Let me tell you a story" and I'd open my eyes to see the ghost of his looming face tinged with what passed in him as guilt. "No, Daddy. Please. Not again."

"I'm sorry, son. I wish there was another way."

"But I see things."

"That is your gift."

I had no choice once the words took over, falling from his lips like water drops, infecting me with the fun-house horror of his imagination:

> Did Keith feel guilt? He did, but only once, with one artistic piece:
> The Magic of Reality. A non-nature work. Its star? His niece.
> A girl of maybe fifteen years, enamored of her uncle Keith
> While he, who hated children (how they're coddled, wreathed
> In un-ironic splendor), invited her to do a show.
> A real show! While Keith had doubts, the Master said
>   he had to go
> And do it, prove that all compunction was a lie.
> Keith watched himself in disbelief, say: close your eyes!
> Her blouse bloomed red from where he stabbed her.

He carried her out to the box; she hardly stirred,
Just moaned as he so gently laid her in and closed the lid.
And donned that magic cape, still feeling pity for the kid
But told himself that it was time
For her to become more, to turn sublime.

He'd encircle me with these words, bending close, watching what they did to my eyes. Here was the great secret to his success: me, a foolproof gauge to heightened terror. He'd keep coming back, retelling a scene in different ways, until my eyes darted around like little mice struggling to stay afloat and he knew he'd nailed it. Then he got greedy, asking what else I saw, what the characters looked like in the tiniest detail. My lips moved of their own volition. The character took on a life of his own. The words just flowed out of me—words that didn't *create* Keith anymore, but simply tried to keep pace with the creation. "*The stage was dark. Red velvet curtains. Gargoyles on either side. A huge brass clock overhead. Keith was wearing his white tuxedo and gloves beneath the cape. He wheeled the box onto the middle of the stage. There were only a few people in the audience. Old men sitting by themselves. They were hunched, bored. Then they saw him. Their eyes shone in the darkness. They struggled to get a better look. They wanted something new, something different. Keith pulled out his saw. Here it was: the magic of no illusions.*"

I saw everything. Not in verse but in even scarier prose, which he'd then translate into his own inimitable style. *Keith, Keith, Keith.* The name was like a curse, whispered into my ear night after night by a man desperate for a bestseller. How had this terrible collaboration begun? Who'd first mouthed that psychopath to life? Father had spoken to me one night of a gardener who dismembers lonely women. This was at a time when female dismemberment was all the rage in fiction. I'd covered my ears, heard myself reply as if from far away: "*He's an artist, he sees beauty where others see only horror.*" Father paused. "*Say more.*" A flurry of pictures littered my mind: Mother's nature paintings, her artistic pretensions, the things I'd seen her do with that ceramist Roland in the Volvo as it was parked outside our garage one moonlit night—odd contortions of limbs that I had as yet no language for. Father kept nodding as I described it all as best I could. He didn't even stop to ask, or wonder, where I was getting such material. He was enthralled, adding his own words until I broke down weeping: *Yes, that's it, that's what I see.* But Father wasn't done. He kept coming back to this tale, fleshing it out night after night with bloodshot intensity, and I kept heightening the horror, hoping it would satisfy him. Only nothing could do that anymore. He was drunk with the power of his story. At first I was afraid—of him, of our creation, of myself. Was I just as responsible for making Keith as he was? The possibility horrified me at the time, and as we hurtled toward the novel's climax I kept groping in the dark for Father, for one shielding embrace that would tell me he still cared about me apart from this terrible partnership. But only when it was over did Father hold me in his arms, promising it would be the last time, that he'd learn to do without my help.

He never did.

In the end I had no choice. I'd suffered long enough for those awful books of his. I also began, gradually, to be less afraid, even indifferent to his menace. Of course this sent him into desperate paroxysms as he tried to draw some reaction out of me, turning his novels into pure splatterpunk schlock. That's when I realized that what he'd given me really was a gift—one that I could do so much more with if I were free of him—the gift to imagine worlds, to be immersed in their unreality and not flinch in the face of the sublime. What I am saying is that I felt myself slowly coming into my own as a writer, full of my own perfect notions. I began to see *possibilities*, the words coming to me with more harrowing certainty than anything before: the real true-life sequel to *A Portrait*—one *based on actual events*. I cut the brake wires, it was true, I can say that finally, because it should be clear by now that this wasn't to kill him. It was to keep him alive. To perfect what he'd begun, to make him a character who'd live forever in *my* book.

And the most astounding part? Father knew it. I'm sure of that. He went willingly to his doom. He must have known it was the only way. Death would immortalize him like Socrates or Jesus, while life would only have made him an object lesson for the evils of parental greed and twisted relationships—would only have ruined his own success. True, he was reluctant at first. He'd braced himself with liquid courage. Mother had to practically pull him out the door. But then, as I watched him trudge across the snow, he glanced back, and in that glance I saw how he really felt.

He was thankful. He was, dare I say, *passing the baton*. He must have known I'd turn his death into something awe-inspiring, a fiction more fantastic than anything he'd ever attempted. Only later did I discover he'd already been planning to drive into that ravine—that that's why he hadn't brought along anything to read. Which had actually killed them? The brake wires or his suicidal intentions? It didn't matter. The important thing, he'd always told me, was the work that emerged from suffering—the blood we draw from the stone.

Be brave, he was telling me in that last glance. *For you are the Master now.*

All this was going through my mind as I responded to my sister. "No," I said again, with even greater conviction. "Henri must have taken the scissors himself. I don't know why. It could have happened anytime. He did have a key."

She didn't respond at first. She was desperate to believe me. I was, as she'd once said, all that she had left. "Yes, I suppose you're right," she said. "Any of his workers could have taken it."

"Or the television people."

She nodded and wiped the tears from her eyes. I could tell this was hard for her. So I sat back and changed the subject. I asked whether she wanted to watch that evening's public television program on the history of the Incas. She nodded again, more forcefully this time, and murmured that she'd always been interested in the fate of lost civilizations.

"Me, too," I said.

She never mentioned the scissors again.

It's springtime now. The birds are beginning to sing. About what? I can only imagine. Worms, nests, the tranquility of flight. Life feels softer after the long, harsh winter. Klara has begun to venture onto the patio again, sitting on her chaise, wearing her straw hat and reading Victorian novels. The white streak is finally fading. I've moved most of my models back downstairs. This way I can be closer to her while I work. I've recently begun a new project—my first civilian vessel, a luxury cruise liner with fourteen decks revealed in cut-away, plus several swimming pools, a casino, a theater, and a full gymnasium. I've become so caught up in it that I even hinted to Klara that we might take a vacation aboard such a ship this coming summer. She laughed in that refreshingly quiet way she's had lately, and said that if I still feel the same in another month or two she'll call a travel agent for a brochure.

The garden didn't survive the winter. Klara couldn't bring herself to do the necessary work. But it's no great loss. She's no longer interested in gardening. She's never even seen our television episode. We were sent a DVD and it's still tucked away, unopened, along with a letter from Leo, in a kitchen drawer. She also hasn't said a word of protest about my efforts to find someone to move the old Roman back to his familiar perch. She occasionally talks to Mrs. Silfer on the telephone, and every once and a while invites her over for tea. But these have been subdued affairs and I get the impression that Mrs. Silfer is becoming less and less enthusiastic about them every time. I heard her snap at Klara once as she was leaving, telling her something along the lines of "buck up" and "you're too young." Too young for what, I have no idea.

Speaking of age, I ought to say that Marta has had a rough winter with her old bones, as she puts it. Now it is we who take care of her as much as it is the other way around. She still comes to the house a few times a week between lunchtime and supper. But Klara does most of the cooking and cleaning, while I sit upstairs with Marta playing cards or watching those Spanish-language talk shows with large-breasted hosts. Klara finally cleaned out Mother's and Father's room. That is where Marta takes these afternoon rests. She looks at me kindly while I sit with her, but doesn't say very much. During commercial breaks she just tells stories about her childhood in Manila. She describes the festivals and street food and vast crowded churches filled with singing and incense and those dark confessionals that wipe away all sin. I nod and smile along, pretending to concentrate on the television—on Rosie with her Bounty paper towels or Ford trucks grinding in slow-motion through waist-deep mud. But I imagine that far-off place—a teeming hive of street children and religious icons and sweaty priests who have seen and will forgive everything. I can almost hear the peal of church bells floating above the filth, like an ideal of perfect bliss that forever eludes one's grasp. She must have very beautiful memories of church bells.

Church bells make me think of the Mormon boy, who returned last week, right on schedule. I shut the door on him again—I think for the very last time. I don't mean he won't be back. I've seen several documentaries showing how persistent Mormons are. I only mean that next time I've resolved to invite him in. We can sit in the living room and Klara can feed him biscuits, or I can show him the basement with its old farming tools. Perhaps I can distract him and slip out, lock him in there for a short while and listen to his screams and scrabbling terror. What will he do? Try to pick the lock? Pry open the door with a rusty hoe? Good luck with that! Still I might falsely cheer him on: *You've almost got it!* Or give him advice, mouthed through the keyhole: *I hear the light switch, but where's the bulb? Oh my. Have you checked those stacks of dusty boxes?* Or just laugh like one of Father's villains and let him figure out that it's all a game—all fear—whether you call it religion or war or a gruesome tale of murder, a game that *someone* is enjoying—the one pulling the strings, the ones being entertained, even when someone *else* is suffering. Or per-haps *because* someone else is suffering? Let him contemplate that in silence, in darkness, with me, his high priest and author, just across the door. Then, when he's calmed down, we can whisper to each other through the keyhole—about what it's like to be a Mormon, or what it's like to have faith in nothing at all.

After all, I don't want Klara to think I'm utterly averse to guests.

THE END

ACKNOWLEDGMENTS

I wish to extend my deepest gratitude to those who helped me write this book. To Michelle Latiolais, for taking me seriously when I didn't, for encouraging me to get back in the chair when I wouldn't, and for being honest about my writing when I couldn't. To Linda Goldman, for always believing and always providing sage advice. To Marlene Adelstein, for exactly the right guidance at exactly the right time. To Meredith Kaffel Simonoff, for enthusiastically and patiently pushing me to make the manuscript the best it could be. To Sarah Knight, for knowing what worked and what didn't. To Melanie Hart, for wholeheartedly embracing this book and for a keen editorial eye. And to Mark Teppo, for making it all happen.

I am also indebted to insightful early readers: Ben Ripley, Jeff Kleinman (who generously picked up the phone and talked me through various issues), Bob Rabin, and Cara Robertson. And to Andrew Donnelly for his Latin advice (any errors are my own), and Michael Hamilton for his many insights.

I am profoundly grateful to have such loving and supportive parents: Jean and Birgit Barsa.

And not a day goes by when I don't realize how fortunate I am to have the love and support of Kim Yuracko, Sacha Barsa-Yuracko, and Katja Barsa-Yuracko.

ABOUT THE AUTHOR

Michael Barsa grew up in a German-speaking household in New Jersey and spoke no English until he went to school. So began an epic struggle to master the American "R" and a life-long fascination with language. He's lived on three continents and spent many summers in southern Germany and southern Vermont.

He's worked as an award-winning grant writer, an English teacher, and an environmental lawyer. He now teaches environmental and natural resources law. His scholarly articles have appeared in several major law reviews, and his writing on environmental policy has appeared in *The Chicago Tribune* and *The Chicago Sun-Times*. His short fiction has appeared in *Sequoia*.

The Garden of Blue Roses is his first novel.